Martha's Notebook:
A Zombie Apocalypse Trilogy

Written by
C. Fulster

I hope you enjoy my book.

C. Fulster

Martha's Notebook

Copyright © 2024 C. Fulster, Independently Published

All rights reserved. This book or any portion thereof may not be reproduced or used in any manner whatsoever without the express written permission of the publisher except for the use of brief quotations in a book review.

ISBN 979-8-9910391-0-9

info@cfulster.com

https://cfulster.com

ACKNOWLEDGMENTS

I want to take this time to thank my cover image creator, Vishal Bhardwaj, my cover designer, Nabin Karna, and my editor, Sydney Rain.

I would, also, like to acknowledge a hardworking friend and a devoted brand, The 6th Clothing, Co, for supporting me. Badi's continued support includes the design and distribution of branded merchandise for Martha's Notebook.

Thank you all so much.

CONTENTS

	Acknowledgments	i
Chapter 1	That Day	Pg 1
Chapter 2	The Neighborhood	Pg 9
Chapter 3	Scoite's Peak	Pg 25
Chapter 4	Not Alone	Pg 40
Chapter 5	Strangers	Pg 55
Chapter 6	New Faces	Pg 70
Chapter 7	Loss	Pg 90
Chapter 8	Memories	Pg 106
Chapter 9	Training	Pg 122
Chapter 10	Sacrifice	Pg 135
Chapter 11	Alone	Pg 150
Chapter 12	Ups and Downs	Pg 163
Chapter 13	The Outpost	Pg 176
Chapter 14	The Search	Pg 189
Chapter 15	True Villains	Pg 212
Chapter 16	Not Alone	Pg 230
Chapter 17	Secrets Revealed	Pg 249
Chapter 18	Epilogue	Pg 274

Martha's Notebook

CHAPTER 1: THAT DAY

Unknowingly, the last day of normalcy began with the chill of the air nipping at my cheeks as Ava and I ambled down the sidewalk. Our shoes crunched through bright, fall-colored leaves. I tightened my grip on the straps of my backpack before two large silhouettes appeared. Two deer startled me before a comforting peace returned. They gracefully strutted across the street before disappearing behind some evergreens.

"They're so cute, aren't they?" I said, unable to contain my smile.

"Sure, if you like things that actually notice you exist," Ava snarled, her tone laced with frustration. Her glare seemed distant, possibly lost in thought about Arlo, a schoolboy that Ava ranted about for the past week.

"Boys are stupid," I declared in support, despite my limited experience in that area.

"Understatement of the year, Martha." Ava's blonde ponytail with its iconic bright blue streak caught the light of the setting sun. Her blue eyes reflected maturity beyond her years.

As we approached our house, we noticed Ms. Walz, a stout, older woman with shoulder-length, marbled gray and brown hair. She chatted away with our mailman, Booker, by her mailbox. It was a familiar suburbia scene for us as they talked frequently. They shared wide grins, obviously discussing an inside joke or the latest gossip. As we approached, Ms. Walz turned toward us with a welcoming wave.

"Girls! How was school today?" she yelled. Her enthusiasm bounced off the white picket fences surrounding her.

I couldn't help but beam at her contagious greeting. "I got my first *A* in writing," I proclaimed as a swell of pride boosted my words.

"Congratulations, Martha! That's wonderful. Is that your first *A* in seventh grade?" Ms. Walz exclaimed, clapping. The mailman nodded, followed by an encouraging chuckle.

"Thanks," I replied, my chest puffed with pride.

Ava, however, rolled her eyes and made her annoyance known as she huffed, "Boys are complicated creatures."

The two couldn't contain their laughter as it filled the neighborhood. "Oh, Ava, one day all this boy trouble will make sense. Highschool boys, especially fifteen-year-old boys, can be confusing."

"Doubtful," Ava retorted with a weary half-smile.

"Well, you two have a good rest of your evening, alright? And tell your parents I said hi!" Ms. Walz waved us off. Her cheerfulness was a vast contrast to the usual tension that awaited us at home.

"Will do, Ms. Walz," I shouted, and we turned to leave. Ava offered a simple nod in agreement.

The brief exchange was a momentary reprieve from the reality that awaited us at home. A reality where Ava's protective instincts were a necessity, not just a trait of her mature personality.

We approached our house, and I glanced at my sister, sensing her switch into that motherly mode she reserved for me. We stepped up to our porch, ready to face whatever anxiety waited for us on the other side of the threshold.

Ava creaked the front door open. The air inside felt heavy, like walking into a room filled with water. "Martha! Ava!" Dad's voice sliced through the tension as he spotted us.

Mom quickly snapped. "Don't you dare try to distract me from this conversation, Peter!"

With his baseball cap that was practically glued to his head, Dad's athletic frame leaned against the bottom banister of the stairs in the same polo shirt and jeans he always wore. I swear he owned one pair of pants and only three shirts, which were different color variations of the same shirt. Mom's rage filled her short, full figure, and as she interacted, her hands danced in the air, causing her golden-diamond bracelet to bounce light everywhere like a disco ball.

"Hi, Daddy," I managed, my voice struggling to reach him.

My close bond with Dad grew ever since he and Mom began fighting. He tried his best to keep Ava and me out of every altercation. Ava blew him a kiss, her eyes reflecting a storm of emotions she pushed down.

She and Dad had their own bond, which replaced the relationship she had with Mom years ago. Ava had a similar figure to Dad, while I took after Mom and her petite figure. Mom's wavy, shoulder-length brown hair matched mine, but I kept a green bow in mine to separate me from the storm we called Mom. Ava's blonde hair, I imagined, would have matched Dad's hair if he had any left under his hat.

"Girls, go on upstairs," he said with a warmth that made my heart ache. His hand ushered us up the stairs, his protective reassurance for us.

We scampered upstairs, their voices fading but never truly leaving our ears. However, once inside our shared sanctuary, Ava's demeanor shifted. Her grin was like the first ray of sunlight beaming through stormy weather.

"I can't wait anymore. Look what I got for you, Martha." Ava shuffled through her backpack until she gently presented me with a leather-bound notebook. When I took it from her, I noticed her eyes glisten, but she blinked away any evidence before I could be sure.

"I got this for you since you're getting more into writing," Ava explained, the corners of her mouth lifting into a bittersweet smile. "You can pour all your thoughts and worries onto paper instead of keeping them bottled up. It could be a good outlet."

"Really?" My fingers traced the velvety cover, already feeling lighter. I grabbed a marker and emblazoned the front with my name, making it truly mine.

"It's all yours." She never broke her vigilant gaze from me.

Downstairs, Mom and Dad's voices rose again, the words sharp and jagged. "—spend more time with your daughters instead of those frequent trips," Dad's voice broke through, his plea raw with frustration. "And those incessant business calls. They don't need you as much as we do."

"Work is important, Peter. You have no clue what I'm a part of," Mom countered. Her tone was dismissive, but her love for power and control bled through every word.

I pressed the notebook against my chest, pretending it shielded me from the chaos unfolding beneath us. Ava leaned against the wall, trying to hear more of the conversation, her pain for Dad written all over her. Dad continually fought for us, for the family. A concept that seemed further from Mom's mind each day.

"Let's just focus on this, okay? On us," Ava murmured, pulling me back to the present.

"Okay," I whispered, clutching the notebook even tighter. Dad was right, though. We needed Mom to be here for us. But, with my sister by my side and the notebook in hand, I realized we also had enough to build a little world of our own.

The muffled shouts from downstairs clawed at our sanctuary's protection, but Ava's voice was a soothing comfort as we both plopped onto my bed. "Martha, that notebook is for you to pour out your frustrations and anger at Mom." Her light blue eyes were earnest about their mission to provide comfort.

"An outlet?" I asked, my voice barely louder than the hum of the heat rattling through the vents.

"Exactly." She nodded. "Everyone needs one. Some people... they eat their worries away, or worse. Me? I've got soccer... and this..." Ava reached into her backpack, her fingers grasping something carefully concealed. With a magician's flourish, she produced a sleek digital camera from one of her soccer socks, cradling it like the rarest of treasures.

"Is that—" My eyes widened.

"Shh, it's our secret. I got it with my saved allowance... and maybe a little 'borrowing' from Mom." A devilish grin danced across her lips.

"Stealing?" I teased, unable to suppress a giggle.

"Let's call it an advance on life's harsh lessons." Ava's smile never faltered. "Promise me, not a word to them. Mom or Dad."

"Cross my heart," I said, drawing an *X* over my chest. "But it is going straight into my notebook, far from their prying eyes."

"Imagine us years from now," Ava mused, gazing at her camera with a sparkle in her eyes. "You, a world-changing author or poet. Me, capturing moments that take people's breaths away. We'd be unstoppable, huh?"

"An unstoppable duo, living in large mansions," I added. Laughter bubbled within me at the thought of a future so bright, so untainted by the present darkness.

Our shared amusement halted abruptly at the sharp rise of Dad's voice. "Monica, you work too much! It's an obsession!"

"Peter, grow up!" Mom's retort was a venomous lash. "Money is power, and I have plenty of both. I am the only strength in this family! This family would shrivel and die without me."

"Strength?" We could hear the disbelief in Dad's voice from our room. "You're just overcompensating for the lack of control in your childhood, Monica."

"Overcompensating?" Mom's voice climbed to a screech. "I am creating something monumental. No one can stop me. Not even you. One day, I'll wield ultimate power!"

Ava slid across the bed to grab my hand, a silent pledge between sisters in the chaos. While their words clashed below, our dreams hung suspended. A fragile bubble waiting to burst. But in our room, with my sister's courage enveloping me, I could almost believe we might just make it through unscathed.

With the dwindling sunlight shining in our room, my fingers trembled as Ava's voice muffled the argument downstairs. "Just let it out, Martha. Everything you're feeling, all that pain, use the notebook to hash it out." Her eyes were a dependable anchor in our family's rocky waters.

I nodded, and my pen danced across the pages of the leather-bound journal. The words spilled out as easily as breathing. Fears, my longing for peace, and the love for my sister transformed into tangible words. Sentence after sentence unraveled, each one silenced the chaos downstairs until I couldn't hear anything except the pen scratching against the paper.

After several minutes, I dropped my pen into the notebook. My hand cramped, although my heart felt free.

"Better?" Ava's voice called out as I capped my pen.

Exhaling deeply, a smile that felt like dropping my heavy backpack after a long school day filled my face. "Yeah, much better." Clutching the notebook, I realized it wasn't just paper, it was a piece of Ava's heart given to me that bore the weight of our family's issues.

Before I could bask in the warmth of our sisterly bond, our serenity shattered. Screams, sharp and terrifying, pierced the air outside. They sliced through the delicate peace of pre-teen girls. Ava and I exchanged a panicked glance before rushing to the window.

Our breath fogged the glass as our desperate eyes searched the twilight. The scene unfolding below snatched the remnants of childhood innocence from my grasp. Ms. Walz, the neighborhood grandmother that constantly greeted us with so much love, as she did earlier, fled from a grotesque figure hot on her heels. Green lights illuminated ominously from the back of the assailant's hands and neck like an electronic toy of death.

Ms. Walz stumbled onto the sidewalk, her cry catching in her throat. Ava's hand gripped mine as we turned from the window and sank to the floor. Our hearts raced. The terror of witnessing a violent attack loomed over us. Additional cries erupted outside, creating a macabre spectacle in my mind. One that promised no returning to the life we wanted an escape from.

Ms. Walz's screams dwindled, replaced by a haunting silence that echoed with the occasional distant cries of others succumbing to the same fate. I buried my face in Ava's shoulder. The fabric of her shirt dampened with tears I didn't realize I shed.

"Shh," Ava's voice soothed as her arms encircled me. "I've got you, Martha. I've got you."

But even as she whispered those words, we understood that the toxic battleground within our home was nothing compared to the horrors beyond our walls.

My mind ran wild with thoughts of the apocalypse, once an impossible concept. In that moment, as darkness descended upon our small mountain town, Ava and I faced the grim reality that our childhood was officially over, stolen from us in the blink of an eye.

A world of survival against the unknown had begun.

CHAPTER 2: THE NEIGHBORHOOD

I held Ava's hand as my fingers trembled, but somehow I found a shred of bravery to stand back up. Our eyes met for a moment, hers fearful but strong like the roots of an oak tree, and I knew I didn't have to face the horror alone. Together, we crept up to the window, and our breaths instantly fogged the glass.

"Stay quiet," Ava whispered, like the world outside could hear us.

The curtains fluttered as we looked out, half-expecting to see Ms. Walz's body sprawled out on her lawn. Or worse. A small pool of blood, where Ms. Walz fell, welcomed our eyes to the mayhem. I could make out a bloody smear across her white picket fence before the trail faded into the shadows of dusk. Her absence added additional horror to the scene our neighborhood had become.

I scanned the street, my heart pounding in my toes. Then, my blood turned to ice. A dark, tattered figure dashed through the yards, its movements too jerky and unnatural to be human. It acted just like an actual zombie, like the ones in those old movies Dad loved, but something was different. It chased three kids that sprinted desperately for their lives. The youngest stumbled over a garden hose, scrambling up before the monster could reach him. My hand flew to my mouth, softening the scream that escaped.

"Martha, don't," Ava said, but it was too late. The terror hypnotized me as it unfolded, bit by bit, right in front of our house.

Screams echoed from every direction, a festival of pure panic. Doors slammed, engines roared, and tires screeched as neighbors tried to outrun their gruesome end. Some bumbled into cars, others fled on foot. Everything from lone adults to groups of children and all the possibilities in between. It was a wild jailbreak, with prisoners replaced by harbingers of death.

"Is this—is this real life?" My voice seemed non-existent among the screams piercing the window.

Ava's grip tightened, and her knuckles turned white. "We'll be okay, Martha. We need to be." Her words were more for herself than for me. The protective shield she always wrapped around us both felt fragile, like a bubble about to burst.

I wanted to believe her, to find solace in her strength. But when I watched a mom shove her child into their car before a creature tore her away from her family, I realized our family issues were diminished to nothing. All that mattered was survival. The world outside wasn't ours anymore. It belonged to death, to the creatures, and to a future so uncertain our safety seemed questionable at best.

My fingers clung to Ava's like a life vest in stormy waters. My other hand clung to my new notebook so hard I feared the entire thing would crumble into dust. Ava's breathing came out in short, jagged pulls, mirroring my heart's frantic pace.

"Enough! Just stop, Monica!" The sharpness in Dad's voice startled me, snapping my attention away from the window. Ava and I exchanged glances. I had forgotten about the chaos unfolding beneath us, which had become more of a minor inconvenience.

Their conversation halted as two unusual blaring alarms emanated from downstairs.

"What is that? Is that one of those Amber Alerts?" Ava looked confused as she listened closely.

"Really, Peter? You'll do anything to get out of an argument, won't you? Put down your phone and pay attention to me." Mom's hate, laced with that familiar edge of contempt she reserved just for him, filled Mom's retort. The world was ending everywhere, for all we knew, while our parents ignorantly bickered like it was just another Tuesday.

Dad didn't wait for another word before his footsteps resonated through the house as he made his way toward the front door. Terror took over as nightmarish daydreams about every terrible outcome bombarded my mind. Wanting to scream out to him to stay inside, my frozen body could do nothing while my brain worked at the speed of the world's fastest computer.

"Mom doesn't understand," Ava lashed out with disdain. "She doesn't understand. He's only thinking about what's best for us."

I nodded, unable to summon words. My throat tightened as each scream outside wrapped around it like a python, squeezing tighter with every scream. But Ava was right. Dad always put us first, even if it meant stepping directly into danger. That's just who he was, a shield against the horrors of the world. And our seemingly unbreakable shield was walking straight into a danger even he didn't stand a chance against.

The front door slammed with a finality that sent shivers clawing up my spine. Was Dad entering the "outside world?" Ava and I launched ourselves back to the window and huddled together. Our wide eyes locked on Dad as my muscles tensed like a full body cramp.

"Finally." Mom's acidic voice exploded throughout the house. "Once this divorce is finalized, I can live happily knowing I did the right thing." Her words slithered up the stairs, a reminder of how toxic our home life had become. "I need to get out of this house ASAP. He better accept full custody, or that will be a new wrench in things."

Ava's hand lunged for mine, trying to squeeze all the rage out of her body. It was a punch in the gut hearing the truth of what our mom thought about us. Even amid the end of the world, she wanted us gone, along with Dad.

"Ah, I mean… I wonder where Peter went." Mom tried covering her tracks, aware of our potential eavesdropping. It was too late for our fractured family, but Ava, Dad, and I could remain a powerful family.

My attention snapped back to Dad, remembering his stroll into imminent danger. Our once-familiar street was a war zone, and Dad had stepped right in the middle of it. Neighbors continued to dart between houses. Screams pierced the evening air, and those… things hunted with a voracious hunger. Dad had that familiar look of wanting to save someone but didn't know where to start.

"Peter!" a voice shrieked.

Dad didn't hesitate to run into the street, attempting to locate the person in danger, until one zombie locked onto him. A man in tattered, casual clothes. Bullet holes and bloodstains covered his body. The sight was absolute horror, and his limbs jerked in unnatural ways as green lights illuminated ominously from its neck and hands. My heart stalled while I scanned the demon of death, wanting to understand the monster as much as I could. I pleaded with the moon that it wouldn't be Dad's last day.

"Please no, please no," Ava prayed as the world outside enveloped Dad.

Dad dodged left when the creature lunged, their deadly dance inches from catastrophe. We sat like statues at the window as we helplessly watched the only other person we loved as much as each other, gamble with death.

"Run, Dad, run!" I shouted through my shaky vocal cords, though I knew he couldn't hear me. My breath fogged the glass even more. The world outside smeared into ghostly silhouettes. Ava slid her pink hoodie sleeve over her hand as she frantically wiped the window.

Each second stretched into an eternity. Dad continued to run, dodge, and fight off the creature. I knew he would fight as hard as he could to get back to us.

My fingers slid up Ava's forearm then dug themselves into her sleeve. Ava focused on Dad so much she didn't even notice. Dad finally sprinted from the street toward the safety of our SUV. The reliable, red SUV that traveled countless road trips with us and stood as Dad's proud vehicle, even if it had its share of dents.

"Get it, Dad," my voice came out as a confident command.

He grasped the door handle with an urgency that mirrored the fear deep in my chest. The door didn't budge. Desperation painted his face as he realized the keys weren't in his pocket.

"Are you kidding?" Ava and I cried in unison as our faces dropped, wondering if we were spectators of Dad's final moments.

The grotesque monster barreled at Dad, and its limbs flailed in its desperation. Dad swung around the vehicle, playing a deadly game of cat and mouse, keeping the SUV between him and the monster's greedy hands.

"Keep moving, Dad!" Ava's voice trembled beside me, her eyes wide and shimmering with unshed tears.

He slipped around the back of the SUV, narrowly avoiding a swipe from the monster, all too eager to tear into his flesh. Then another figure darted past them, barreling down the middle of the street. A stranger sprinted from a female zombie with a mangled leg, in utter desperation to escape.

"Look!" Ava pointed, and I followed her finger to witness the zombie's attention snap to the new prey. Its bloody head swiveled with a sickening crackle of vertebrae.

The words spilled out of my mouth. "Go. Go. Get away from him!" My plea for both the stranger and Dad.

After jerking and tweaking, the zombie changed course, sprinted after the stranger, and left Dad alone. Its speed was relentless, and it became a blur against the backdrop of fleeing neighbors and abandoned homes in the twilight.

Ava exhaled sharply and I followed. We were still far from safe, but Dad was out of immediate danger.

"Thank God," Ava murmured. Then she finally noticed my nails buried in her arm and smacked my hand away like a mother would her child. "Ow! Knock that off." The brief exchange created a dash of normalcy.

"Let's hope that stranger ends up safe," I said as I rubbed the back of my hand. A guilty feeling filled me when I envisioned the stranger most likely still running for their life, but it was someone else's turn to watch helplessly through a window.

Our focus returned to Dad, remembering he was still in a dangerous world. Dad's selflessness and unwavering determination radiated strength, the same strength I hoped to find within myself when the time came.

Then, our selfless father took off to help a fellow neighbor. His strides long and determined across the lawn toward Mr. Morrow's house.

"Martha, Dad!" Ava's voice stumbled with a mix of pride and terror as we peered through the windowpane. Our breaths fogged the glass, again.

There he was, Mr. Morrow our neighbor, who always wore a luxurious sweater with matching jeans and his iconic cornrows. Dad and he had been close friends for a long time. They watched football games together as often as possible.

He struggled in his driveway a few houses north of us. Mr. Morrow flailed in defense against another relentless, green-glowing zombie-thing. The ghastly figure pinned him to the ground, its jaws snapped like a crocodile, dying for a bite. I wanted to scream for Dad to be careful, but my body turned to stone.

"Come on, Dad," I breathed through gritted teeth. I begged for hope among the screams that hung in the air.

As if ignoring my silent plea, Dad launched at the zombie with the force of a semi-truck. Time warped into a slow trickle and almost stopped as they collided. A gut-wrenching scream echoed from the altercation. A cry of pain that cut through the muffled shuffling and growling of the skirmish.

"Mr. Morrow!" Ava cried, her face pressed against the window, eyes wide with horror.

I watched helplessly as Mr. Morrow clutched his cheek. Blood cascaded down his dark skin from three deep slashes created by the vile creature's nails. The dark streaks painted his face as I wondered if zombie wounds in this world mimicked zombie wounds from the movies. Would Mr. Morrow suffer an excruciating fate and become one of those monsters?

"Is he going to…?" Ava couldn't bring herself to finish, the question hanging between us like a boulder on a precarious ledge. It felt as if the mentioned outcome would bring it into existence.

"Shh," I hushed Ava, not wanting to know the answer to the question she couldn't ask, though it nagged at both of us. We continued to look on helplessly. Did the movies differ that much from real life? Were we in real life, or were we unknowingly caught in a movie? Terror and chaos had entered our neighborhood and affected people we knew, like our dad who risked it all for a neighbor and a friend.

Dad stood between Mr. Morrow and the fallen zombie the same way he stood between Mom and us, allowing Mr. Morrow time to stand. Every breath became visible as he panted, peering down at the creature. Even in the apocalypse, Dad's instinct was to save, to protect, to stand as a shield for humanity.

"Please be okay." My words shattered against the window. Dad's form loomed menacing and brave, still oblivious to Mr. Morrow struggling behind him.

"Let's get some things together in case Dad wants to leave or something. I don't want to stay here with those things outside." Ava broke the tension, pulling me away from the window. "We have to be ready the minute Dad comes in the door."

"Okay," I said, my voice steadier than I felt. As much as I wanted to continue watching, to see Dad make it to safety, I knew our time at home dwindled. We had to prepare if we wanted to ensure our survival, knowing we couldn't use our home as shelter forever.

I mindlessly threw a few things in my backpack and sprinted back to the window for proof of Dad's well-being. "Look, Ava," I whispered. My voice trembled as much as my hands. "The lights… they're going out."

We stared, unable to tear our eyes from the scene. The eerie, emerald glow that had once illuminated the zombie's neck and back of its hands, flickered erratically before dimming into nothingness. They became as dark as the night sky. A collective sigh escaped our lips, a momentary relief from the constant terrors that had transformed our quiet neighborhood into a horror movie scene.

Dad turned, and I witnessed his face drop like an anchor when he noticed Mr. Morrow's face. Their gazes locked on the injury. My stomach churned at the sight. I couldn't imagine what was going through Dad's mind, let alone what Mr. Morrow might have been thinking and feeling. Was it the end of Mr. Morrow, even after being saved from a gruesome death?

"Do you think he'll be okay, or will he turn into one of those horrifying things?" Ava's questions felt like she read my mind.

I wanted to assure her, to tell her everything would be fine, that Dad wouldn't let anything happen to Mr. Morrow. But the words caught in my throat, strangled by the uncertainty clouding every thought. The two of us sat in silence and the question lingered in the air without an answer.

Dad's hands trembled, and he gingerly moved Mr. Morrow's fingers away from the scratch. The raw red gash was a saddening contrast against his skin, and it spelled out a silent verdict neither of them wanted to face. A bite or scratch, that's all it took in the movies. Unlike the family movie nights, when we huddled together under blankets, blissfully unaware that fiction wasn't far from reality.

"Martha, what does this mean?" Ava's voice shook with every syllable. Terror kept me silent.

Their heads bowed in unison and an invisible weight settled on their shoulders. It was a defeat that didn't just knock you down, it kept you there, holding you with a grip stronger than fear itself. Ava's hand grasped mine. Her nails dug into my palm this time. Dad grabbed the back of Mr. Morrow's neck, and they pressed their foreheads together. A gesture of respect and farewell as the moment needed no words to describe the gut-punch of sadness shared between two close friends.

From our second-story vantage point, the message shared between them was clear as Dad stepped back before he reached out, his hand enveloping Mr. Morrow's in a firm shake before pulling him into a second, last hug. Ava and I shed tears at the brotherly bond Dad had with his friend. A bond stolen without warning.

They parted ways and Mr. Morrow jogged toward his home, a retreat filled with defeat. It hurt to watch, to know no matter how brave or powerful Dad was, there were things even he couldn't stop.

"Think we'll ever see Mr. Morrow again?" Ava's question broke through my daze. Her blue eyes searched my brown eyes for answers.

"We'll just have to wait and see. Maybe Dad knows more from their conversation."

Ava nodded, but doubt flickered behind her eyes. Ava and I learned a devastating lesson that this world planned to teach everyone. Sometimes good people succumb to a darkness that lingers over everyone.

Dad stood alone in the driveway for a moment. His shadow disappeared as Mr. Morrow's house lights became dark. He turned and glanced at our house as his eyes ascended to our window. A wave of love and fear reached us. An unspoken promise that he'd fight until his last breath to keep us safe.

Dad broke into a jog, urgency propelling him home. Each step was heavy, laden with defeat, yet driven by a will that refused to buckle. With everything, he returned to us because that's the dad he was.

The pride swelled in my chest with a confusing mix of love and sorrow. Ava and I had always seen Dad as invincible, but in that moment, as he hurried for the safety of our home, I realized being a hero wasn't about being fearless or untouchable; it was about getting up again after each fall, about returning to fight even after a devastating defeat.

"Come on," Ava said as she yanked herself away from the window. "We need to move. Dad is coming back, and we should be ready for whatever he needs us to do."

The world outside had fallen into a haunting hush, like the terror itself had to catch its breath. I stayed at the window until Dad reached the door, watching over him as he had always watched over us. And once the door closed behind him, shutting out the brief silence that blanketed our street, I knew no matter what came next, we were not alone. We had Dad, our trusted protector against the encroaching nightmares.

The thudding of boots on the stairs jolted us. Ava's eyes met mine, wide with fear. The sounds grew louder, more desperate before Dad's voice pierced the door with absolute urgency. "Girls! Pack what you need, now! We're leaving immediately!"

Adrenaline surged in my veins, and I grabbed my backpack. Ava's expression mirrored my panic. Her eyes darted to our necessities scattered around the room.

"Where have you been?" Mom's shrill voice snapped at Dad from the kitchen with a tone that cut through the house like a knife.

"Outside, Monica! Do you have any idea what I just went through? We need to go somewhere safe. Maybe the mountains." A desperation I had never heard before oozed from Dad's voice.

Mom's scoff echoed in response. "Leave? And abandon this house? Do you have any idea how much we've invested in this place?"

Martha's Notebook

I ignored their arguing, and grabbed my stuffed penguin, Mr. Woddly, and shoved him into my backpack along with the gummy worms from my dresser. Ava's face held a determined scowl inches away from the door. She understood the stakes just as much as I did. This toxic arguing downstairs was nothing compared to the horror outside.

Ava moved swiftly, her purple backpack hit the floor with a soft thud. She emptied its contents in a swift motion and removed a few textbooks, notebooks, and pens that she scattered across the carpet. Her movements were efficient, practical, as she retrieved her camera and wrapped it carefully in a pillowcase. With reverence, she nestled it into her backpack amongst her survival essentials.

"Monica, this isn't about the damn house!" Dad's plea faded among the neighbor's screaming and screeching tires. Neighbors who had waited for the lull to flee for safety like we were about to do.

"Do you know how much money is invested in this property?" Mom retorted, her voice rising in pitch.

"Enough, Monica!" There was a steel edge to Dad's voice, one that stomped out any arguing. He became an anchor in the storm, the one who held us together when everything else threatened to tear us apart.

"Martha, come on," Ava urged, tugging at my sleeve as I tossed my notebook into my backpack and zipped it up. We slipped into the hallway, our steps quick and light.

"Are you girls ready?" Dad's face appeared at the bottom of the stairs, etched with concern and love. It was the same look that had comforted me through scraping my knees on my bike to middle-of-the-night nightmares.

"Ready!" Ava shouted as I tried to muster confidence I didn't feel.

"Good." Dad's lips twitched into a grim half-smile, and he turned back to confront Mom's incessant protests.

"Peter, you can't be serious—"

"Monica! Come with us or don't. I don't care anymore. I need to get these girls to a safer place. If you want to stay in this house with whatever craziness breaks in, be my guest. We're leaving." Dad was stern and final with his words.

"Martha, Ava." Dad's voice softened in tone, just for Ava and me. "Stay close. No matter what happens, it's going to be okay."

The fear in his eyes betrayed his words, and though I nodded, clutching my backpack straps, I couldn't shake the dread that settled heavy in my stomach. We descended the stairs to join Dad on this adventure.

"Peter, what in God's name is so terrible out there that we have to abandon our home?" Mom's voice rang sharp with ignorance.

"I saw things so bad you'd leave all this behind if you were in my shoes?" Dad zipped up Ava's pink hoodie and prepared us to leave like we were toddlers preparing for a snowy day.

"Monica, it's not safe here. We need to go now." Dad's insistence met with Mom's scoff. Her faux concern barely hid the glint of dollar signs in her eyes.

"Peter, this house is solid. It's worth a fortune. We can hunker here and wait out whatever is going on." Mom's words put money over everything, including us.

"Mom doesn't get it," Ava whispered, her eyes burning with animosity.

"Money won't matter if we're dead," Dad shot back, exasperated.

"Are we really going to throw away everything for some… some panic?" Mom continued. Her persistence grated against the situation's urgency.

"Everything, Monica? Is that what matters to you now?" Disbelief colored Dad's response, and he glanced at us, meeting my gaze with a silent understanding.

"Peter, think about the money!" Mom persisted. Her voice tinged with desperation.

"Do you think those creatures care about money?" Dad mocked, possibly trying to inject some humor into the situation to comfort Ava and me.

Ava and I scuttled toward the front door. We turned in unison, waiting for Mom and Dad. Dad's voice cut through the tense air. "Monica, we leave now, or you're staying here!"

Mom's eyes darted between the staircase and the front door, a storm of indecision brewing. With a huff that could bend steel, she charged upstairs, her footsteps an unpleasant retreat. Dad's eyes rolled skyward before he transformed his expression into a reassuring smile for us.

"Are you girls ready?" he asked, kneeling before us.

"Ready," we whispered. Smiles broke through our worry like shy sunbeams.

"Listen," Dad's voice softened, again. "I don't know what we'll face out there, but I need you both to be brave. Can you do that for me?" His hands enveloped ours.

"We can," Ava said, and her words empowered me into giving a confident nod.

"Promise you'll do whatever I say? It's all to keep you two safe." The urgency in his voice enveloped us.

"We promise," we chorused, our voices mingling with our fear.

Dad kissed each of our foreheads, a gesture so tender it felt out of place in the harsh reality just outside.

He stood, squared his shoulders, and grabbed the doorknob. "Let's go. We're going to run to the car—" Dad patted his pocket, and a worried look grew. He hurried toward the kitchen.

In a jovial saunter, Dad returned. "Got 'em," he chuckled, clinking his set of keys. "Can't forget these for a second time." He winked, pressed the 'unlock' button, and a faint orange light flashed outside.

"Are you two still ready?" Dad's attempt to lighten the mood stirred faint giggles from us, the first since the nightmare began.

"Ready, set, go!" His countdown released my anxiety.

Dad flung open the door and ushered us into the night. We sprinted to the car, each hopping into our designated seats like magnets. When I settled into the back seat, the silence of the neighborhood pressed in on me like the calm eye of a relentless storm.

"Come on, come on," Dad muttered, checking the rearview mirror. Every moment was dire, and we couldn't afford to waste any time.

"Monica!" Dad's voice strained with impatience, but he held back from honking the horn.

Don't wait anymore, Dad. I wanted to yell, but my words were prisoners of my throat. Could I say that about our mom?

The front door burst open, and there she was. Mom clutched a fire-safe like the cure for some terminal disease. "We can't leave without this!" she shouted, half-tripping as she stumbled toward the car.

"Always about the valuables," Dad mumbled, shaking his head as she clambered into the passenger seat with her clumsy companion.

He shot us a quick smile in the mirror, then threw the car into drive. As we pulled away from our home, the streetlights leap-frogged above us, casting an eerie glow on the empty road ahead.

The SUV hummed beneath us, weaving through the side streets where shadows danced under sparse streetlights. I pressed my forehead against the cool car window to give a soothing comfort to my anxiety.

"Martha, keep your head down," Ava warned softly from beside me, but I couldn't tear my eyes away from the scenes outside.

Every few blocks, we encountered pockets of horrid groups of monsters staggering after frantic residents. Most of the creatures were grotesque. Their flesh torn and bloody, while others might have passed for neighbors if not for the hunger in their eyes and the green glow emanating from their necks and hands.

"Look at their hands and necks!" I whispered to Ava, my voice trembling. Each creature, no matter how decayed, had something glinting from the same spots on their skin. It was a microchip-like implant, shining with an unnatural green glow against their mutilated flesh.

"Monica, keep that thing in your lap," Dad growled with his focus split between driving and the cumbersome safe Mom clutched.

"Peter, you don't even know all the important paperwork sitting inside. This safe will be worth millions!" Mom snapped, oblivious to the terror outside her bubble of greed.

"Money will be more than meaningless in an apocalypse, Monica. That's now an anchor for our family!" Dad's knuckles turned white as he gripped the steering wheel.

A shiver ran down my spine as we passed another group of creatures. A scream cut through the night, and I flinched, burying my face in Ava's shoulder.

"Martha, it's okay, we're going to make it," she soothed, wrapping her arm around me. But her voice wavered, showcasing her own fear.

"Everybody hang on!" Dad swerved the SUV as a creature lunged at us from the darkness. The vehicle shuddered, and we all let out a collective gasp.

"Peter, be careful!" Mom shrieked, and her grip tightened around the safe.

"Better the safe than us, right?" Ava said under her breath.

"Quiet back there." Mom's scowl searched through the darkness for something to divert her attention. "Where are we even going?" she asked, acting as if this were an unplanned vacation.

"Somewhere safe. Somewhere isolated," Dad replied with a note of uncertainty in his voice.

"Scoite's Peak?" Mom asked, annoyed at the possible answer.

"Exactly," Dad confirmed, giving me a quick glance in the mirror and a thumbs up. When his eyes met mine, for a moment, I saw the determination that had always made me feel protected.

"Whatever happens, remember, I love you both."

"We love you too, Dad," Ava and I said together, gripping each other's hands tightly.

Mom, undeterred by the exchange excluding her, focused on her only love perched in her lap.

As we continued our escape, the suburban echoes faded into the background, replaced by an eerie silence that filled the car as we left civilization. We left everything behind, but we were together, and at that moment, it was all that mattered. That and the nagging question of where did those microchips came from that suffocated our familiar neighborhood with a cannibalistic shadow. One that almost stole our dad from us.

CHAPTER 3: SCOITE'S PEAK

A fog crept around me like a shadowy snake made of nightmares. Its coils suffocated the world beyond my sight. A single green glow pulsated within the fog, elusive and random. It was like the mist itself hid secrets too monstrous to reveal. I spun, trying to find a recognizable face or item. My eyes darted everywhere as the green glow seemed to follow my gaze, mocking my search for safety.

"Dad? Ava? Is anyone here? Please..." My voice revealed my fears, and my heart yearned to break free from the nightmare I became trapped in. Ava, my protector, my rock, was gone. Dad, our guide through the shattered world, was missing. Their absence became a void more terrifying than any creature the apocalypse had thrown at us.

The green glow intensified, swirled, and merged into a beacon amid the smog. It beckoned me. A siren call I knew would lead to disaster. Then, the single light split into three distinct orbs, morphing into a triangle of terror that watched me from the shadows.

A guttural growl rumbled through the air, vibrating the very particles in the mist. Stepping out from the dark, a grotesque mass with gnarled limbs and a gaping maw appeared, staring into my soul. It lunged with its jaws unnaturally wide, attempting to swallow my soul.

I stumbled backward, my breath caught in my throat, and it felt like the shadows reached out to snatch me up.

"No!" I screamed. A fight-or-flight instinct boiled inside me as I realized I couldn't look to anyone else to fight for me. It was only me and the monster, and I couldn't let it steal me from the world like the many others it had.

"Stay back!" My words erupted with ferocity, a battle cry that rang out from the depths of my soul, echoing Ava's spirit. My legs quivered, but I stood my ground, determined to face the horror, to be the strong woman I knew I could become. Dad had always told me I could be as gentle as I wanted, but even the gentlest animals can bite.

With every ounce of willpower, I braced myself for the onslaught. I prepared to fight, to cling to life with all the tenacity a girl who had witnessed the end of the world could.

My heart slammed against my chest so hard it startled me awake. My eyes flew open as remnants of the nightmare clung to me like cobwebs. A little groggy, I scanned my surroundings as maple trees whizzed by and a sun prepared to break through the horizon that replaced the dark mist. The hum of the engine and the white noise of the tires on the road lulled me into a soothing comfort. I glanced around, waiting for my pulse to not feel like a heavy metal concert.

Ava curled up in her corner of the backseat, breathing steadily and peacefully. In contrast, Mom's slumber looked uncomfortable, her head slumped awkwardly, buried in her crossed arms that protected the safe even as she slept. The sight of them both, so close and safe, eased the tremor in my hands, but it was the genuine smile on Dad's face that calmed my hands and my nerves completely.

"Hey, sleepyhead. Did you get a little rest?" Dad's voice pushed out the remaining pieces of the nightmare through the silent car like thunder rolling off in distant fields.

I rubbed my eyes, still heavy with residual terror. A sleepy nod was all I could muster. His concern added another layer of comfort, warming me more than the stale air circulating through the car. "Yeah," I mumbled through a yawn.

"We don't have long until we'll arrive at Scoite's Peak." Dad seemed at peace and much more relaxed than he had been hours ago.

The words sparked curiosity as I rested my head against the cool window. Scoite's Peak was the place Mom and Dad took me when I was about six, during one of Ava's soccer tournaments. The world outside appeared to be back to normal. An internal voice crept up, asking if everything involving those green illuminated zombies was just a dream. A sleepy half-smile settled in as I admired the view. Towering trees created a frame around each scenic view as we ascended the spiral road. Zombies or not, I needed to appreciate the serenity of the car and the landscape while I had the chance.

As the mountain road unfolded, ushering us into Scoite's Peak, a flicker of hope lit inside me. Perhaps, just maybe, we'd find what we hoped for. Whether it was safety, strength, or separate condos for Mom and Dad, I had a strong feeling that we would discover something significant in the small mountain town.

The nightmares continued to dance through my mind as I watched the distant stars fade into the light of morning. The crunch of paved roads transforming to gravel under our tires jarred me from my drowsy state, and two quick potholes under the car acted as alarms for Ava and Mom. Their eyes fluttered open as our car jostled over the uneven road with ancient cobblestones peeking through in places where the gravel layer had worn away. The town that emerged from the mountain's peak simulated a page torn out of a storybook. Old European style buildings, eerie and enchanting with their high peaks that reached for the clouds, welcomed us as we entered the desolate town.

Mom stirred before she clutched at the safe on her lap. Relief washed over her after realizing she still possessed it. Ava's eyes darted between Dad in the driver's seat and back to me. She frantically spun around, checking every inch of her surroundings for danger, before a relieved smile rolled across her face and she melted into her seat.

Realizing she and her loved ones were safe, she snuggled against her backpack, the familiar fabric offering security.

"We're here," Dad announced with a note of triumph. His voice lifted above the rumble of gravel beneath us. "Girls… welcome to Scoite's Peak."

I pressed my face closer to the glass, taking in the buildings left untouched by tragedy. Several two and three-story structures protected us from the outside world, each one mimicking the mountains themselves.

"Wow," was all that escaped my lips, unable to keep the awe to myself. For a moment, I allowed myself to be a wide-eyed twelve-year-old again. I took that moment to go back to where I could be a kid before the apocalypse stole it away from me again.

"Beautiful, isn't it?" Dad's voice oozed with nostalgia. He glanced in the rearview mirror where his reflection met mine. The same childlike wonder filled his eyes.

Scoite's Peak seemed like a sanctuary, a fortress against the zombies and the darkness they brought. However, as we drove deeper into its heart, the stirrings of unease grew. I felt hope and safety, but also a subtle sense of impending doom.

The car rolled into a parking spot parallel to the sidewalk. Gravel crunched beneath us as Dad brought the car to a stop and shut off the tired engine. Silence seeped into the car, a deep contrast to the hum of the engine and the crunch of the gravel. European charm turned to fear as the eerie stillness peered down at us like gargoyles perched high above.

"Okay," Dad broke the silence, his voice steady as he surveyed the street through the windshield. "Let's just get our bearings before we head out." His hand slid over the horn before he slammed it down.

The shrill blast of the horn sliced through the quiet town like a cannon fired in a library. Every muscle in my body cinched. The sound ricocheted off the stone buildings.

"Peter! What the hell are you doing?" Mom's voice tore through the car. Her left hand cocked back to slap his arm. "Are you trying to alert all the psychos that there's a new meal in town?"

Beside me, Ava's presence both comforted and reminded me of the danger we faced. She didn't seem to mind or understand that the horn could bring those things sprinting toward us.

"Easy, Monica," Dad replied. "It's a precaution. If anything's lurking about, better to know now than when we're out in the open."

Mom wasn't having any of it, as her face turned red. "Precaution? You call that a precaution? Do you want us to be trapped in here? You're willing to put your family right in the path of whatever attacked you?"

The brief shock of the horn's blast dissolved back into silence, and Dad flashed a triumphant grin at Mom. "See? It's like ringing a dinner bell. If any of those things were here, they'd be right on top of us by now," he said confidently, with a twinkle in his eyes.

Dad's joking loosened the tight knot in my stomach when I realized he had a plan all along. Ava and I shared a moment of comfort as our bodies relaxed in sync with each other like balloons deflating. We both had to remember Dad knew what he was doing. Someone in the family had some control over this chaos.

Mom's lips pressed into a thin line. "Great, Peter," she snapped, throwing him a scalding look that could curdle milk. "But did you think about it echoing through the mountains? We're on top of a mountain. That sound could roll for miles. You might as well have lit a beacon for every infected in the area!"

His smile faltered, the realization tugged on his face. My heart sank as I realized what Mom meant, but it sank for Dad realizing he did, in fact, put his family in danger. Despite understanding her point, I couldn't help but feel a sting of annoyance at how she always cut him down. Glancing at Ava, I could tell she wanted to raise a white flag for them to just be civil toward one another.

"Let's just—let's be quick about this," Dad said, his earlier confidence replaced by a newfound urgency. A small crack in the armor he wore so well.

I wanted to say something to ease the tension, to bridge the gap widening in our toxic family, but words failed me.

We opened our doors in unison by mere coincidence. The gravel beneath us crunched like brittle bones underfoot. The blanketing silence was heavy with the weight of imagined threats in every building.

"Stay close," Ava whispered to me. The whisper felt loud in the empty town as she clutched her backpack to her chest. She offered me a reassuring glance, but her eyes were pools of concern.

Dad surveyed the desolate town with every inch we moved. The keys jingled softly in his hand. Such an ordinary sound felt so alien in an apocalypse. Dad crept at the helm of the family, vigilant of every movement and sound.

Mom struggled at the rear, clutching the safe like it contained the cure for the creatures, which maybe it did. Her priorities had always been different, skewed by what she believed mattered most. To her, the contents of that safe were more than survival, they were her future. A future which Dad, Ava, and I weren't a part of.

Scouring the deserted street, Dad's gaze landed on a two-story structure topped off by a rooftop balcony. "There," he pointed, "That could give us a good vantage point to see any trouble coming."

"Shouldn't you lock the car?" Mom's voice cut through Dad's plans for safety. She continued to glance back at the car like her eyes could lock the car on their own.

Dad chuckled dryly, the sound carrying a twinge of sadness. "I'll leave it unlocked. Might be someone's last resort to escape those things." His eyes briefly clouded, possibly remembering his narrow escape. I understood his haunting look. Dad's earlier brush with death had imprinted on him more than we knew.

Mom, however, was far from satisfied. "Great. So, when we come back, will we find the car stolen because of your charity? We're already scraping by as is. Let's leave the house behind. Let's leave the car behind. What are you going to leave behind next?"

"You?" Dad whispered and chuckled to himself. "Do you ever think about anything besides money?" Dad made sure those words were loud enough to hear. His head shook in disbelief. "What next? Are you afraid we're going to run up a tab in one of these bars?" His tone, light and mocking, was an uncomfortable relief to the silence. "Maybe they won't even let us in. You know, dress code and all. We have two minors with us." He turned to Ava and me and shared a loving wink.

Ava and I exchanged glances, stifling giggles that threatened to burst out. We didn't want to fuel Mom's rage, but the absurdity of Dad's humor amid the apocalypse was its own brand of comedy.

For a moment, Mom just stared at him, probably envisioning a horrible fate for Dad. Then silence fell, and no one was brave enough to break the tension.

"Come on, before someone or something sees us," Dad urged us, gesturing toward the building with the balcony as we approached it.

As we shuffled closer, we moved as a unit, a family set on safety and the glimmer of hope the building provided. Maybe we could build a new life inside.

We cautiously tiptoed to the door of the hotel that loomed before us. Its glass panes reflected our disheveled appearances. With methodical caution, Dad wrapped his hand around the metal handle and eased it open. The hinges whispered as he slipped inside. The door sealed behind him with a gentle thud that resonated in the hollow town. We three girls waited with patience and fear from outside.

My heart pounded a rhythmic dance inside my chest, mirroring the tension that buzzed through Mom and Ava. We waited for any sign of life, inside or out, to show itself as we all held bated breath.

Dad returned and eased open the door. "Coast is clear," Dad proclaimed. His voice barely rose above a whisper, but it thundered to us.

We shuffled forward, our steps hesitant as we followed Dad into the dimly lit confines of the lobby. His eyes never stopped moving, scanning every shadow, every corner where danger might lurk.

The chill of the lobby's marble floor seeped through my shoes as we shuffled inside. A hotel that was once bustling, reduced to a distant memory. Luxury surrounded us, haunting reminders of what was once valuable that now sat abandoned. I wondered if any of the lavish paintings on the walls or the extravagant fixture dangling from the ceiling would ever hold value again, or if they were just relics of a past that would eventually succumb to history.

Mom didn't hesitate, and her eyes dripped with an ego against the world. She shouldered past Dad with the same indebted attitude she had since she yelled at a barista for putting too little espresso in her coffee when I was eight.

"Stay close," Ava shouted at Mom, as hushed as she could. Mom beelined for the reception desk, the heavy safe acting as an anchor until she chucked it onto the counter. She sidled behind the desk and rifled through drawers with a thief's desperation. It didn't take long before she let out a small, triumphant grunt. She emerged with three bills pinched between her fingers and a necklace. The sixty dollars and the diamond necklace had Mom acting like she won the lottery, but to us it felt like she was holding Monopoly money and a child's necklace.

"Jackpot," she crowed, waving the cash like a flag of victory.

"Monica," Dad's voice lingered with frustration. "That stuff isn't worth anything anymore."

She spun toward Dad, the fire of defiance lighting her face. "You're not worth anything anymore," she snapped. "While you play the hero, I'm securing our future…" Mom's voice tapered off. "Or my future."

The tension grew in the room and within Mom. Ava squeezed my shoulder reassuringly, her eyes telling me without words that it would be okay. But the question lingered. Was there truly any security to be found in our new world? Or were we all grasping at false dreams?

My fingers wrapped around the straps of my backpack as Mom's hand hovered over a crystal dish next to the computer. It cradled three sparkling wedding rings that seemed to scream out in the deathly quiet lobby. Her grin spread like she'd stumbled upon a treasure chest that someone forgot to bury.

"Look at these beauties. They could easily be worth ten grand each, if not more." She gloated and leaned over the counter to flick open her safe with practiced ease. She tossed the rings, cash, and the necklace into the safe. "I might have just made tens of thousands of dollars while you've been honking horns and lollygagging around."

All Dad could do was shake his head. "Keeping the girls safe is the only thing I care about," he replied. The pride in his voice wrapped around me like a warm blanket. "And the girls will always be worth more to me than money."

I wanted to believe him, to feel that security he radiated, but doubt nibbled at my insides. We were alive, but for how long? Would wedding rings ever mean anything again?

Trying to divert the animosity, we turned to the grand spiral staircase of twisted iron and polished wood beckoning us upward. Dad, Ava, and I ascended the stairs in single file while Mom gathered her safe and struggled to not leave it behind.

As we climbed, the air became thick, and the silence of the building pressed against us. We reached the second-floor landing where a sign hung in the broken light of morning: "This way to The Peak's Peak."

A barely suppressed chuckle escaped Dad's lips as he caught my eye. "Hey girls, should we take a peek at The Peak's peak?" He couldn't contain himself at the dad joke hanging between us as we continued upward.

I couldn't help the small giggle that bubbled up. His jokes were terrible, but they were what we knew Dad for. The joke lifted the current struggles of this world and gave all of us a glimpse into normalcy.

As usual, Mom was quick to douse Dad's entertainment. "Stop screwing around, Peter, and get us to safety." She struggled to venture up the stairs as the safe clanged against the metal railing.

I glanced at Ava, who rolled her eyes at Mom's dour demeanor. Despite the circumstances, I couldn't stifle the smile that had spread across my face. "That was a good one, Dad."

"I liked it, too," Ava said with an enormous grin. We relished the rare moment, not knowing when, or if, another one would occur.

Dad transitioned back into hero mode and surveyed the next landing as we narrowed in on the third floor.

The last steps illuminated in a soft glow as sunlight streamed through the glass double doors at the landing. The warmth of the rays trickled through the cool darkness below. It was like the world above was untouched by the horrors that plagued our childhood.

Dad cautiously poked his head through the doors, scanning the rooftop for any movement. My heart pounded, half-expecting some horror to tackle him to the ground like Mr. Morrow, but the coast was clear. He flung the doors fully open with a shove and stood aside, ushering us into safety.

"This way, ladies," he welcomed us, like a guard announcing the queen.

Ava went first, but I followed closely. Mom trailed behind, clutching the safe like usual. And just for a moment, as we stepped onto the rooftop bar, the apocalypse felt distant.

We shuffled our belongings against the door. Mom tucked the safe against the door and immediately re-stacked our backpacks on top. A barricade of backpacks and the weighty safe gave us some additional security, so we could immerse ourselves in the incredible landscape.

Instinctively, we gravitated toward the railing, as if we were on vacation, grabbing a bite with a gorgeous view. The air felt thinner, crisp, and cool, biting at my lungs in a way that felt strangely cleansing. I closed my eyes, letting the wind's gentle caress sweep away the dread from my body.

"Feels good, doesn't it?" Ava muttered beside me. Her voice was relaxed, like she was copying my actions.

"Feels like it's washing everything away from the last twenty-four hours," I agreed, though I knew it was only temporary.

Dad stood tall and inhaled a lungful of the mountain air. His chest expanded deep, and I felt compelled to mimic him. He followed with a gaze that swept over the endless stretch of peaks and valleys that bowed beneath the town.

"Girls," he began, and rare emotions bled through his words. "This is a special place to me, a place where I always got a new perspective on my problems. No matter what I went through, this place always helped me. I'm hoping this place can help me one more time."

His eyes held a distant sparkle of memories that perhaps not even Mom knew. Memories that helped him not only escape the apocalypse thrusted upon us, but to escape the stresses of his impending divorce. For a fleeing moment, I pretended we were just a family on vacation since we didn't get many of those over the last few years. I hid the realization that we were banished survivors, running from an unstoppable evil.

"How many times have you been up here, Dad?" I had to ask, curious how much the spot meant to him.

"Since my parents first took me up here when I was about thirteen, wait—no, I was twelve—probably about twenty times. I've tried to come up here at least once a year. But lately…" Dad glanced at Mom. "I've been up here a few times this year." Mom glared at him, knowing she couldn't say much because of her constant absence.

Ava, I, and the mountains stood silent before we all turned to stare into the tranquil sunrise, ignoring the awkward toxicity of our family that didn't falter, even from the world ending. Taking in the view, my eyes followed every mountain's edge, wondering if they could weather storms for millennia. Then perhaps we, too, could find the strength to endure the new, hostile world along with our old, harmful one. With the wind whispering promises of triumph in my ears, I allowed myself a sliver of hope.

"Stay still," Dad hushed, and he placed his hand on mine and Ava's shoulders. The mountain breeze drew attention to the severity of his tone. His eyes fixed on something across the street, narrowing like an eagle eyeing its next meal.

I held my breath, and every muscle froze. Afraid that even the faintest creak of the wooden patio planks could shatter the fragile peace. A tremor of anxiety quivered through me; the sensation was familiar, yet no less frightening.

I saw a movement out of the corner of my eye. Oversized drapes parted, and the fabric rippled. The silhouette of a man's face peeked into the sunlight. His intent was clear as a finger pressed against lips, the universal signal for silence.

Dad's confusion mirrored my own, his forehead creased with concern and intrigue. Was the stranger a friend or foe? He raised his hand to convey friendship, but the drapes fluttered, and the face vanished into the shadows.

"Back away from the railing," Dad instructed with terrifying authority. Ava and I obeyed without hesitation, stepping back toward the entrance. Dad dropped to his knees, scanning the quaint facades of the town with renewed intensity.

"Did you know there were other people here?" I whispered to Ava. She shushed me, but her eyes were wide with the same curiosity and terror. Were we too preoccupied with zombies to not notice other people?

"Quiet," Dad murmured, more to himself than to us. "That could have been a warning or a threat, but either way, we need to get inside." Dad was determined to move all of us to safety. Crouching,

Dad waved all of us inside while he never broke sight of the street as we gathered our things and crept through the door.

A single gesture transformed fresh relaxation into utter fear. Our illusion of safety shattered, and we returned to reality and the truths we had to accept. This predatory world would continue to hunt the living. Dad had always taught us to dream, but never at the cost of our safety.

The next few minutes would require us to put our hopes and dreams aside to keep what little safety we had. Dad's instincts had kept us alive this long, and despite the chill from a stranger, I trusted him to lead us through whatever lay ahead.

Ava remained silent beside me, clutching her backpack like a life vest. We stood in the unknown. The eerie silence of Scoite's Peak wrapped around us like a python, squeezing the air of safety from our lungs.

Without warning, a guttural scream shattered the tranquility. It bounced off the buildings and mountains with an unnatural ferocity. It wasn't entirely human, but more of a synthesized human sound created with electronics. The sound pierced every muscle fiber of my body and radiated into my bones.

"Inside," Dad hissed, motioning us all inside as he joined. We scrambled as our hearts raced, minds reeling at the possibilities of what could have created the sound. It continued to vibrate through the town like a bomb had exploded.

Dad quietly shut the door and peered through the glass, scanning what he could see of the streets below. He desperately wanted to find an answer to the question we all had.

"Is that... one of them?" Ava whispered in a trembling voice.

"I don't know," I replied, my fear on full display. "But Dad's got us."

Dad's silhouette cut a sharp figure against the emerging daylight. An ounce of doubt filled my head, questioning if Dad was a big enough hero to battle the darkness that could have come from a place deeper than hell.

I pressed my back against an icy wall, not feeling anymore safe inside than outside. The air grew thick with a tension that seemed to suffocate us as I realized Mom had snuck past me in the stairwell and was hiding in the second-floor hallway.

"Girls, don't move," the stern whisper helped ease some of my fear.

The scream erupted a second time. It appeared more desperate in distress. The electronic distortion in the voice was more prevalent this time. A sound that had no place in the natural world, a harbinger of something far worse than we could imagine.

"Stay quiet," Dad uttered. His gaze never left the streets. "We don't let it know where we are until we know what it is."

Everything settled for several minutes, but Dad never altered his surveillance.

"Is it gone?" Ava's whisper with fear.

"I don't think so," I shrugged and glanced down at Mom, who hadn't moved an inch.

"Whatever that thing is, it has the green lights on its neck and hands… but it can scream?" Dad's confusion gave me chills. He glanced back at us with a look that conveyed a tear in his superhero cape. It was fear tinged with curiosity, a look that proved Dad wasn't as invincible as we wanted him to be.

"Is it one of those… things?" Ava's voice cracked on the word. The monsters of our new world were too horrific for her or me to comprehend.

"Could be," Dad admitted. "Or something else. Something worse." His words carried a heavy implication that the terrors we encountered could be just the start. The thought of evil gaining power in this world scared me to the very essence of my being.

"Then what do we do?" My voice sounded small. A child's plea to be saved.

"We survive," Dad stated with the strength of steel. "Like we always have."

The wind picked up, carrying the scent of dead leaves and a chill that seeped into our bones as it slipped through the cracks around the door. I closed my eyes, trying to find solace because we were together, but for how long?

CHAPTER 4: NOT ALONE

The stairs creaked under my feet, even as I tiptoed with more care than I'd ever taken in my life. My heart hammered against my ribs, trying to break free from my chest. I followed my family further into the building, moving lighter than a fall breeze, trying not to rustle any leaves.

We reached the second floor, the air thick with silence. Once, the place had buzzed with life, echoes of laughter trapped in the walls. But even our breathing was too loud, too alive for the desolate space.

"Martha, stay close," Ava quietly called as I fell behind. I nodded, though the action felt clumsy and irrelevant. Each door we passed could harbor our worst nightmares. Undead creatures hungry for what brief life remained, or humans who had turned feral in their desperation.

We approached an open door and the tension it created seeped out into the hall. Dad held up a hand, signaling for us to halt. I tried not to imagine what lurked within that room, ready for us. But imagination is a wild thing, especially with fresh fears running amok.

"Stay here," Dad whispered, not removing his eyes from the wide-open door. Mom's expression tightened, a rare glimpse that she still worried about Dad and still held feelings for him.

Martha's Notebook

"Peter, be careful," she said, but the quiver in her voice betrayed her usual bravado. Her eyes never left him as he edged closer to the unknown.

I snatched Ava's hand, seeking courage in her touch. She was always the brave one, at least more than I was. But even protectors get scared, and there was a slight tremor in her touch.

"Whatever happens," Ava murmured so only I could hear, "we stick together, okay?"

"Okay," I agreed. My voice felt like a shout in the hotel's stillness. Whatever lurked behind those doors, whatever monsters awaited us, I knew if we had each other, there was hope. And in our new, twisted world, hope was perhaps the rarest commodity of all.

Dad's silhouette edged forward, a quiet warrior through the dim shards of light piercing the hallway from the scant windows. My breath hitched as he paused next to the door. His gaze fixed on something at his feet. A suitcase, abandoned during a hasty escape. With each step he took into the room, his body tensed, ready for an impromptu battle. He disappeared into the room, I can only assume to clear it from corner to corner.

I crept forward, trying to keep within sight as he disappeared. My heart pounded in a frantic rhythm. Ava gripped my shoulder, which reassured my frantic chest, a reminder that she stood by my side.

"Clear," Dad's voice echoed through the hallway, ceasing my ghastly nightmares.

When Dad's words hit our ears, Mom surged into the room. Her ego propelled her to safety without a thought of our well-being. For a moment, I wondered if she even remembered Ava and I existed, whether our safety even crossed her single-minded determination to secure her own comfort first.

"Let's go," Ava sighed as Mom disappeared into the room. We followed her into our temporary sanctuary, or prison. The line between the two was perilously thin.

The stagnant room greeted us with messy sheets on one bed while the second bed remained unused. A bathroom light illuminated as much as the sparse sunrise. Untouched by the chaos that reigned outside its walls, the room felt typical aside from the discarded suitcase. It was a pocket of normalcy high in the mountains.

Dad nudged the suitcase aside and gingerly shut the door.

An unusual scream rang out, a terrifying second reminder that we weren't alone. Dad's protective presence gave me a scrap of confidence, a sense of security in our continued nightmare.

Dad shuffled toward the window, his movements slow and deliberate. The muscles in his back tensed, a testament to the burden of our survival that he shouldered every waking moment. His fingers barely disturbed the heavy, gray fabric of the curtain as he peered out, searching for the source of the soul-piercing, distorted wail.

"See anything?" Ava whispered, and her words echoed ominously in the hushed room.

Dad didn't respond, his focus locked in on the desolate street below. I could feel the weight of his focus, as if finding the creature could rid the world of them.

Meanwhile, Mom, with a grunt of relief, let her precious safe thud onto the carpeted closet floor. Dad snapped a glare at her careless act before returning to his perch. She nudged it with her foot, but it didn't budge at all. Following that, she closed the door with a decisive click. I wondered if shutting the door was more to protect the safe than to protect us. The monstrosities surrounding us wouldn't matter if the precious safe had protection.

Ava and I claimed a bed, the messy mattress giving a comforting creak under our weight as we both bounced onto it. Our minds were weary from the endless hours filled with nightmares that bled into reality. We gained solace in the simple act of sitting side by side, shoulders touching in unity.

"Anything, Daddy?" I asked, as I reverted into an innocent child for a fleeting moment. I wanted him to say no, that the streets were clear, that we could breathe easy even if just for today. But part of me, the part growing up too fast in my fractured environment, knew better than to expect such pity.

He shook his head slowly, but kept his eyes trained on the scene below. Bated breath was an understatement, since he didn't seem to inhale or exhale for several minutes.

"Not yet," he murmured. "But we must always stay alert. Rest while you can," Dad encouraged, still glued to the window.

"Will we be okay?" I asked, the words escaping like a plea.

Ava wrapped her arm around me, pulling me close. "As long as we're together, we're more than okay. We're a family. That's what matters, Martha."

Mom plopped onto the untouched bed as she untucked the edge and slipped underneath.

"Who did you hide that safe from?" Dad's voice sliced through the tense silence with a sarcastic tone, maybe taking a jab at Mom for including the bulky item in our search for safety.

Mom just smiled, a wry twist to her lips. "From the poor, desperate people of the world, of course." Her tone mocked the gravity of our situation.

Dad's sigh felt like a volcano on the verge of erupting. His disgust at her selfishness was palpable, a thick cloud of disapproval that darkened the room. Without another word, Dad kept his precautions focused on the street. I never knew people could continue their bitterness toward one another, even as impending doom lingered around us.

Mom stretched her arms above her head, groaning with the effort. The heavy safe had burdened her muscles since we left. An anchor of wealth she couldn't leave behind, even when speed and movement meant everything for survival.

"Let's get comfortable, girls," she said, patting the mattress next to her. Ava shot a look at me, one that spoke volumes of her tolerance being tested, before she carefully hopped up and sat down beside Mom.

I could almost believe we were safe. We could make it work, wait out the monsters like a terrible storm. Ava and I could mediate between Mom and Dad. Maybe there was hope of some semblance of a future.

But we still couldn't escape our reality, not when Dad remained vigilant by the window. His silhouette, a constant reminder of the dangers that lurked beyond our sanctuary. He sat perched like an eagle soaring through the sky, eyes locked on any hint of movement or any sign of a threat. It was both reassuring and terrifying, knowing he braced himself for whatever came next. Ready to defend us.

"Try to rest," Mom said. Her voice felt nurturing, which was unusual. Perhaps exhaustion overtook her ego. The room felt too energized for sleep, though. Every one of my muscles tensed for the next unknown scream.

"Will things ever be normal again?" I whispered. The question slipped out into the separated light, but I didn't expect an answer.

"*Normal* is nothing more than a setting on a dryer, sweetie." Mom's attempt at humor fell flat, absorbed by the fear swirling through the room.

The light of dawn crept through the crack in the curtains, casting eerie shadows of buildings harboring an unknown number of people, either friend or foe.

Dad's demeanor quickly transformed. His stare deepened as his face inched closer to the windowpane. The muscles in his neck popped out like rigid iron bars. "Is that what made the noise?" His voice was hardly above a whisper, but it cut through the serenity of the room like a knife.

Ava, Mom, and I shot up from our relaxed positions, jarred by Dad's words. We knew better than to rush to the window and expose ourselves, but the need to see the face of our enemy clawed at us with desperate fingers.

"There's someone out there," Dad said without turning away from the window. His voice vibrated with a low growl of concern and disbelief. "It's a woman. She's just... just walking down the middle of the street. No concern or fear whatsoever."

My imagination painted a picture more fear inducing than any reality my eyes could have witnessed. One of those zombies with elongated arms and disfigured legs, limping down the street with blood drooling from its enlarged mouth filled with broken shark teeth. Eyes like pools of evil as it hunted for its next meal.

"Does she look... like one of them?" Mom's voice trembled with the question we all dreaded the answer to.

"There's a green glow on the back of her neck and hands. And she's limping on a mangled leg." Dad confirmed our fears, though far tamer than what I had imagined. That unnatural luminescence became a warning of the plague encroaching on us.

"Is she heading toward us?" Ava's voice cracked and she crumbled under the sheets for protection.

Dad didn't respond immediately, his eyes still trained on the lone figure outside. Finally, he shook his head in a subtle gesture. His body language did little to ease the tension that gripped us. "Can't tell yet." His shoulders hunched as though bracing against a storm only he could see. "But we need to be ready for anything."

"Ready for anything" could be our family's unspoken motto. A mantra we could live by in our toxic, common world that translated well to our new environment. Readiness couldn't quell the terror that gnawed at my insides. It couldn't soothe the ache of longing for a past we could never reclaim.

Ava wrapped her arms around herself, a self-protective gesture that conveyed both strength and vulnerability. Mom bit her lip, a line of worry etched between her brows. And me? I clung to the hope that

Dad, our protector, would keep the horrors at bay for as long as he had the strength to.

The urge to see the outside world tugged at me. I knew Ava felt it, too. We whispered to each other, seeing one another itching to sprint toward the window. "Let's just take a quick look." Ava's blue eyes screamed with curiosity and terror.

"No." The word broke through our conversation like a runaway semi-truck. Dad's voice was firm, leaving no room for argument. "We can't risk moving the curtains too much. It could draw their attention. And I'm not sure I want you two to see… what happens out there if anything does?"

His words were a cold bucket of water on our fiery curiosity. With a heavy sigh, I settled back onto the bed. As much as I wanted to ignore Dad, I understood. He was our only shield against anything outside, and his desire to keep us safe fueled his caution. Dad turned to us as a look of empathy washed over him. "I'll explain everything that's happening outside, okay?" His eyes scanned mine, then Ava's, searching for understanding.

We nodded, hungry for every scrap of information he would share. While Ava and I were all nerves and eagerness, Mom flopped back into her bed. She closed her eyes like she could shut out the apocalypse with her eyelids. Not a single worry seemed to thread through her mind, or if it did, she was an expert at hiding it.

"Outside," Dad shared in a hushed tone. "The woman is still limping down the middle of the street." His words confused. Nothing had changed since he spotted her. "That green glow on the neck and hands, that's how you know they're not… not human anymore."

My grip on the bed sheet tightened, knuckles whitening. The image of that eerie, unnatural glow invaded my thoughts like my dream.

"Is she dangerous?" I knew they were, but maybe the mangled leg depressed her lethality.

"Very," Dad replied. "But not just her. All those things are dangerous, and we must always assume they are dangerous.

"Thanks, Dad…" Ava said, mustering a smile to mask her fear. "For keeping us informed and for protecting us."

He nodded, and I glimpsed a smile cross his face. Then he returned to his watchful vigil at the window. The weight of a family's survival rested on his shoulders. "Try to get some sleep, girls," he mentioned without looking back. "I've got this."

I glanced at Ava, who offered me a small, reassured nod. Relaxation filled us as we snuggled into our beds. Even with my body taking a break, my mind continued to race. As much as I yearned for the comfort of sleep, I knew the specter of the woman with the green glow and the mangled leg chasing me would haunt my dreams.

As my eyes closed for a moment of tranquility, it shattered just as quickly. "She stopped," Dad mumbled to anyone who wasn't asleep. "She's in the center of town, not moving a muscle."

Ava and I sprung back up, staring at Dad with the blankets still wrapped around us.

"Her head it… it just snapped backward." The words fell from Dad's lips in disbelief. "Like a puppet with its strings yanked too hard."

I imagined it, a gruesome marionette jerking in ways only a marionette could, and I shivered. From the corner of my eye, Mom's chest rose and fell with an oblivious rhythm, her worries locked away with the safe.

Another unnatural scream reverberated in the city. Dad shivered in disgust. "She created that noise." Dad appeared like he didn't want to be the lookout anymore, but didn't want any of us to watch. "That scream… It's not human, not anymore. It's screaming with no one around, though. Is this some sort of trap, or disfunction of whatever is controlling this thing?" Dad continued to talk to himself as we listened.

My heart raced. Ava and I exchanged glances, sharing a wordless conversation of fear and curiosity. We didn't need to see it to feel the horror that crept along the edges of our sanctuary.

"Is it done?" Ava's voice quaked, and her innocence begged for the correct answer.

"Yes," he nodded slowly, swallowing hard. "For now. She lowered her head to 'normal' and started walking, again, like nothing happened."

"Like she's not a monster…" My voice released some pent-up anger at them.

"Exactly," Dad confirmed. His eyes drifted back to the window. He absorbed the terror outside, so we wouldn't.

"Will we be okay, Dad?" I knew he would tell me what I wanted to hear no matter what.

"Always," he replied without hesitation. His silhouette in the sliver of morning sun became a comforting sight. "As long as I'm here, you'll always be safe."

My breath caught in my throat as Dad mumbled in desperation. "No. No. You idiot, no. Go back inside." His words blended into a whispered chant. Ava hopped back into my bed and her hand squeezed mine like we were watching a horror movie.

"Dad, what's happening?" Ava's voice couldn't reach Dad through his quiet chant, repeating over and over.

Then a deep, manly voice echoed off our walls, pleading for mercy. "No! Don't! Please don't! Please… stop!"

Dad jerked backwards away from the window as if yanked by an unseen force. He crashed to the floor with a thud that shook our fragile room. My heart thumped wildly against my ribs, fear spreading throughout me like wildfire.

Mom awoke in a violent thrust, peering around the room at the creator or the noise until she noticed Dad slumped on the floor in a trance.

"Is he—is he okay? What happened?" Ava's questions trickled out of her terrified mouth.

I ran to Dad and kneeled beside him. He remained in a state of shock, motionless. "Dad? Are you okay?" I pleaded for a response.

He remained motionless. His eyes wide open yet unresponsive, like the horror outside had reached in and stolen his soul. Silence overtook the room aside from our anxious breaths. We waited for Dad to break the heavy and oppressive silence.

"Peter?" Monica's voice cut in like a raft thrown into the void. We hoped she could snag a piece of reality we could hold on to, but even her words seemed to dissolve in the thick air, unanswered. We were alone with our fears and the world outside continued its descent into hell.

The silence bore down on us in a harsh contrast to the earlier cries of terror. Finally, Mom's voice cut through the stillness of the room again. Her voice oozed with a desperation I'd never heard before. "Peter, what happened? Tell us!"

Dad's response was barely audible, yet it thundered in my ears like a clap of lightning striking my brain. "There's... more of them," he mumbled, lips barely moving. "It wasn't just the girl."

Mom's sharp intake of breath mirrored mine. Our eyes fixed on Dad, wanting him to explain.

"More of them?" Mom questioned through curiosity and anxiety.

"Six... there were six others," Dad whispered in a hollow tone. "They came out of the alleys and buildings. They ambushed him." A mask of horror covered his face, pale and injected with dread.

I couldn't stop myself from asking, even though I feared the answer. "What do you mean, *ambushed*? Is the man okay?"

Dad's head slowly turned as his eyes pierced the haunted look on my face. "It doesn't matter, Martha." His voice gained strength, but it was the strength of despair. "We need to secure this room now."

Ava launched from her bed in response to Dad's words. She shoved furniture against the door with a determination beyond her teen years. Dad struggled to his feet as every movement seemed to cost him pieces of his sanity. I wanted to help and prove a strength I knew I didn't possess. I wanted to become the strong woman I always dreamed of being, not just for myself, but for Ava, Mom, and Dad.

I grabbed a chair and dragged it across the carpet to pile onto our makeshift barricade.

"We need to be quiet," Mom cautioned, her usual self-centered demeanor momentarily overtaken by the instinct to survive.

We all came together. The urgency of the situation forced us to create safety in a hushed manner. Each thud of furniture against the doorframe called attention to our survival. The Noirytzs were going to survive, no matter what we had to do.

Without understanding her actions, Mom shoved everything away from the door just enough so she could toss the unknown suitcase across the hallway.

"Stupid Thing," Mom mumbled as the suitcase smashed into the adjacent door, unleashing a thunderous bang as it fell to the floor while the thud ricocheted throughout the hotel like a scream in the Grand Canyon. My heart skipped a few beats as Mom, Ava, and I froze, wondering if the zombies could hear the sound. Dad knew better and immediately sprinted to the door and, as quietly as possible, shoved our barricade against the door again.

"Are you trying to get us killed?" Dad hissed, shooting a glare at Mom. She fired a smirk of arrogant confidence right back.

I ran and dove into bed and pulled the comforter up over my head, a poor protection against a potential onslaught waiting outside. I peeked out and noticed Ava copied me on the opposite bed. Dad remained still, a statue of shock with his stare burning through the door.

"Stay quiet," Ava whispered, pulling the covers over her eyes. "Maybe they didn't hear that."

For a moment, I believed we were lucky enough for the sound to not reach the street. Then the shattering glass below snapped me back to reality, fracturing the fragile hope Ava tried to cultivate.

Safety fell away fast as an icy chill hit my body through the thick blanket. Stampeding rushed the stairwell like an earthquake on a mission. It was the sound of doom climbing the stairs for us. I couldn't move, couldn't breathe. Dad, Mom, Ava, no one moved an inch. The four of us barely released a breath.

Please, please, please, I chanted in my head, too scared to speak and not wanting to draw extra attention.

Seconds stretched into eternity. The rumbling roared down the hallway. The herd of nightmares rushed past our door, but our relief was short-lived when destruction began feet from our barricaded door.

The crash of a door being obliterated echoed through the building. All I could do was pray nobody was hiding in the adjacent room. We heard glass shatter and furniture smash across the hall. Then, a distinct sound rang out from the street.

"Was that a gunshot?" Ava whispered, then immediately covered her mouth.

Dad's rigid posture broke as he tip-toed toward the window, like a shadow gliding across the wall. We watched, holding our breaths as he slid the curtain aside ever so gently. Curiosity pulled Dad's attention back to the street.

Another thunderous boom split the air, followed by a distant, triumphant shout. "I think I got one dem sum-bitches!" The male voice bellowed through the town with a raspy tinge.

As if provoked, the horde outside our room erupted in a second frenzy. Once again, the earth-shattering rumble stampeded down the stairs after the survivor that fought back against the new evil. We could almost track the monsters down the stairs. Then more glass shattered as they reached the street. Dad recoiled from the window, squeezing his eyes shut hard, like he was trying to extract the images from his mind. His body betrayed the steel nerves he'd always shown us.

"Is it over? Did the stranger win?" I whispered as female screams rang out that answered my question. Dad remained motionless with his hands pressed hard against his closed eyes as if he could hide from the horrors.

"Peter, please. What happened this time?" Mom's voice cracked with sincere concern.

"I can't... don't ask me to explain it," Dad choked out the few words he could manage as he tried to preserve his sanity.

"Stay with us, Dad," Ava begged softly as she reached out toward him from the covers.

But there was no comfort to give, not when every echo of shattered glass and every cry that seeped through the walls told us a monstrous truth. These new apex predators were relentless monsters that had transformed from the earlier creatures we'd seen in our neighborhood. We never witnessed traps or anything like Dad described.

I felt the room close in. Claustrophobia strangled my sanity. Like the comfortable hotel rooms we enjoyed many times on trips to Sio Chain, Aillacht, or Foscad City, transformed into a small jail cell where we had the keys, but terror chained us to the room. Dad's frame shuddered as he crept back to the window for one more glance. He shuttered so violently it seemed to rattle his bones.

Whatever horrors played out beyond the glass were enough to drive him from his perch at the window, and he crawled into bed like a snail. Without making a sound, he vanished beneath the blankets.

Climbing into our adjacent beds, Ava and my eyes connected. Our eyes screamed in absolute terror without either of us creating a peep. I nodded mutely, understanding the weight of Dad's burden. Ava had always been a brave one, but with Dad lost in his own silence, her role became even more pronounced. We were two sisters in a broken family that had become a broken world. We clung to the fragile hope that behind the walls, we might somehow remain untouched by the death that roamed freely outside.

Mom gave up on Dad and nestled into bed.

"Promise me, Martha," Ava whispered, pulling the covers over her shoulder. "Promise me we'll always look after each other."

"I promise," I whispered back. Promises felt like flimsy things, too easily broken by the creatures we shared the air with. But I'd say anything to see a glimmer of reassurance in Ava's eyes. Maybe we could survive together and still become famous photographers and poets.

As I rolled over to stare at the ceiling and attempt to get some rest, the chaos of the outside world seemed like an impending nightmare, ready to pounce on my motionless body. Bringing the blanket up to my chin, its warmth enveloped me. A relaxing sensation ran down my body.

I melted deeper into the mattress as exhaustion overtook my body and adrenaline dissolved. The familiar scent of Dad mixed with the musty air of the room reminded me of soccer trips for Ava or my Spelling Bees. It was a scent that spoke of safety, of a time before the madness began. It was an uncomfortable feeling to become so relaxed as my mind dove into memories just moments after what I thought was certain death. I shut my eyelids as each blink became a struggle. For a moment, a fleeting second, I allowed myself the luxury of peace, letting the world fade away as slumber claimed me.

I closed my eyes as the softness of the pillow cradled my head. An eerie, calm silence overtook the town, like night had fallen in the middle of the day. Dad's quiet breathing beside me was the gentle rhythm that kept my thoughts from capsizing into panic. It lulled me to the brink of sleep.

My body, weary from the relentless tide of adrenaline and fear, surrendered to exhaustion. Each muscle relaxed, every tense fiber unwound, and my mind drifted. The safety of the blanket allowed me to slip away from the horrors that prowled beyond the walls of our sanctuary.

Just as I teetered on the edge of consciousness, a voice sliced through our walls, unnatural, but familiar at the same time. A distorted female voice laced with electronic undertones a human couldn't create alone. A fresh wave of terror created from a single word. "Hello?"

My eyes snapped open simultaneously with the pounding of my heart. I held my breath, straining to hear more, but there was nothing. The ghost of that single word hung in the air. A new variable that sent ripples of fear across my mind.

I remained motionless under the covers. Was that voice generated from the same creature that had just removed more people from this world? Exhaustion weighed heavier on my eyes, and they shut once again. My mind slipped away into dreamland as the same voice rang out. I couldn't decipher if it originated from reality or my dreams, but it haunted me either way. "Please come outside."

CHAPTER 5: STRANGERS

Sun light danced across my eyelids as the Sun peeked through the crack in the curtains. I woke to an eerie silence except for the soft breaths of my family enjoying their naps. It was about mid-afternoon when I remembered the terrifying voice that intertwined with my dreams. I peeked at Dad, his light snoring implied rem sleep had him hostage. It was my chance to peek at the streets below. A chance to see the haunting images that tortured Dad.

I slipped out of bed and snuck over to the window. The gateway to visions that caused my hero to become catatonic were within reach.

The window grew closer until I could almost see objects through the sliver of light in the window. A voice whispered to me in an uncompromising tone. "They're all gone. The zombies left. Get back in bed." Dad's voice contained more life than seconds ago, but it wasn't the time to test his seriousness. I immediately turned around and hopped back into bed.

Climbing back into bed, my fingers fumbled for the familiar leather-bound spine in my backpack. I nearly forgot about my notebook, but I updated it amid the chaos of our overwhelming life. As I opened it, the blank pages yawned wide, ready to swallow the terrors seared into my mind from the past days. I hadn't written about the nightmare during our drive to Scoite's Peak, the one that had my heart ensnared in the jaws of fear, the time we almost lost Dad, or all the appalling times Mom made it clear she was the only one who mattered. I needed to engrave every detail into the pages before new ones entered our haven.

My pen skated across the page, and the terrifying images clawed their way back into my consciousness. The zombies' eyes were bloodshot and vacant, like their microchips had devoured their souls. That infamous light we feared with its unholy green glow. Those hands that clawed for Dad, hungry for the life he clung to.

My head screamed in terror as my pen screamed in excitement. Each word helped me step away from the darkness that loomed in my mind. The scratching of pen against paper was a soothing rhythm in the silent room that gave me company.

"Martha?" Ava's soft voice struggled as she rubbed her eyes. I looked up to see her blinking away the remnants of her own dreams, or nightmares. Her smile shined, but her watery eyes revealed a nighttime battle with demons. "Couldn't sleep much either?" she whispered as she sat up in bed.

She scanned the room until she noticed Mom and Dad entangled in the sheets like fast food burritos partially coming undone. Dad's chest rose and fell in the steady rhythm of deep sleep, even after his brief words. Mom, oddly asleep but ready, seemed like she could spring out of bed at any moment to run to work. Her arms bent at angles reminiscent of the safe she guarded our entire journey. A grim symbol of her self-serving nature.

"Nightmares," I admitted, trying not to disturb Mom or Dad.

"Putting that notebook to good use, eh?" Ava smirked as her eyes lit up and she nodded at my notebook. "You probably have a lot to write about with everything we've been through. Keep writing and I don't doubt your words will help somebody one day, even if it's the last person on Earth."

We chuckled, and her encouraging words lifted me. It was more than just recounting terror; it was exorcising demons. Banishing them to the pages where they could no longer haunt me.

As the last sentence trailed off, an enormous weight dropped from my shoulders. Perhaps Ava was right. Perhaps I could survive the world where society crumbled before our eyes. Outlets were the only armor we had against the darkness, both imagined and physical.

"Let's hope today is zombie-less," I stated and closed the notebook with a gentle thud and tossed it between my legs on top of the covers.

"Every day we're alive and together is a good day," Ava replied. Her optimism hit as a stark contrast to the bleak reality beyond the walls of our haven. She glanced at our parents, probably remembering the toxic life we desired to escape. Little did we understand the nightmares outside our hotel bubble.

Ava stretched, causing the bed to creak. The sheets rippled as Mom tussled in bed. Immediately, she mumbled, "Where is it? Safe? Where's the safe?" She launched herself to a sitting position and her stone-cold eyes searched the room.

"Mom, you *hid* the safe in the closet." Ava said as Mom stretched her arms upward before diving back into the bed.

With the violence of a storm, Dad flung himself upright and his breath shot out in sharp gasps. Dad's panicked eyes scanned the room just like Mom's did, but with a sincere concern buried behind them. He exhaled deeply, then laid back down with a confused smile. It appeared I wasn't singled out with sleep nightmares after the day we had. Dad's eyes softened as he spotted us sitting in bed. His love radiated an unspoken promise in the blinding chaos of existence. I felt it wrap around me even as silence reclaimed the space.

As my family awoke, I tried to cover my notebook. Then, I leaned toward Ava and asked, "Where's your…" I forced a couple fake coughs as I glanced past Ava at Dad. "Well, you still have *it*, right?"

Her eyes lit up when she remembered her camera. "Oh, yeah!" Her hand flew to her mouth, muffling the sound too late. Her eyes widened with the realization that our safety hung by a thread, not knowing Dad had verified the zombies vacated the town.

I chuckled as I put her terror to rest. "Don't worry, Dad said we're alone in town again."

Mom's eyes erupted in annoyance in Ava's direction. "Can't you two just keep quiet?" Mom lashed out with zero concern at the volume of her voice.

Ava dissolved into the bed, her usual confidence deflated like a punctured balloon. Although she had disdain for Mom, she still loved her and hated upsetting either parent. She crept with exaggerated slowness and reached under her pillow with a deliberate caution. Her fingers located her camera and freed it with uncontained excitement.

As the camera emerged, Ava instantly shot a picture of our hotel room. The shutter echoed like a jackhammer in the silence of our room. She must have forgotten how loud the shutter on the camera was. Unlike my outlet, hers was a little more expensive and warranted a harsher reaction from our parents.

Ava's lapse might have been minor with other parents, but in our family, with our mother, money mattered more than life. I held my breath, waiting for the fallout from the stirring of rogue undead outside or Mom inside.

Mom's brown eyes turned red as they attempted to evaporate the camera from Ava's hands. "Where did you get that from, Ava Pyu Noirytz?" Mom's voice felt like an eruption bubbling below the surface.

"Monica, we don't have time for petty things like a camera." Dad cut in to keep the peace.

"Did you know about this, Peter?"

Martha's Notebook

"No, but it doesn't matter right now. Even if she explains how she got the camera, what are you going to do, return it? I don't think any stores are open for returns or will even care about returns right now."

"Stop with your sarcasm." Mom's penetrating stare never left Ava as she responded to Dad. "You, missy... we will discuss this later and you will explain where you got the money for that camera."

"You two can discuss the camera when the apocalypse is over." Dad made one more attempt to soften the rage boiling in the room. Mom's glare transferred to Dad, then she slid out of bed in frustration.

The following silence felt like glass, fragile and clear, and each breath felt loud enough to crack it. Ava's camera sat in her lap. Dad's eyes narrowed with intrigue, not anger, as he stared in Ava's direction.

Ava crumbled under the weight of the words, her shoulders curved inward as if she could fold into herself and disappear. But then, with a courage that made my heart swell, she lifted her chin. "I bought it!" she exclaimed. "I needed an outlet... something for myself. With everything going on between you two—"

"Your parents' divorce, you mean? So, it's my fault you have this expensive looking camera?" Mom cut Ava off, her glare shifting between us like a lighthouse beam, warning us of rocky times ahead. Mom's eyes narrowed on my partially covered notebook. "And what about you, Martha Priom Noirytz? Is that your outlet?"

My mouth went dry. Ava had saved, planned, and bought my notebook to provide the same savior she had. I couldn't leave her on an island of Mom's rage all alone.

Something built up inside me. For the first time, I felt a flash of Ava's strength lift me to bravery. "I bought mine, too. I needed something to help me with the... divorce."

"Saved up," Mom scoffed, turning back to Dad. "Well, what are you going to do about this, Peter?"

Dad's eyes met mine, and there was an understanding. A silent agreement that some battles weren't worth fighting. He chuckled, a sound that seemed out of place in our tense situation. "Should I ground them? Tell them they can't go outside, or they must stay within sight? Monica, look around. They're already being punished for something. I think we can let this go."

Mom snorted, realizing Dad was right, but hating it all the same.

"The girls could hide way worse things than notebooks and cameras as their outlets," Dad said, empathizing with us.

As Mom's anger simmered to a boiling stovetop pot, Dad stretched and emerged from his bed. Ava and I desperately tried to hide our "outlets" before Mom's rage could begin a second round.

"We should head out soon," Dad called out as he peeked through the curtains and focused on the path ahead. Dad's leadership powered the family as we all grabbed our things and prepared to leave like warriors preparing for a battle.

Ava and I exchanged glances, and her lips curved into a frightened but grateful smile. No matter what happened with Mom and Dad, we were two sisters against a world that had transformed into a silent hell. We tucked our emotional lifelines into our backpacks in a flash and hoped Mom wouldn't notice. She was too busy removing her financial lifeline from the closet.

"Alright, everyone. Ready for our first day of vacation?" Dad's joke cut through the tension. A classic dad joke that amused everyone but Mom, but they were never for her. Ava and I giggled despite the bleak future in front of us. Mom rolled her eyes so hard I could almost hear them spinning in their sockets.

"Really? Because we're hiding in a hotel room? Are you kidding me?" Her dry questions hit the room like a wet blanket.

Dad replied with an exaggerated nod. "Better go grab a bite from the continental breakfast before we head out. Save me a waffle."

Our laughter rose a pitch higher with a twinge of sadness at the absurdity of it all, knowing we could never go back to those days. They were officially distant memories.

We lined up at the door like children waiting for recess. A pang of fear built from us, leaving the security of the walls, even if something could tear that safety away at any moment.

Mom finally wiggled the safe out of the closet and jerked it up off the ground.

"Monica, are you going to lug that safe everywhere?" Dad asked, and each word oozed with frustration. He stood in front of the door like a bouncer about to deny Mom and her safe entry into the outside world.

She flashed a crooked smile that chilled me until I physically shook. "I must. There are things in this safe that I need to keep secure. Things that could destroy our world."

"Things? What 'things,' Monica?" Dad's words hit heavy as terror weighed them down. "How could whatever is in that safe *destroy our world* any more than it already is?"

"Obviously, it contains money and several things like the girl's birth certificates and our passports, but there are things from work I just can't leave anyone else in control of."

"Like what? What's in the damn safe, Monica?"

She ignored his probing while her fingers wrapped around the dark metal. His anger simmered, threatening to boil over, but the contents of the safe remained a mystery as Mom threatened to shove the safe straight through Dad's chest. "I'll replace your heart with this chest if you ask what's inside again."

"Can we just go?" I tried my best to diffuse the tension, but a shock ran through my body when my parents turned toward me. I wish I could be as strong as Dad or even Ava.

Somehow, I did enough that Mom and Dad stopped arguing, and Dad focused on the door again. His body stiffened, accompanied by a deep sigh of fear. The door handle squeaked as Dad inched it downward. A small rush of air flowed in as a gap formed and Dad peered through the slice for a view into the hallway.

I snatched Ava's hand from her backpack strap and squeezed it in terror. Were zombies waiting for us on the other side of the door? Ava's hand tightened around mine as Dad eased the door open and a sliver of morning light cut through the dim hotel room. His body stiffened when he slipped into the hallway and shut the door behind him. A soft whistle broke the silence, Dad's signal that the coast was clear.

As Mom swung the door wide open, my breath hitched at the sight across the hall. A reminder of the devastation the zombies could create, laid at our feet. An obliterated door left a gaping view into the devastation of splinters and shredded fabric. A testament to the horrors that transpired feet from where we hid. A chilling reminder that death could remove us from this world at any moment.

"Let's go… quietly," Dad whispered in an urgent tone.

We scurried down the hallway, then down the stairs.

We strolled through the lobby as complacency came over us until Dad's arm shot out like a security barrier, separating us from a danger we weren't aware of.

Two figures strolled down the street, a dark-skinned man in a black hoodie and jeans hand in hand with a pale woman wearing a light pink hoodie that covered her brown hair and black yoga pants. My heart ceased mid-beat, and my brain followed suit. Something was different about the couple. The characteristic green glow that instigated terror was absent. Their movements lacked the jerky marionette dance of the zombies we became familiar with.

Dad crept toward the entrance and motioned for us to hide. His eyes never left the pair. There was a calculated risk in every decision, and I trusted his instincts implicitly. Like a lion hunting its prey, every step was lighter than air as he cautiously stepped between broken pieces of glass. He reached the shattered glass doors, then continued to watch the couple from a crouched position. With the subtlety of a ninja, he inched it open to steal a better view as they continued down the gravel road.

Mom, burdened with the safe she insisted on carrying, decided she would make a run for the car. Mom's stubbornness launched her into Dad, and their tumble flung the door and Dad into the open. The safe caught on the door with a metallic screech before tumbling to the ground in a thunderous commotion. Ava and I sprinted toward Mom, trying to stop the decision she had already put into motion.

Time seemed to stop as everyone froze. The couple whipped around with the man's shotgun aimed directly at Mom and Dad. A standoff between the living amid a world filled with the dead.

"Monica, what have you done?" Dad whispered in terror as his body remained frozen. Fear boiled up in our family, along with the strangers. Would it be our last minutes alive, or would these people become allies?

"Please…" Dad struggled to ride the line between whisper and scream as he raised his hands in empathy. "We're not a threat."

My heart rode the line between a million beats and none, a frantic Morse code pleading for safety. The standstill stretched on, a taut wire threatening to snap with the slightest movement.

"Lower the gun," Mom demanded in her stern, motherly voice. A familiar tone she used on Ava and me whenever we would play catch and I missed the ball, causing it to break whatever expensive flowerpots were near us.

"Mom…" Ava's hushed, but it carried the weight of our shared anxiety.

The man hesitated, his eyes bounced between us and the woman by his side. Slowly, ever so slowly, the barrel of the shotgun lowered. The man pointed the shotgun at the ground and released one of his hands from it. It was an unspoken language of truce in a world with few words.

"Thank you," Dad exhaled. Our relief was palpable, but the echoes of the dropped safe still rang in my ears. Luck was on our side for the moment, but we had to remember that a selfish mistake like that could cost us everything.

The woman whispered urgently to the man. His shotgun clunked against his thigh as he motioned us forward, then placed a stern finger to his lips.

"Quiet," he mouthed, eyes darting to the bulky safe Mom protected like a newborn. With a shake of his head, he signaled its abandonment.

Dad locked eyes with Mom as he whispered in agreement with the stranger. "Monica, leave it. We got lucky this time, but I will not risk our safety a second time."

Mom's face twisted in disdain. The veins in her neck bulged with silent protest. Yet, she surrendered with a loud eye roll. "Fine but give me a minute." Mom's rage mixed with understanding, but everything had to be on her terms as usual. Mom lugged the safe back inside, leaving us suspended in uncertainty as we stared at the gouge left in the gravel sidewalk.

Hours dragged on, then I realized it was only minutes before Mom emerged. The absent safe felt like a missing member of our circle until relief washed over me. We would have far fewer issues without it.

Dad's expression vibrated between relief and concern. "Where did you hide it?" he probed.

An evil smile hit Mom's lips. "Let's just say I secured my secrets. If you ever hope to uncover them, I'd suggest protecting me as much as the girls."

"Why am I not surprised? Always looking out for number one." Dad's disappointment seeped through his words as his resentment grew.

"I'm looking out for the ones I care about." Mom's icy retort hit us all. Did she not care about any of us anymore?

Two strangers looked on, our toxic family on full display. Mom and Dad's fighting pulled us back to a familiar scene that acted as a moment of relief from the threats of this world.

Our cautious steps crunched the gravel as we approached the strangers. Their anxious eyes pleaded for silence. Tension radiated from Dad as he scanned our surroundings. His protection ramped up as we neared the strangers. The mountain road between us felt like a mile as we scrutinized every movement of danger.

Barely daring to breathe, we met the unfamiliar couple. The tension exploded without warning as the serene landscape shattered. A guttural, electronic roar reverberated through the air. The mocking, unnatural scream of the creatures. We froze, immediately connecting with the strangers over a life-threatening warning that came for all of us.

Dad's eyes met the man's in a silent exchange of terror and strength. With a swift hand gesture, the man ushered us toward the woods just a few buildings away in the direction they walked.

Branches slapped against my face as we plunged into the underbrush while the forest swallowed us whole. We didn't stop until the world we knew vanished behind a curtain of leaves and shadows. A ravine gave us safety as we took a moment to breathe and introduce ourselves. Our voices shook in the weight of our situation.

"So, who are you two?" Dad asked in a cautious tone, unsure if an answer would follow.

"I'm Samuel. This is my girlfriend, Jordan," the man replied quick and blunt.

"Samuel," Dad acknowledged, "and Jordan. Nice to meet you two. I'm Peter. These are my daughters, Martha and Ava, and my wife, Monica." Monica scoffed at the word "wife."

Samuel nodded. His story unfolded in a whisper, painting a grim picture of the previous onslaughts in town. First, rogue zombies had devoured families, businesspeople, and much of the city. Next, dozens lost their lives to relentless investigative zombies. After that, they'd hoped silence would spare them, but Dad witnessed how that played out.

"We thought by staying quiet, maybe they would think the town was deserted," Samuel concluded, weighted down by defeat.

My breath came out in short, frosty bursts as we huddled close to the earth's cold embrace. While the ravine offered a natural hiding spot, we discussed other related horrors. Dad's eyes fixed on Samuel, who had the same forged look of steel from similar soul-shaking events. Dad and Samuel's similar protective instincts radiated outward.

"Samuel, what have you seen them do?" Dad's question hung in the air. A question our family was curious and terrified to learn the answer to. I could see Dad's own visual horrors filling his mind.

Samuel's eyes glazed like he visualized the nightmares he was about to recount. "It wasn't much different from what you saw." Samuel's exhale released some of the terror in his voice. "About twenty unarmed or lightly armed humans against a horde…" His voice trailed off, but the silence gave a terrifying backdrop for our imaginations to run with.

A shiver ran through me, not from the icy fall breeze, but from the truth behind Samuel's words. All the books, the late-night horror movies I used to watch, they were nothing compared to this unstoppable nightmare.

"Is there any way to stop them? To fight back?" A fragile hope filled Dad's eyes. He leaned in closer, as if trying to will a positive answer into existence.

Samuel licked his lips, a gesture of nervousness or perhaps contemplation. "They act like zombies from the movies we've all watched, except they consume everything. Flesh, bone… nothing remains. We've seen them stand up to guns, knives. Nothing seems to stop them." His words stole the air from my lungs. My mind flew through all the possibilities that zombies could withstand.

"But there are rumors. Some survivors say you can kill them by destroying a microchip. Neither of us have gotten close enough to confirm that, though." Samuel glanced at Jordan and her horrified eyes as she slowly nodded.

Dad's hand instinctively went to the back of his neck, his fingers brushing over skin and muscle as if searching for something that wasn't there. He momentarily lost focus, and I knew he remembered the zombie he'd fought off. The way it crumpled to the ground when the microchip shattered.

"Microchip? It only takes one?" Dad asked, more to himself than to anyone else. "I've seen one taken down... but only once. That rumor seems to match what I witnessed."

"These are only rumors, though," Samuel reiterated, his voice tinged with skepticism. "I've never witnessed it, though."

We sat in silent contemplation, each of us grappling with our own thoughts and fears. Dad's blue eyes met mine. Did we have a weapon of knowledge against these creatures?

Dad broke the silence. "If there's even a slim possibility we can beat these things, we need to take it."

The weight of his words felt like an anchor, giving us something to cling to in these treacherous times. As he spoke, the model father-figure rose within him. A man who would do anything to shield his daughters from the darkness that crept up all around us.

"Samuel, listen," Dad's voice erupted with an idea. "We have a car stashed back in town. If we can just make it there, we could get out of this hellhole and find somewhere safe for all of us."

Laughter spilled from Samuel's mouth. It felt out of place in the grim woods and chilled winds that cut through us. He shook his head, eyes glinting with a knowledge that set me on edge. "You drove that red SUV, right? You didn't see it when you left the hotel, did you?"

Dad's eyebrows raised in confusion. "No, I... I didn't look. I focused on you and Jordan and whether you were friends or enemies." Dad's face wore a twinge of guilt for not being more observant.

"Exactly," Samuel nervously chuckled again. I couldn't fathom what was so amusing. "You didn't see it because it wasn't there, Peter."

Confusion tightened its grip on us. Dad pieced together a simple but loaded question. "What are you trying to say, Samuel?"

"The Chippers," Samuel said like the word explained everything. Seeing our blank stares, he continued, "That's what we call them and what we've heard others refer to them as. The infected, it seems, are all controlled by some sort of microchips. The more survivors we found, the more the title seemed to circulate. But those Chippers destroyed your SUV, just like they've destroyed every car we've seen enter town."

A chill crawled up my spine, but I masked it with a nod. It was hard enough to keep Ava from sensing my fear without letting Dad see it, too. Dad mumbled with a chill in his tone, "They destroyed the car? Do they understand cars?"

"Yes. They understand cars give us a way to escape. So, whenever they find one, they tear it apart or something. Finding a car in this world is rarer than finding a unicorn."

Disbelief and dread seeped into my bones. It couldn't be true. Then Samuel leaned in closer, lowering his voice as if sharing a forbidden secret. "Have you ever heard the zombies talk before? Seen them do anything besides mindless killing?"

"I heard the screaming one in town," Dad answered.

"They didn't do that before. That's because they're evolving. At first, they were erratic, mindless, but now? Now they hunt in packs, ambush, and even use tactics like feigning injury or danger to lure us out of hiding. They're learning."

The world tilted on its axis as I processed Samuel's words. I turned to look at Ava, her wide-eyed terror a deep contrast to the steely resolve on Samuel's and Jordan's faces.

"You two don't seem scared by any of this," Dad stated.

Samuel shared a glance with Jordan before she finally spoke. For the first time, her voice emerged eerily steady and chilling.

"We're not scared of what the Chippers can do. We're terrified of what they will learn to do."

CHAPTER 6: NEW FACES

The crunch of dried leaves and twigs underfoot became a familiar melody as we trudged through the dense forest. Days blended into one another as we searched for a new haven to call home for as long as possible. My boots, once pristine so I could show them off at school, now wore earthy shades of dirt from our travels.

"Careful," Dad's voice cut through rustling leaves and distant birds chirping. His hand reached back to steady Ava as she stumbled over a hidden root.

The trees thinned as we ascended. The elevation stole the air from our lungs and our breathing grew heavy. Samuel, the group's weary optimist, pressed ahead with an unbreakable persistence.

"There." Samuel muffled his voice, as we all did with zombies lurking about. He pointed at a break in the trees that framed a sheer cliff. A protective perch high above the chaotic world.

After hiking for an hour or so, we emerged from the trees to a welcoming campsite overlooking the valley below. A collective sigh escaped our lips. A view lay before us that compelled silence, a precious moment of beauty amid the chaos. The spot left us open to the elements and zombies, but we didn't have the luxury of being picky anymore.

Samuel and Peter shared a silent exchange of relief and child-like wonder. They stepped closer to the edge, hands on hips, surveying the land with a sense of ownership. A reward for the days of travel through a zombie filled valley.

"Would you look at that?" Samuel's voice erupted with a joy I hadn't heard yet. "You can't beat this view."

Dad nodded with a grin. His shoulders relaxed for the first time in what seemed like forever. "Yeah," he replied. "The perfect location to stay for a while. Trees for protection, plenty of room to sleep… and that view…" Dad's words trailed off with his stare.

The two men stood in triumph with a picturesque backdrop. Two men who had seen the best and worst of humanity. Their strength gave me hope, and, for a fleeting moment, I allowed myself to believe that maybe, just maybe, we could carve out a semblance of life, away from the gnashing teeth and mindless hunger of the Chippers.

The rest of the group spread out along the crest, each lost in their own thoughts as they took to the panoramic sanctuary we'd stumbled upon. For a moment, the apocalypse escaped my mind, giving me an unfamiliar peace. The sun peaked in the sky, which gave everyone a warm hug like a blanket during a snowy day.

A murmur of excitement buzzed through the air like electricity, igniting a spark in my bones. Samuel and Dad stood over a patch of ground and mapped out a campsite with animated gesture after animated gesture.

"Right here, we can build the campfire and easily fit six tree stump stools around it." Dad exclaimed and crouched down to pat the earth. "We'll have this view behind the fire, and just over there…" he pointed to a spot nestled against the mountain that formed a slight, shallow cave. "that's where we'll set up the sleeping area. Not much protection from the elements, but more than nothing."

"A perfect spot to watch for Chippers… and maybe some sunrises with Jordan," Samuel chimed in, his eyes glistened with a rare spark of joy. "We can take turns scouting the valley below."

"What a terrible gig. We *have to* take turns staring at a gorgeous view?" Dad and Samuel shared chuckles.

I couldn't help but giggle at their enthusiasm. Dad and Samuel allowed themselves to be lost in childhood memories of camping that they wanted to share with their new makeshift family.

"Come on, Martha!" Ava's voice called from above. She scaled the rough bark of a nearby tree and perched herself on a sturdy branch. Her light blue eyes danced with mischief, beckoning me to join her.

With a glance back at the men who were debating the merits of two different spots for the fire pit, I darted toward the tree. My fingers found grooves and notches in the bark, and I hoisted myself up, feeling a rush of adrenaline as the ground fell away beneath me. Ava reached down to give me a hand, pulling me up beside her. At that instant, it felt as if I was escaping the contaminated world and reclaiming a shattered fragment of my stolen childhood.

We sat like birds watching over our fledgling nest. "Who would've thought climbing trees would be a break from the apocalypse?"

"Definitely beats running from zombies," I managed between breaths, the exhilaration catching in my throat.

Below us, Mom scoffed at our newfound sanctuary. She had claimed a chair-shaped rock for her throne, distant from the rest of our group. With arms crossed against her chest, Mom frowned like her face knew no other expression.

"Shouldn't she be helping?" I whispered to Ava, nodding at Mom.

"Let her be," Ava replied, brushing a strand of dirty blonde hair from her face. "She believes the world owes her something. But right now, let's just enjoy this moment. We're safe."

"Safe," I echoed, a word that felt foreign to my mind.

"Hey, you two gonna build a treehouse up there or what?" Dad's voice floated up to us, tinged with humor and affection.

"Maybe we will!" Ava called back, her laughter cascading down like a challenge.

"You'll need someone to help with the foundation. I'll be there in a jiff!" Dad's grin took me back to days of building wintery forts and snow sculptures.

For a precious few minutes, I indulged in the fantasy, envisioning rope ladders and secret hideouts. I snapped back to reality when visions of green luminescence and shredded bodies crawled their way into our treehouse. They cornered us with nowhere to go and yanked Mom and Dad from the tree into nothingness.

"Peter," Mom's voice snapped, her tone filled with discontent. "Is this really it? This is where you want us to live?"

"Monica," Dad replied while he continued to draw lines in the dirt. His sarcasm was forefront and obvious. "Where else do you suggest we go? A hotel?"

"Somewhere… nicer than this," she gestured vaguely at the untamed forest around us. "We deserve more than sleeping in the dirt with who knows how many bugs around us. Don't we?"

Samuel stopped chopping a tree into sections for chairs with Jordan's hatchet. He stood up straight, then wiped his hands on his jeans. "Monica," he began with a cautionary note, "right now, any building is a beacon for the Chippers. They're hunting and they're smart enough to know survivors hide out in buildings. Hell, they're smart enough to know we use cars to escape. We need to do things they may not understand."

A flicker of understanding flooded Mom's eyes, but her stubbornness wouldn't let her concede. "Well," she retorted, narrowing her eyes on Dad, "you'd think the man leading us would've thought of that sooner."

Dad shrugged and continued chopping tree stumps for everyone's chairs. It was obvious he heard the insult, but brushed it off.

Samuel glanced at Dad. "Who says he's in charge?"

Dad snapped back and shot Samuel a sly smile. "Do you really think we'd let you be in charge?" The two chuckled like college roommates sharing a joke after years apart. Mom, satisfied with her attempt to maintain the upper hand, turned her attention elsewhere.

Jordan, meanwhile, had amassed a small pile of firewood, piling it up next to Samuel's firepit. I could see the practical gears turning in Samuel's head, strategizing the best way to keep us warm without drawing unwanted attention as the sun crept closer to clocking out for the day.

"Martha…" Ava whispered, and her eyes didn't break away from Mom. "Do you think she'll ever get it?"

"Get what?" I humored her, but I knew what she was about to ask.

"That this is how it is. That we need to stick together and make do with what we can to survive."

"Maybe," I sighed, not entirely convinced. "For now, let's just hope these trees and that firewood keep us safe." My gaze lingered on Dad's stoic figure. A flickering hope bolstered my belief that if anyone could lead us through this, it was Dad.

I scaled further up the rough bark, my fingertips brushing against some sticky sap of the tree. Ava followed with practiced ease, her arms strong and sure as she hoisted herself onto a sturdy limb parallel to mine. We settled in, our legs dangling, watching from our new perch as the adults continued their scurry, trying to create a campsite before nightfall.

"Look at them," Ava commented with a trace of amusement in her voice. "It's like they're playing house in the middle of the apocalypse."

A snap of twigs yanked Ava and my attention to the surrounding trees. Her body tensed, and my muscles coiled in unison. Eyes wide, she turned her head so sharply it could've been robotic like the Chippers.

"Did you hear that?" she whispered. We both tried to catch a better view but were too terrified to make a sound.

Shuffling and rustling seemed to vibrate through the air as everyone below froze in terror.

"Martha?" Ava whispered through clenched teeth.

I swallowed hard. "We're not alone." The words came out strangled. Fear wrapped its icy fingers around my vocal cords.

"Could be an animal," Ava said, but we both knew the lie for what it was. Animals wouldn't stroll up to human voices so nonchalantly.

"Or Chippers," I added.

"Samuel mentioned witnessing an ambush by the Chippers." My voice froze just as the last word fell from my lips.

"Maybe... maybe they don't know we're here yet," Ava's voice shook with terrified optimism. "Maybe they're just passing through."

I wanted to buy into the thought. Our eyes locked, a silent conversation passing between us. This could be it, the exact moment our luck ran out. When the cruel world finally caught up to us.

We pressed our backs against the trunk, wishing we could become one with the tree for safety. Our eyes darted between the shadows created by the setting sun. "Stay silent." Ava's words were barely louder than the breeze. "We have nothing to fight back with."

The expected glow of malevolent green never appeared. Instead, a glint of metal winked at me from the dense foliage. An unexpected calm shot through me at the sight of a gun in the tree line.

"There! Look!" I pointed out the gun barrel to Ava, who squinted to locate it.

"Those aren't...?" Her question trailed off as another metallic shimmer caught the dying light.

"Elu! Calian!" The words erupted from Samuel's lips. A jubilant spectacle vastly different from the potential outcome we imagined. His voice wobbled, treading a fine line between relief and the necessity of stealth.

The tension evaporated from Ava's posture as she exhaled. Her body slumped against the trunk in brief exhaustion. Below, Samuel's arms spread wide, welcoming the strangers into our joint home. Mom and Dad's eyes darted between the new strangers.

"Friends?" I asked. The idea felt foreign to me, seeing as we were lucky enough to meet two friendly strangers. The world could still offer surprises that didn't involve teeth and ravenous appetites.

"Should we go down?" Ava asked, mid descent.

I nodded. "Yeah, let's meet them."

We descended as the sun did the same. We shimmied down the tree, bark scraping against our palms. By the time my feet hit the ground, the sun disappeared, and Jordan ignited her impressive fire.

"Everyone..." Samuel announced, gesturing to the indigenous woman beside him. "This is Elu, and her son, Calian." The pair shared an air of resilience etched into their very stance. Both had a survivalist appearance, with rugged boots, jeans, and jackets that proved they came prepared and ready for this world. With pistols in their hands, the boy, Calian, wore a dirty baseball cap that radiated a fearless energy.

A curious light danced in Ava's blue eyes as they met Calian's. He matched her gaze. His own brown eyes reflected an unspoken curiosity and interest. They were about the same age, but something about the way Ava held herself seemed more mature.

"I'm Peter," Dad blurted as he approached Elu with an outstretched hand. "That bundle of joy over there is my wife, Monica," he continued, a slight tilt of his head at where Mom still sat on her stony throne. A solitary figure out-of-place amid the camaraderie.

"And these..." Dad's arm swung in our direction, "are my daughters, Martha and Ava." I offered a small wave, the weight of eyes on us.

Ava's lips curled into a shy, flirtatious smile. Obviously, a subtle playfulness directed at Calian. It was rare to see innocent love amid the backdrop of our shattered world. I briefly imagined what her life could have been like without the burden of an apocalypse ruining her paradise.

As the others exchanged greetings, three more figures emerged behind Elu and Calian. Despite their hesitation, they couldn't resist the allure of human connection. They were all that remained of a family of five. Their numbers dwindled as they fell victim to the very things we had all grown familiar with and grown to hate.

"Welcome." Dad's jovial attitude reached out like a welcome carpet to the defeated family, making sure no one felt unwanted. His voice acted like a warm blanket that wrapped around everyone's shoulders.

As they mingled, I couldn't help but feel the shift in the air. Each survivor brought stories of their last several days. Some filled with death, others filled with close calls. Elu and Calian even seemed to thrive in this world after they told us they lost a member of their family.

As everyone conversed, I took the moment to unleash my thoughts and stories in my notebook. Our family had close calls, but it amazed me that death had kissed every family and group except ours. A sense of panic set in my body and my hand trembled so much I couldn't write. Were their stories giving us a glimpse into our future?

The forest hummed with a life that seemed untouched by the apocalypse. Wings beat against the chilly night sky and I wondered whether it was a bat or a bird.

The broken family of three opened up as they huddled for warmth and security. The mother, Jenn, remained petrified, but tried to stay strong. Short, messy hair covered her tired eyes, and an over-sized jacket enveloped her. I wondered if the jacket belonged to her husband, one of the lives lost in their struggle to escape. Jenn kept a tight grip on her remaining two children, Thomas, who had short spiky hair beaten down almost as much as him, and Whitney, who mimicked her mom in every way except height. I watched their faces try to mimic Jenn's feigned bravery.

"Guess we're gonna need more room around the fire," Dad quipped, attempting to infuse a little lightness into the heavy air. Samuel and Dad rolled a sizeable rock toward what was slowly becoming our circle of safety. "Can you tell Samuel and I love rock and roll?"

Samuel laughed so hard at Dad's joke he fell over the top of the rock, while Dad laughed just as hard. Aside from the two, the circle remained quiet, with some eye rolls and Mom growing enraged at Dad's enjoyment.

The flickering campfire cast a warm glow across every face. Dad threw his thoughts into the fire. "Has anyone else noticed we haven't seen or heard a Chipper in a few days?" He poked at the logs with a stick, sending sparks swirling up like tiny fireflies as wood crackled in the smoky air.

"I wonder if this is a new evolution. Maybe they won't need to feast on humans anymore," Jordan added, giving deep thought to the idea.

I glanced at Jenn and her kids, huddled like lost birds. Their eyes, vacant and hollow with grief. Thomas clung to his mother's arm, while Whitney's head rested on Jenn's shoulder. Then her compact frame shuddered with silent sobs. Their relative silence reminded me of the cost to survive. Defeat carved itself into their faces just like an ancient statue.

"Maybe Jordan's right." I added, hoping these monsters could venture away from consuming humans.

That's when Calian and Elu, who had been listening intently, exchanged a glance. "We once encountered an... unusual survivor," Elu began, her voice steady but tinged with uncertainty. "This survivor was a true survivalist type. He'd found a government outpost just outside the mountains."

"A True Survivalist, huh? So, a crazy, whack-nut conspiracy theorist?" Dad chimed in. A joke backed by his honest opinion.

"An abandoned government outpost?" Ava's voice shook. Her eyes jumped to Calian, begging for his attention.

"Whatever he is, I think it's worth checking out." Calian's youthful voice dripped with excitement at the challenge. "He said there were Chippers inside, just two of them, though. At least he thought only two."

"Only two?" Monica scoffed, her dismissive tone mocking the comment. But she couldn't mask the flicker of fear that touched her eyes at the mention of Chippers.

"Could mean something," Samuel said, stroking the stubble on his chin. "There were two Chippers inside a government facility? Either the Chippers are searching every building possible..."

"Or it's a trap," I finished Samuel's thought. My pulse quickened at the thought. How many Chippers were hiding deeper inside the facility, or what else could they be hiding? The government always hides more than we know.

"Exactly," Elu affirmed, nodding gravely. "We need to be extremely cautious. If there's one thing we've learned, it's that nothing is as it seems anymore. With these things and their 'upgrades,' we can't allow ourselves to get complacent anymore. That's what happened with..." Elu glanced at Calian with a sorrowful smirk. "Dad."

"Then we'll be careful," Dad assured her, his determined gaze swept across our small band of survivors. "One wrong choice, and who knows how many of us will have to pay that price."

The fire crackled and popped while we digested the implications of our discussion. Each upgrade, each trauma, was another piece of the puzzle in understanding the horrors of the Chippers. And with every revelation, the weight of our reality pressed harder on us, trying to create diamonds that could withstand this world. Diamonds that could withstand the undead and the unraveling of everything we once knew.

The flames danced like ballerinas in the dark, casting an eerie glow on the faces huddled around the fire. A log rolled off the top of the pile and sent sparks up into the night sky as Elu continued the tale told to her by the Survivalist.

"There were documents scattered everywhere," her voice cracked as she focused on the story. "But… the documents told a story we couldn't have imagined." Her eyes filled with tears that reflected the fire's light. "The beginning of all this madness… it wasn't some bioweapon or a disease like the stories we've read or watched. It was all started for… AI entertainment."

"Entertainment?" I shouted in disbelief before everyone glared at me and I had to reassert myself on my tree stump. My brow furrowed in confusion and disbelief. Realizing our current hellish reality stemmed from something so benign, felt like a punch to the stomach that crawled its way into my heart.

"AI? Like Artificial Intelligence?" Samuel's voice waited for an answer we didn't want to hear.

"Yes," Elu answered. She leaned forward as if sharing a forbidden secret. "Teens and avid gamers were lured in with promises of the *ultimate virtual gaming experience.* They had microchips implanted into their skin, hoping it would lead to gaming like the world had never seen before." Elu's hand clutched the back of her neck, as if she were checking for a hidden microchip. Most of the group mirrored Elu's neck check.

"Microchips for a gaming experience? Sounds more like someone wanted—" Ava's words were cut off, but her eyes dilated with horror.

"Control," Elu continued. "You're right. Ava, was it? They wanted to play God. Some people will never be content with what they have and will always want more. That's where egos come in."

"Some people don't feel complete unless they have a puppet to control," Dad added grimly, and his jaw clenched. "And the government was the base for all of this?"

Elu nodded solemnly. "That's what the Survivalist gathered from other survivors and the government facilities he infiltrated. The government is using a company as the front for all of this, to give more credibility to the idea that it's just an entertainment system. The one thing he couldn't figure out was why. Mind control, of course, but why mind control? For military purposes? For testing? Just because they can?" She let out a frustrated sigh. "He couldn't find more than that. It's like he vanished, leaving only shadows and silence."

"Mind control..." Mom spat out the words like they were poison. "...do you really believe all that? The guy probably was a conspiracy nut and just wanted something to believe in. None of you truly know the when, where, why, how... or the who of how this started."

"Do you?" I whispered, as an icy dread settled over me. "Whoever did this either had good intentions with a dangerous plan, or bad intentions with an evil plan. Either way, someone lost control while trying to gain control."

"So, what do we do next?" Ava's voice rang out. Her hand inched closer toward Calian's. "We've survived this long. The reasons behind this and who is responsible won't matter if we can't survive."

"We must survive," Samuel added, his eyes scanned the forest behind our group. "But the question is, for how long? If someone released these demons into the world, who knows what other horrors they've unleashed?"

"Or will unleash," Dad added as he shot up from his makeshift chair. "As much as we'd all like it to be, we can't count on this spot being a sanctuary forever. We need to keep moving, find answers, and maybe stop whatever is going on."

Mom interjected, "I told you we should have gone to a hotel."

"We need answers," I said, staring into the flames. "But can we find answers if this survivalist conspiracy guy is gone?"

"We can try. Tomorrow let's search for a more secure place to call home and then work on finding answers," Dad declared, meeting everyone's stare with a leader's resolve. "For now, let's rest. Tomorrow's a new chance to get a win in this nightmare."

As the fire crackled and conversation dwindled, I leaned back, staring up at the stars desperately peeking through smoke and the canopy of trees. It was a perfect time to continue writing all my feelings and update my notebook further under the eyes of the sky, staring down at me.

Elu's voice carried a soft undertone as she recounted more of the survivalist's tale. The campfire provided a gentle accompaniment.

"He said he saw a *Test Area* in one of the facilities." Her voice sliced through me as my imagination ran with images of terror. "Blood splatters everywhere, bullet holes riddled the walls. Whatever the government tried to do to stop the Chippers… it didn't work."

As the flames flickered, faces illuminated with a growing realization of what we were up against. Dad's eyes ceased to blink, reflecting the orange glow, like he was trying to burn the imagined images out of his mind.

Jordan chewed her lower lip, her brown eyes lost to the dancing flames.

Ava twiddled her thumbs in a catatonic stare as I noticed Mom. Still perched behind the group, she, once again, seemed out of place. As everyone dealt with our terrifying truth, Mom didn't seem to have a care in the world while she snatched twig after twig from the ground and slowly plucked every dead leaf from the branch. Was the information too much for her to grasp, or was she too wrapped up in her financial anxieties to care?

"Can you believe it?" Ava's voice broke the frozen air that ensnared us. "All of this because of a video game?"

"More than a game," I replied with a blank stare I couldn't shake. "It's like we're living in someone's twisted version of reality, or maybe this is the game and we're nothing more than extras."

"Guys," Jordan spoke up, breaking our collective trance. "We need to come up with a plan. These things were too much for the government and they're evolving all the time. If the government's attempt to stop them failed before they could improve themselves, what chance do we have unless we figure something out and quick?"

"We need to 'upgrade,' too. We need to learn as much as we can about the Chippers and find a weakness."

Samuel responded to Jordan as they exchanged a loving and protective glance. "There is a location we need to find. It seems like this government facility has lots of answers we need and maybe a way to stop these things."

"Speak for yourselves," Mom muttered under her breath as she focused her hatred on the dirt. Her voice dripped with sarcasm, like she found our resolve foolish, or perhaps inconvenient.

"Mom," I snapped back. "We're in this together. We need to—"

"Martha, please," her voice hit like a slap. "Save your speeches. I'm not interested in playing the hero. I just want to stay alive."

"Survival works out better if we stick together and work as a team," I shot back, my patience fraying. "And maybe look for something beyond just yourself!"

"Enough," Dad interjected, his voice stern but calm. "We're all scared. But turning on each other won't help. We need unity now more than ever."

A heavy silence, thick with unsaid words and collective fears, settled over the group. The campfire appeared to shrink as if it grew fearful of the surrounding darkness. And in that moment, between the embers and the encroaching shadows, we understood the fragility of our situation.

The revelation about the Test Area had barely settled in my mind when Calian, with a look of sudden remembrance, leaned into the circle. "The Survivalist," he began, drawing all eyes to him, "he mentioned that the facility just outside the mountains contained most of the information he gathered himself. He thought if he could explore it further, he might get more answers... maybe figure out how to stop these Chippers."

His words hung in the air like a promise to end the apocalypse. A spark of hope ignited within me as the campfire smoldered into a red glow. Hidden somewhere out there sat the potential to end this nightmare.

"Was he certain?" Dad asked with the excitement of a child on Christmas morning.

"Pretty sure," Calian replied. "He planned to search the facility further within a day or two of us seeing him. Said he heard rumblings that this facility held all the answers. He believed this main government facility was the place."

Could we dare to dream of a future without the constant threat of being devoured by those creatures?

Calian continued, "Before we left the Survivalist, he had one last bit of information." His voice faltered as his head dropped. "The Chippers... their upgrades don't just affect how they hunt us. They're becoming harder to kill."

"Harder to kill?" Samuel's voice shook as the words fell from his mouth. "Did he say why or how? Is there anything we can do to stop that?"

Elu interjected with a deep sorrow. "He was about to divulge more about the resilient upgrades and how to battle them. Then an electronic scream cut through the area and drowned out his words as we scattered. We haven't seen him since."

My mind raced back to hiding in the hotel in Scoite's Peak before the Chippers showed us, or Dad, what they were truly capable of. At least what they were capable of before any recent upgrades.

"Sounds like they just continue to evolve," Ava whispered beside me, her body trying to crumple into a ball of fear.

"Or adapting," Dad added as his grim eyes soaked up the last flickers of the campfire.

"Either way," Samuel joined in, "we'll need to be even more careful now. If they're 'upgrading' or whatever, we don't know how many upgrades they've received or how long they will receive them."

"Could their ambush skills have improved? Or do they have new tactics to implement?" Dad asked as his eyes glazed over, and I watched the same terror from Scoite's Peak replay in his mind.

"Maybe," Samuel countered and stroked the stubble on his chin, "but what if that survivalist guy never realized you need to destroy the microchips? That's the only sure way to stop them, right?" His hand fell into his other hand, slicing the air as if to sever the invisible wires of our predicament.

"Could they be adapting to how we fight? How are they learning?" I offered my thoughts, but the idea alone made my stomach churn.

"Do the microchips send and receive data? Where is the data sent to?" Ava's thoughts blew everyone's minds as the realization grew along with their eyes.

"Smarter zombies or not, does it really matter? They can still kill us," Mom scoffed at our conversation with her first words in a while.

As theories and ideas bounced around the circle like a volleyball, a rustling tip-toed through our words. My heart hitched, silently hoping for more allies against an increasingly unstoppable foe. At the same moment, Elu and Calian's heads turned and their eyes narrowed. Their bodies tensed like coiled springs.

"Did you hear that?" Ava's voice stopped the rogue conversations in their tracks.

Then, every member of our group stared at a singular spot in the tree line. Even Mom paused, her thumb-twiddling ceased as terror froze her body. Her expression morphed into one of alert wariness.

A blur of russet fur darted through the underbrush, startling us into silence. A fox, with its ears pinned back and eyes wide with fear, charged past our circle. It scurried so close I could have reached out and touched its bushy tail.

"Wow, look at that!" Jenn's voice broke the silence. Thomas and Whitney peeked their heads from Jenn's shoulders. "Isn't it cute?" she whispered to them, a rare moment of comfort after the hellish conversation.

"Never seen a fox before," Mom admitted with a child-like glee. Her tone was surprisingly soft, tinged with wonder. Yet, as quickly as her moment of vulnerability appeared, it was gone, replaced by her scowl.

Where we were relieved and relaxed by the fox, two others varied. Elu and Calian exchanged a loaded glance. Their expressions were a mix of concern and understanding. They had an entire conversation without a word between them.

"Mom, you thinking what I'm thinking?" Calian's voice shot out like a soldier discussing strategies in an enemy territory.

"Yep." Elu nodded slowly. Her eyes never left the spot the fox emerged from. "That fox wasn't just out for a stroll. It was fleeing something."

A chill dripped down my spine. The playful chatter that had warmed the evening air became thick with freezing terror. Anticipation lurked in the shadows of the trees.

The smoldering wood created an ominous lullaby in the encroaching darkness. Then our nightmares turned into reality. An electronic fox call, distorted and unnatural, filtered through the trees. My heart seized as no one in our circle dared to move an inch.

Dad attempted to ease everyone's fear by saying, "Everyone, stay calm," but his voice oozed with fear.

Elu rose beside him, her posture transformed into a soldier preparing for battle. Calian stood as an equally intimidating foe, preparing to fight by his mother's side. They knew the wild too well to mistake the signs at our feet.

Samuel, whose laughter earlier had filled the night, prepared to fight our usual opponent. Jordan scrambled up and clutched Samuel's hand as she feigned strength.

I glanced at Ava, who crept closer to Dad. She grappled with conflicting emotions as her mature instincts clashed with the impulsive desire to rely on his protection. Her blue eyes frantically searched the tree line for answers to the unseen.

Then, the creator of the sound appeared. A single green glow illuminated the tree trunks as the Chipper paused at the edge of our camp. It was like the very forest itself presented us with a demon. The light didn't waver, an unblinking symbol of the apocalypse.

"Stay behind me," Dad commanded to me and Ava, but also to hype himself. His fatherly presence was on full display.

"We can get through this, together," I couldn't stop myself from adding. My own attempt to gain strength.

"Let's not give it the chance to call others," Elu whispered. We knew what she meant, but with their upgrades and hunting tactics, could there be more already, or was it a rogue Chipper?

Calian shifted from foot to foot, the muscles in his jaw clenched with his unrelenting stare off with the creature. In his eyes, the reflection of the green glow flickered like a warning beacon.

"Here, right now, this is our ground," Samuel shouted, and a fire built inside him with Jordan's hand resting in his. Their joined energy fueled his need to defend her. "We will not budge."

The green glow remained motionless, but the tension swirled around us like an encroaching fog. Our breaths and the fire's remnants mingled with the icy night air, creating a physical fog seeping across the dead foliage.

"We're stronger than this Chipper. Let's take it down." Jordan's strength mirrored Samuel's, and the two became a formidable force.

Ava clamped onto Dad's arm as both a lifeline and a shield. Her motherly instincts for me gave way, and she reverted to a timid daughter who needed her father's protection.

I swallowed hard, unable to rise from my temporary seat. The world seemed to shrink to that lone green glow.

As a collaborative courage built through the group, Calian's voice shattered our hopes. "There's no way it's alone."

His words challenged the Chipper, and on cue, more lanterns of light pierced the darkness. A constellation of doom approached us. My breathing ceased as the green illuminated our campsite and everything surrounding us.

"Can we even win this?" Ava's quivering voice asked Dad. Winning or losing meant life or death. For one of us, for all of us, we weren't sure how many would walk away from the standoff. And yet, the adults stood in defiance against demons that wanted to extinguish our lives as the campfire finally succumbed to the chilly night.

"Focus on the now," Elu commanded with the ferocity of a lion preparing to defend their pride. "We will survive this. We fight together and we stop these creatures here and now."

Calian gripped a pistol attached to his right hip, still locked on the menacing horde. He nodded a single time with the same determination as his mom. Ava's resolve faltered for just an instant as her motherly heart tore between her fight-or-flight instincts.

"Stay strong and fight together." Samuel raised his shotgun and aimed it directly at the first Chipper that emerged from the woods.

The green lights created a line of eerie spectators observing us, contemplating their next move as we did the same.

"We stand together," I whispered. For a fleeting second, there was a glimmer of pride in my heart, a lion-like resolve that wanted to mimic Elu and Calian's.

The crack of a stick ended the standoff, and the first Chipper sprinted directly at Samuel and Jordan.

CHAPTER 7: LOSS

Elu and Calian, who seemed prepared for our exact apocalypse, drew their pistols like a synchronized dance. Their movements mirrored each other, showcasing how tight-knit their family truly was. They aimed at the lunging Chipper and unloaded several rounds each. Every bullet hit its left hand, shredding it and the attached microchip. The zombie collapsed to the ground, sliding to a stop at Samuel's and Jordan's feet.

Samuel and Jordan, in utter shock, could only mouth the words, "thank you," accompanied by enlarged eyes.

As if stunned, the remaining Chippers stood motionless. None of them moved or reacted to the takedown of one of their own.

"Are they… are they waiting for something?" The words leaped from my mouth as my mind played tug-of-war between jumping for joy or running in terror.

"Could this be a trap?" Samuel grunted with a puzzled look scrawled across his face, matching everyone else's. "No one get too comfortable yet."

"Maybe they're… studying what just happened?" Elu suggested. The idea instilled more terror than the Chippers' presence. Could they be that advanced and quick?

"Doesn't matter." Calian's eyes scanned for the slightest twitch of movement. "We stick to the plan and protect each other. No one gets left behind."

"Mom?" I frantically searched for her, but all I saw was a woman wrapped in her own fears, glued to her rock with no way to defend herself. She could only hope the brave men and women in front of her would do their jobs.

"Martha, focus!" Ava's command snapped me back to the terrifying green wall.

"Right." I steadied myself. I wanted to help in some capacity, but knew there was nothing I could do except hope and pray like Mom.

The silence extended for so long it seemed like it had stretched time itself. An eternity compressed into a single minute, a standoff where hell could overwhelm us in a fraction of a second. The moment grew more daunting as I realized how eerily quiet the woods and mountain became. No animal calls or whistling winds. It felt like even nature stopped to witness what would happen next.

I picked up a branch, wanting to go down fighting if it came to that. I tightened my grip on the stick, its rough bark pressed into my palms. Beside me, Dad and Ava had done the same. Makeshift weapons clutched with strength generated out of fear and desperation.

"Stay close." Dad's protective nature tried to hide his fear of losing one, or both, of us. He flashed a loving, jovial look that reminded me of his true self, even if it was the last smile I ever received from him.

Behind us, Mom trembled, her usual bravado extinguished by the suffocating fear. It was odd seeing her stripped of the arrogance that always seemed to overwhelm anything around her.

A guttural snarl broke the silence. One Chipper lunged with a jerky, swift motion as its eyes locked onto Jordan with predatory hunger.

"Jordan!" I screamed, unable to contain the panic. A wave of terror enveloped Jordan, and every joint became cemented in place.

Samuel raised his shotgun in an instinctual protective movement. The shotgun roared with a thunderous blast that shattered the quiet forest. Time became irrelevant as the shell connected with the zombie's leg, slowing everything around us as parts of the zombie shredded apart. The force sent the zombie sprawling to the ground amid a spray of dirt and torn foliage.

"Nice shot, Samuel!" Dad bellowed and gripped his branch with renewed vigor. Samuel's figure vibrated with a warrior's energy, ready for the next threat without an ounce of fear.

Samuel pumped his shotgun, ready for another shot. Mom's demeanor, along with everyone else's, softened as they realized we could battle these demons and win.

A second Chipper lunged from the shadows of the tree line. I braced myself behind Ava as she raised her stick above her head. Inside my head, I battled with myself about wanting to be strong like her, Dad, Samuel, or any of them.

Another blast rang out, and the ground shuddered under the impact of the Chipper slamming face first into the dirt. I spun around to see Samuel's grin as he lowered his shotgun. Jordan wasted no time smashing the zombie in the neck with her branch as she parried to the side. Her stick came down with a force that vibrated through the crisp night air. Jordan quickly landed a second blow to the microchip on its neck with the butt of the branch. The sickening crunch of technology giving way under brute force was oddly satisfying.

"Babe! I got it!" Jordan cheered in subtle joy mixed with victory and disbelief. She stood triumphantly over the twitching zombie's form.

For a moment, hope flickered within me like the last embers of our campfire. We appeared unstoppable against an unyielding threat. Could we survive the nightmare? Ava loosened her grip on her branch as I emerged from my hiding spot behind her.

"Nice job, Jordan! Keep smashing those Chippers!" Dad called out. His encouraging words became eclipsed by the rustling leaves as the remaining five Chippers shifted into an evenly spaced circle around us like the AI watched our interaction and meticulously placed each one for maximum effectiveness against us.

The Chippers' next move dwarfed every horrifying thing we had been through, as a sound so alien and disconcerting rooted me in place. Another Chipper, an especially gaunt figure with eyes like blood-filled voids and missing a chunk of its stomach, arched its back grotesquely and flung its head skyward. The noise that spilled forth was not human nor animal, but a series of non-linear screeches and whirs. The sound mimicked a broken radio signal mixed with a loose serpentine belt. It was like the AI system spoke to us directly, warning us we weren't leaving the campsite alive.

"What the?" Ava whispered, as absolute terror enveloped her voice.

The noise sent razor-sharp shivers down my spine. It felt like an icy knife being dragged down my back. I grasped Ava's hand, seeking warmth to combat the icy chills swimming through my body.

"Stay close," she murmured, her stare never left the contorted figure that created the eerie siren. "Martha, whatever happens, stay with me."

I nodded, unable to tear my eyes away from the spectral display. Around us, the forest held its breath. Even the nocturnal creatures hid among the shadows.

The Chippers' coordinated assault unfolded before our eyes. No longer one at a time, but an all-out attack like racehorses released from their gates. Time crept through the thick air as each second stretched into hours. The forest alternated between feral footsteps trampling the dead leaves and thunderous claps from gunshots.

Elu and Calian, side-by-side, danced with the undead as their guns played a metallic symphony.

Entranced by Elu and Calian's synchronous tactics, I barely heard Ava. "Martha, watch out!" I jerked back just in time to dodge a clawing hand. A rush of air startled me as a Chipper whizzed past where my head had been.

Next thing I knew, there was a thud and a grunt as Dad grappled with a creature. The muscles in his arms strained. His paternal instinct to protect focused on the blood-thirsty zombie as he lost his grip on the tree branch. Ava tried to find her opening to strike the killing blow while Dad kept the Chipper occupied. She sat like an eagle, watching over the battle rolling across the forest floor, patiently waiting to assist in the life-or-death struggle.

"Now, Ava! Strike hard!" Dad yelled, struggling beneath the weight of the undead beast.

Ava swung with precision, but the Chipper thrashed too wildly. The blow hit the Chipper's shoulder blades, just missing the target, and my lungs seized. Fear gnawed at my insides, yet I couldn't look away. I couldn't force my body to move as my mind was in "fight mode" but my body was in "flight mode."

Why can't I help? I screamed in my head.

"You need to nail this next one." Dad screamed to Ava between breaths as his battle continued, neither side gaining an advantage. Dad was visibly tiring as the zombie tried to capitalize.

My vision blurred with the onslaught of emotions. Around us, battles raged on. The night air filled with the stench of gunpowder and decay. I forced myself to keep my head on a swivel. My eyes darted from shadow to shadow, watching for any sign of the next attack.

I noticed Jordan wrestling a Chipper. Her branch was the only thing that kept the gnashing teeth and desperate claws at bay. Her muscles were taut beneath her dirt-stained shirt. With a heave, she pinned it against a tree mere inches from her flesh.

"Jordan!" My voice was hoarse, but she didn't need my warning. In one fluid motion, her hand shot out, fingers wrapping around a hefty rock from the ground. Her arm drew back, and with all the force her slender frame could muster, she brought it crashing down on the microchip implanted in the zombie's neck. The sickening crunch echoed through the forest and the Chipper crumbled down the tree trunk.

The relief at Jordan bringing down a Chipper was short-lived as a harrowing scream pierced the night. I whipped my head around and saw Jenn clutch a rock as if her life depended on it, which it did. The last two Chippers had found their prey.

"Run, kids! Run!" Jenn's voice shattered into sobs as the decaying body of a Chipper bulldozed her petite body. She hit the ground hard, and the stone slipped from her grasp. She desperately tried to cover her face as the creature clawed at her forearms and crimson red covered her torso in seconds.

"Mommy!" The children's cries tore through me with a pain deeper than any zombie bite. Mom stood and froze with the same cemented feet I had. Her self-centered facade disintegrated as primal fear took hold. She wanted to help Jenn, but the sight before her had paralyzed her from her toes to her face.

"Get them out of here!" I yelled at Mom. Her maternal instincts kicked in and she rushed the kids to a trail leading down the mountainside.

As Jenn's screams faded into whimpers, the cruel truth sunk its teeth into my heart. We were losing. We were losing our hope, our confidence, and our lives.

A deep sorrow briefly lifted as I glimpsed Whitney and Thomas scamper out of sight. Their small hands clasped together as their screams pierced the chaotic night. I glanced back at the grim inevitability of our situation. Jenn's struggle ended quickly as the ravenous Chipper enjoyed its meal, feasting on her forearms.

"Run faster!" I screamed to the children, hoping they could hear.

Then, a Chipper sprinted at Mom, who stood at the tree line, then it quickly changed its trajectory. Its dead eyes locked onto the fleeing siblings, trying to dispose of any strays. The jerky movements of the grotesque creature lurched into the darkness where the kids disappeared. Like a baby needing its mother, Mom bolted back to her rock chair for safety. Her ego was nowhere to be found, replaced by raw, unfiltered fear.

Another commotion caught my attention as I hid behind tree trunks. An outline of a savage shadow smashed the back of a fallen Chipper's neck as the moonlight illuminated Samuel's determined face. The sharp sounds of technology shattering against a dense wooden buttstock echoed through the forest. The momentary win overpowered the cries and snarls that filled the night.

Nearby, Elu and Calian stood back-to-back, pistols emptied and replaced with desperation and mother-son hatchets. Elu brandished a small hatchet and fierce resolve as she swung at a Chipper. Calian grappled with another zombie as his hatchet tumbled from his grasp and his face dripped with sweat and concentration, knowing any wrong move could end his life.

A wounded Chipper, possibly having lost its legs to Elu, dragged its body along the ground, driven by the relentless microchips. Its severed limbs painted a gruesome trail in the dirt, which reminded me they were still humans beneath their green glow. But its relentless pursuit, even in such a damaged state, sent shivers down my spine.

"Martha, help!" Calian's voice snagged my attention back to him.

"I got you!" I grabbed the biggest branch I could and took off toward Calian. As Calian restrained its neck, I cracked the Chipper on the side of its head. Its body tumbled into the dirt.

Behind our skirmish, Samuel's shotgun roared again as it silenced another raging Chipper. His eyes scanned the ground for any sign of life from the fallen zombies.

A short-lived accomplishment turned into devastation as Samuel pivoted to check on the rest of us. The sight that met him tore his heart out through his ribs. Only ten feet away lay Jordan, motionless in the dirt. She had lost her battle with the relentless undead. The Chipper that bested her sat perched on her chest, greedily tearing at her flesh.

"Jordan…" Samuel's fierce stance folded into a broken man staring at his love's lifeless body. His shotgun slipped from his grasp and landed in the dirt as he sunk deeper into sorrow and collapsed to his knees. Every Chipper seemed to ignore Samuel, like they wanted him to drown in his agony.

Everyone continued to fight the Chippers as tears flooded their eyes. Paralysis shot through my body like electricity, unable to tear my gaze away from the raw grief etched into Samuel's face.

"Samuel," I called to him, but my words couldn't break his catatonic stare. He disappeared into the sounds of gnawing flesh and crunching bones.

"Martha, stay focused!" Elu's sharp command jolted my attention off Samuel and back to the continued threat. She was right; we couldn't afford to lose ourselves to grief while the battle raged on. Our survival was still questionable, and with the truth of Jordan losing her battle right in front of us, how many more of us would join her in the afterlife?

I forced myself to look away from Samuel's figure, hunched and cemented to the ground. As I readied myself to rejoin the fight, the image of his torment lingered in my mind. It was a haunting reminder that the world sympathized with no one.

Returning to the darkness of the battlefield, I glimpsed Dad's hand as it snatched the neck of his nemesis. The creature's eyes, once human, showed Dad the hollow emptiness their technology injected into them. But there was no time for sympathy. Our survival hinged on swift, merciless action. Would it be them or us?

"Now, Ava!" Dad shouted in desperation.

Ava cocked the heavy branch back and brought it down on the zombie's nape. Dad held the zombie's head above his body with all the strength he could muster. The microchip shattered with a satisfying crunch and the monster fell limp in Dad's hands. A moment of triumph illuminated Ava's features. It was her first kill, a rite of passage none of us wished upon her.

Dad threw the lifeless, mutilated body to the side and popped up, but our brief victory evaporated at the sound of Samuel's heart-wrenching sobs. The sound resonated deep within our bones and brought us back to reality.

Dad's face dropped with empathy. He flipped from protector to brother and took off to comfort Samuel as the Chippers' numbers declined. I don't know if Dad remembered it, but the memory of our neighbor, Mr. Morrow, flashed through my mind and the comradery he and Dad had. Would this situation have the same outcome?

"Come on, Samuel," Dad said in a strange mix of tenderness and urgency as he gently hoisted Samuel from the dirt. "This isn't the end for you. You're still one of us and we're going to make it out of here."

Samuel's response was nothing more than a catatonic stare. His eyes reflected a soul punctured by loss. But Dad was relentless, steering him toward the support of a nearby tree. His protective instincts applied to more than just his daughters. They extended to every fractured soul in our makeshift family.

"Stay with me, Samuel," Dad's words attempted to penetrate Samuel's comatose mind. "We need you."

The surrounding apocalyptic madness marched on around us. From cracking branches to the thud of bodies hitting the ground and the brief joy that followed a successful strike. Dad's act of kinship rebelled against our death filled forest.

"Martha, help me over here!" Dad glanced back at me as he settled Samuel against the rough bark. I sprinted over, wanting to mirror Dad and his absolute compassion for what was a stranger only days ago.

"Martha, Ava, take care of him," Dad told us as he put his hand on the back of Samuel's head and stared deep into his vacant eyes before he whispered, "We've got you, brother." He spun around, grabbed Samuel's shotgun, and joined Calian and Elu in the fight.

Ava wrapped her arms around Samuel, trying to warm his cold, emotionless body. It was my time to step up, but my mind blanked on how to help. Then the words burst out of my mouth, "Samuel, Ava and I are here for you. What can we do to help?"

"Help... please... Jordan..." The plea was a ghost in Samuel's mind. Fragility radiated from his words as Ava and I glanced at each other. Maybe we could pull Samuel from his vacant state.

From the corner of my eye, I saw Calian and Elu standing over the remnants of their battle as Dad jogged back to us. Accomplished faces worn by all three. A headless Chipper sprawled across the ground and another one crawled aimlessly. Feeling the battle won, Calian dashed after the orphaned siblings and his figure disappeared into the trees.

"Stay with us, Samuel," Ava continued to plead. Her voice was laced with the steel of someone who refused to let despair win.

Dad and Elu approached, and I noticed a sense of relief fall over them. Elu crouched next to Ava, placing a reassuring hand on Samuel's knee. "We've got you."

"Mom!" Ava's single word vibrated with such terror. I turned just in time to see the crawling zombie sink its teeth into Mom's calf, right below the knee. The crunch of bone and tear of muscle ended with the bottom half of Mom's leg tumbling to the ground as the Chipper bit straight through it. Her blood-curdling scream shattered our reality again. The icy arrow pierced my heart, bringing the realization that Mom had been snatched away from our lives.

"Monica!" Dad's shout was almost inaudible as he charged toward her. His arms were outstretched with love we hadn't seen between them for years, but it was too late. She grasped frantically at where her calf should have been. Her body crumpled to the leaf-littered ground as she screamed and locked her eyes onto her missing limb. The Chipper continued its assault, as it clawed up her stomach and began clawing away at her arms as she attempted to protect herself by flailing.

"Don't do it!" Elu barked and stepped in front of us with her hatchet raised. Her eyes darted between us and the unfolding horror. She knew Mom had already lost her battle, and she stood by for protection as we mourned.

I could only stare, frozen, as Mom's cries filled the night sky. Dad ran as far as he could before the weight of reality crumbled him into the dirt. Our family fell apart, and we could do nothing but watch Mom lose her battle.

"Run… we need to go…" Ava sobbed beside me.

Dad's head bowed to the ground. His body shook with silent sobs. The pain etched on his face told a story of love once whole, shattered beyond repair. The impending divorce faded and one last look of love shot between Mom and Dad. It was like Mom could no longer feel the pain, but accepted her fate as her mind reminisced about the love she had for Dad and their shared memories. Her eyelids succumbed to her loss and closed with a twinkle of light that flickered out.

"Peter, stay here," Elu urged, her voice attempted to breakthrough the sorrow.

"Mommy!" Ava's childlike wail tore my attention back to her. I wasn't alone in the tragic loss. Dad, Ava, and I shared this horrific pain. It felt like we were miles away from each other in our despair. Our broken family had shattered in front of us all, in a way we could never repair.

"I love you," Dad choked under his breath. His struggle broke me even further, even though his words weren't for me. "Goodbye, honey."

In the eerie lull that followed, I realized the apocalypse had taken more than my childhood. Mom's fate fulfilled as her screams disappeared into the night sky. I was alone with my thoughts, a shattered group, and my father and sister, who fought their own catatonic despair.

Among the soul-crushing loss, I noticed the decapitated zombie laid motionless among the carnage. The Chipper missing its legs continued to devour Mom's body, but we were too distraught to intervene in the lost battle. The Chipper that defeated Jordan had eaten almost half her body as it gnawed on her femur. And somewhere down the slope of the mountain, Calian chased down the siblings, and we internally prayed he would find them before the Chipper.

My ears rang with Ava's cries when, out of the tree line, Calian emerged. His hunched silhouette told us all we needed to know. My lungs tightened, waiting for the kids to appear behind him, but the woods remained empty.

"Calian! Where are the kids?" Elu's voice shot out. Every muscle in my body tensed as I waited for his answer.

He didn't speak. He only shook his head, his eyes outlined in a red sorrow of his own. The message was simple, words were unnecessary, and they would have been too cruel, anyway. A chill vibrated my spine as my imagination painted pictures of what he witnessed, but I was quick to shut them out.

Stumbling forward, he made his way to where we had slowly gathered around Samuel, the one person left we could save. As Calian reached us, Elu enveloped him in a tight hug as I heard his whimpers. A rugged survivor brought to tears over two strangers.

"Samuel," Ava whispered as she continued to wake him from his stupor.

Dad kneeled beside me the same way he kneeled beside my bed when I was a toddler. His hand found mine, and he gripped it tight enough to remind me we were still alive. We had to hold on to each other, even as the world tried to tear us apart.

"Martha, Ava," Dad said, his voice laced with an edge of desperation, "you will survive this, you hear me? You two will survive."

I nodded, swallowing the lump in my throat.

Elu walked up to Dad and placed a hand on his shoulder. "Peter," she began as her eyes scanned the two feasting Chippers, "Calian and I will take out these last two, then we'll handle the one with the kids." Her tone was almost cold, but the pain boiled behind her gaze.

"Easy pickings," she said, but even those words felt saturated with unspoken grief.

Dad's face, streaked with dirt and tears, nodded to her. His arms tightened around Ava and me as a second wave of despair and anguish tried to pull him under. I peeked out from under his arm, eager to witness justice served upon the monsters.

Elu and Calian crept forward like soldiers moving in for the kill. As they inched closer, the Chippers froze as if obeying a silent command. Their grotesque heads snapped upward, necks bending at impossible angles to stare into the abyss as they took a break from devouring Jordan and Mom. The eerie green glow of their microchips shifted to a chilling pale blue, changing the clearing from an illuminating bright color to an ominous pale nightlight.

Ava's hand grasped mine as Elu and Calian exchanged a glance that spoke volumes of uncertainty. That moment seemed to stretch on with confusion. The pastel, blue illumination chilled the air as it froze the Chippers. Then, the chilling blue faded back to their ominous green.

"Do it!" Dad yelled to Elu and Calian, wanting justice just as much as I did, if not more.

Hearing Dad's words, Elu and Calian advanced. Their determination was still prominent, but unsure of what had just occurred. As they approached the headless zombie, it did the unthinkable. It rose. No head, no logic, just the relentless drive of whatever hellish technological parasite possessed its body.

"Impossible…" The word slipped from my lips.

The figure standing before us defied logic and tossed our idea of the new world upside down. The headless Chipper became a symbol for everything the world could throw at us that we weren't prepared for.

My breath hitched as Calian approached the headless Chipper. "Kill it," Elu hissed to Calian, bitter revenge seeping from her words.

Calian closed in with grim, precise movements. He flipped his hatchet around and brought the blunt backside down. With a sickening crunch, the microchip on its right hand shattered like glass. For a moment, the creature's body went limp in defeat. Then, like some unholy puppet, it jerked itself upright again.

"That can't be! Hit it again, Calian." Elu shouted as a shock of disbelief pierced our entire group.

Elu shot Dad a glance that mirrored my terror before turning her attention back to Calian. With a furious yell, Calian smashed the other chip on the back of the creature's left hand. The creature stumbled again, then continued its mindless stroll.

"Impossible..." Ava murmured beside me and her voice trembled.

"Check its neck!" Elu called out, her voice desperate for answers.

Calian glanced at us. His determination rolled into utter fear. We watched as a captive audience to the macabre dance as he noticed the microchip on the back of its neck remained attached, just below the decapitated cut. He cocked back and landed another blow, another glass shattering sound echoed through the forest. The headless Chipper finally collapsed into a tree trunk and sank to the ground.

"Is it... over?" Ava asked.

I couldn't tear my gaze from the crumpled form. Calian's chest heaved with exertion and fear as he poked the Chipper with his hatchet, but the eerie silence of the night was all he heard. Silence descended upon us, punctuated by Dad's soft whimpers, the crunching of bones and tearing of flesh.

How did that Chipper survive two microchips being destroyed? Will we ever have the upper hand, or will we need to sacrifice ourselves to get rid of these creatures? The questions lingered in my head, unanswered, as I clung to the hope that we would learn more about the Chippers and, one day, rid the world of them.

Elu sprinted toward the Chipper devouring Jordan's legs. Rage filled her body as she swung her hatchet in a wide arc, connecting with the microchip implanted in the creature's left hand. The hand lost its grip on the calf as the zombie attempted to rise to engage Elu.

"Watch out!" I cried, but Elu already sidestepped the erratic swings of its arms. With another determined chop, she completely severed the entire right hand, slicing straight through the microchip. The zombie twitched a few times before it gave one last attempt at ending Elu's life. Like a ballerina from hell, she twisted around the Chipper's desperate arms and sliced the back of the zombie's neck, causing its head to flop to one side as it shuddered before it collapsed. Its last spasms sent a shiver down my spine.

Calian, meanwhile, charged like a man possessed at Mom's attacker. An animalistic cry escaped him as he tore into the distracted zombie. It didn't stand a chance, either. Calian's hatchet came down hard, slicing its neck vertically, extinguishing the green glow from one of the three microchips. Another fluid strike on the right hand followed by a windmill like strike on the left hand made quick work of the creature.

A sad sight to see, wishing Calian and Elu's talents could have dispatched the Chippers like that sooner. But when the odds were stacked so far against us and none of us knew how to fight, I realized we needed to learn how to fight like them.

Calian and Elu returned to our makeshift sanctuary around Samuel, who remained lost in his catatonic grief. Dad's voice sliced through the eerie calm that followed the carnage. "Elu, have you ever seen anything like that? A blue light?"

His question felt like a stone thrown into the still waters of our despair. Ripples of "the unknown" expanded with each word. We all waited, holding our breaths for an answer none of us truly wanted.

Elu's stony features faded into childlike fear. She wiped her hatchet on her tattered jeans, leaving a streak of dark red fluid that shone eerily in the dim light as her knees buckled and she plopped onto the ground.

"Anybody know what the hell that was? As if these things weren't hard enough to kill." Calian's words proved even Elu and himself were naïve to the twists and turns being thrown at us.

Elu shook her head. Her gaze swept over us before her eyes locked with Dad's. "I don't have a clue," she admitted, and the raw honesty in her voice was more unsettling than any lie. "But I've heard rumors among other survivors."

"Rumors?" Dad's curiosity couldn't quell his sorrow.

"Yes. Rumors about them... changing. Evolving." Elu continued, and I felt a chill despite the warmth of the sunrise peeking through the trees. "They're becoming more lethal so they can eradicate us."

"More lethal?" Dad's voice rose in disbelief.

Elu leaned in. "I think we just witnessed... an upgrade?" Her question hung heavy in the air, along with the words "more lethal."

The words tasted bitter on my tongue as I realized I had clenched my teeth together so tight my jaw hurt.

"God help us," Ava murmured as she shimmied over toward Calian.

"Alright," Dad said after a tense moment through tear-filled eyes. "We need to leave. Get somewhere safe and far from here. We can't stay here." Whatever had just happened, it had shifted the game again. We had learned to survive, but the rules changed again. We had to change as well.

"Peter's right. Let's gather what we can carry and leave immediately," Elu commanded with sincerity.

I looked up at the disappearing stars, wondering if they were watching us scramble for survival, and I couldn't help but wonder if the next time those microchips turned blue, would we be prepared?

CHAPTER 8: MEMORIES

The sun warmed my face as I clutched the worn notebook to my chest. We shuffled into a clearing where the sounds of rushing water ricocheted off rocks and the smell of fresh mountain water welcomed us. Each step closer to the creek washed away the previous day's horrors and heartaches. I noticed Ava and Calian hand in hand again. Dad was nearby, guiding Samuel along the creek as he seemed to flicker between our reality and his own private abyss.

"Let's rest here," Dad's voice broke through the haze. He slightly shouted to be heard over the flowing water.

Everyone found their own lonely spot to endure their personal battles. I watched Samuel, his body coiled up like a tense spring. His glassy eyes darted around as if expecting the Grim Reaper to take him next. Calian sat side by side with Ava as they shared secretive whispers. Elu sat alone on the palms of her hands. She attempted to get lost in the serene beauty around us before the darkness snatched her.

Ignoring their pain in their individual ways, I opened my notebook. The pages crinkled, worn and weathered, like our group. My fingers hesitated over the paper as the visuals of the last twenty-four hours shot through my mind.

"Martha?" Ava's voice cut through my hesitation. "You okay?"

"I'm working on it," I answered honestly and forced a smile that barely broke through my sorrow. She nodded, understanding without further words, then turned her eyes back to Calian.

The moment my pen touched the paper, it was like a dam inside me broke. Words poured out, incoherent and raw at first, then shaping into the semblance of memories and loss. I wrote about last night, how the stars vanished behind clouds of terror, how Chippers bathed my childhood in blood and screams. The realization that a technologically advanced movie monster stole my mother and others, but in this world, the loss was permanent.

"Take your time, Martha," Dad called out. His words were a balm to my heartache, though I knew his heart ached just as much, if not more. He sat beside Samuel, still comforting him, but his eyes stared at the ink on the pages of my notebook from afar.

"Words can't bring them back," I answered between scribbles. Tears rolled down my cheek as Mom's face popped into my head.

"No," he agreed as his voice trembled, and he held back tears. "But remembering everyone who's gone gives them extended life. They can look down on us as we look up to them."

"But we can never make any more memories with them, Dad." I glanced at him, wanting his words to prove me wrong.

"Maybe that's the point. You and Ava… and even I haven't had too many good memories lately with the divorce and everything going on. Now, you can reminisce about all the good memories you had over the years with Mom." His words caused even more tears to well up in my eyes, and his eyes did the same.

Tears fell onto my half-smile as the tremor in my hand steadied. I let the stories flow through me as a tribute to those lost. With every word, I crafted everlasting memories not even the undead could take away. I became the record keeper for our small group's memories of the loved ones we'd lost.

"Hey Ava," I shouted. "Remember what Mom used to say about why we needed to study and do well in school with reading and writing?" I recalled a sliver of normalcy. Ava and I shouted in unison, "Words create power."

"Indeed, they do," Dad replied.

I wrote of the past for the future, penning a tale of survival and fractured hearts slowly being stitched together.

Ava's slender fingers curled around her camera. I had forgotten she even had it as she flipped her dirty blonde hair with its blue streak out of her face so she could frame a shot of the stream. The click of the shutter was a subtle reminder of our former life. The shutter repeated over and over and I heard the frustration in her voice after each click.

"I can't do this," Ava's frustration boiled over. She allowed the camera to tumble from her hand as she continued to stare at the creek. Her voice quivered with a loss images couldn't replace.

"Every picture feels hollow now. Like a lie I'm trying to tell myself."

The weight of her words slammed against my chest. I paused as my pen hovered above a story half-told. "Mom would've wanted you to keep doing what you love," I attempted to soothe Ava's pain.

"Mom…" Ava's light blue eyes disappeared behind tears as clear as the creek. "She loved things that sparkled like jewelry and trinkets… even her precious luxury watches. I guess… even if we never understood her, she was still our mom."

I agreed and refocused on the half-blank page in front of me. A memory tugged at the corners of my mind, pulling me back to younger days when excitement twinkled in Mom's eyes as she unpacked treasures from her travels.

"Remember the wooden, hand-carved statues she would bring home from that island?" I asked Ava. "The rare native looking ones with the funny faces, and the interesting, God-like backstories."

"The Huna Island statues," Ava said though a painful smile.

"Right, Huna Island." I smiled, too, imagining the row of wooden statues strewed across our mantlepiece. The silent audience to the good times and the bad times of our childhood. "It always felt like our birthday whenever she returned from a work trip with a new statue. Until one day... she stopped bringing them home." A single tear stumbled down my cheek.

"Maybe that's when everything changed. When the statues stopped, so did the part of her that cared about bringing them home for us." Ava replied.

"Maybe," I conceded, but the thought felt like a stone in my stomach. I turned my attention back to my notebook, scribbling down the memory and the feelings before it slipped away. I wrote about how the statues stayed strong even when we weren't. How they endured everything while bringing us so much joy. I needed to find the secret behind their strength, behind Dad's, Ava's, and everyone else's strength.

"Maybe we can discover new things to treasure," I tentatively suggested, holding onto the idea that not all beauty had been destroyed in this world.

"Perhaps," Ava replied, then glanced at the muddy camera. Something changed inside her. The stream continued to flow, nudging us to move forward.

The creek's murmur was a subtle mentor for our grief. It reminded us that the world moved on even if we couldn't.

Dad's voice rose over the serene roar of the creek, hoarse and shaky from the hours of mourning over Mom. "I remember getting the job offer," he started, with a distant stare as if viewing back through time. "Monica... Mom, handed it to me personally. She had a radiating energy to her that made you feel like everything to her."

I watched how his hands fidgeted with a stray twig. Dad always had a way of fixing things and protecting the family, but this time, he could do neither.

"Did you two celebrate?" I asked with intent curiosity. I knew he needed to vent, to let it all out.

A weak laugh escaped his mouth, as if escaping the aura of sadness surrounding him. "We did. I held a door open for her, much longer than I should have, because I wanted to be a gentleman. We went out for sushi, her treat, as she joked I wasn't allowed to buy dinner until I got my first paycheck."

"Mom paid?" Ava couldn't contain her shock. Her eyes enlarged with a shimmer of happiness at the thought of Mom and Dad being happy together.

Dad nodded slowly, and a hard smile grew on his face. "Then we sat in my car for hours just chit-chatting. Mom loved music, so we took turns playing DJ and playing snippets of our favorite song before the other one couldn't contain their excitement about the next song. She was a big fan of punk music. She told me how she was very selective in her style, but once she found a band she liked, she would listen to their songs on repeat until the song became overplayed. Oh, and country music for some reason? She'd argue it was true, feelings music, but I never got on board with the twangy-ness she liked."

"Sounds like her," I said. The heaviness in my chest couldn't stop the corners of my mouth from rising.

"We spent every night together after that and kept it a secret from everyone at work. Mom was terrified they'd fire her for fraternizing with an intern." His fingers paused on the twig, before his grip tightened around it like a boa constrictor. "So we lied. Said one of us was sick whenever the other took vacation. We cherished those secretive moments like they were rare gems from a hidden mine."

"Sounds like you two really loved each other," Ava gushed over the memories as new tears formed in her eyes.

"We did," Dad agreed as a cloud darkened the forest. "But those memories are all I have now. The secrets we kept from everyone around us just to protect each other."

"Would you keep those secrets if you had to do it again?" I asked, thinking of the weight secrets could carry.

"Of course. We always looked out for one another," he replied as his voice got quieter. "But that was before the divorce began."

"I love you, Dad." Ava hopped over to Dad like a toddler before giving him a hug.

"Thank you for telling us all of this, Dad. I never knew," I replied, feeling a strange sense of peace among the chaos. The memories weren't mine, but they felt like mine. Learning about the life that led to your life felt like a gift.

"Of course, Martha," he said, squeezing Ava's arm before letting go. Dad instinctively returned to staring into the water, lost in the memories of love and a time without the overwhelming darkness.

"Then, one day, came Scoite's Peak," he continued. "I took her up there to reminisce about my childhood when we found a new bar. After a few drinks, my liquid courage kicked in and I led her outside. We strolled down Main Street until, under a flickering streetlight, I stopped her..."

I gushed over hearing Dad choke up as he wrote the first chapter of our family.

"And I got down on one knee, right there in the gravel," he explained. "And I asked her to be my forever partner. To build something money couldn't buy."

Ava mirrored me, and we hung on every word. It was like discovering a hidden room in our house. "There was a time when you and Mom were happy?" Ava asked the question on both of our minds.

Dad's face contorted into something we'd never seen before as his composure faded and his eyes hung heavy. "I've always loved her, Ava," he choked on the words. "Even when—even when it got tough." Dad's body slumped as my heart shattered into pieces. *Dad always loved Mom, even through all their problems and the divorce?*

Martha's Notebook

My hands shook as I snapped my notebook shut. The words I'd been writing suddenly seemed trivial and hollow. I mindlessly tucked the notebook into my backpack, and my eyes never lost sight of Dad in his broken state. My feet carried me up and over to Dad before I knew what I was doing.

"Dad..." I whispered and threw my arms around him. His chest stuttered against my hands as I clung to him. For once, I wanted to be his anchor.

"Dad..." Ava whispered from behind me. Her arms enveloped Dad and me. The gravity of our family yanked her into a bonding embrace.

We stayed like that, a tangle of limbs and tears under the twilight sky. No words passed between us or anyone else. In that embrace, we were a tight-knit family, healing from our shared pain.

As we broke from our family hug, each wiping the sorrow from our eyes, Ava looked at her muddy camera lying next to the creek. She sprinted to it, picked it up, and in one motion, chucked it as far as she could down the stream. The splash of the water indicated the end of her camera.

"Beauty doesn't mean a thing when it can be yanked from your life in an instant," she screamed without a care of any Chippers that could be nearby. Her eyes fixed on the ripples that spread through the rushing water. A cold resolve hardened within them. "Survival is all that matters now. Cold, lifeless survival."

The first person she locked eyes with was Calian. A fire burned in her eyes, one of love and ferocity. She shuffled over to him, a chink showing in her new armor. She bowed her head into his chest and he wrapped his arms around her.

"Jordan and I... we met at a friend's house... during a game night," Samuel broke from his catatonic state and jumped right into the conversation without missing a beat. "There was this buffalo-queso dip that was out of this world. After I took the first bite... I swear I shouted, 'Are you kidding me? This should be illegal!'"

Love filled Samuel's eyes as he reminisced while staring at the ripples in the creek. A weak chuckle escaped his mouth as his eyes welled. "Next thing I knew, Jordan walked up to me with the biggest grin I'd ever seen." Another weak chuckle followed by more tears. "She asked me if I liked the dip and admitted that she made it. We couldn't stop laughing, and well, the next thing I knew, we were scheduling our first date."

Samuel's voice trailed off as he retreated into his grief. My heart ached as he curled into an upright fetal position, drowning in his heartache.

We all waited on bated breath for his next words as the creek emphasized the silence with its echoing trickle. "After that night," he continued, "the flirting just... it was irresistible. She was the drug I became addicted to."

I wanted more of Jordan and Samuel's love story. It reminded me of a romance novel, except I knew the grim ending.

"Our first date comprised of beer, wings, and pool tables. A cliché first date, but one I will never forget." His eyes lit up with a flicker of pure joy. "Chatfield's Sports Bar engrained itself in our lives. We watched hockey and played games until the bar closed. No ulterior motive, no trying to impress... just two people genuinely enjoying each other's company."

I visualized the ruckus of the pool balls and the cheers of drunken patrons. I could almost feel the sticky floors beneath my boots from the few times we'd stopped at some sports bar to grab lunch with Mom and Dad. It was a stark contrast to the love life of a teen.

"She beat me at every game we played, even when I tried. Darts, pool, shots..." he chuckled, filled with emptiness. He reached into his front pocket. His hand trembled as he searched for the contents. The rest of us stared vigilantly.

Struggling, he yanked a small box from his jeans. Everyone gasped at it. Samuel flipped the box open as a glint filled our eyes. "I was going to ask her to marry me," he whispered to himself, loud enough for us to hear.

"To marry you?" Ava prodded gently, maybe envisioning her own fairytale moment.

"To marry me," he affirmed. His thumb caressed the small diamond with affectionate care. "I wanted to wait for the right moment, you know? When the world wasn't falling apart, or at least not as bad. I just needed a moment when we weren't fighting for our lives…" His voice trailed off into deeper sorrow.

"Samuel…" I tried to reach out to him, but what could I say? Words seemed trivial to someone's loss I could never relate to.

He looked up and his eyes met mine. "I know marriage doesn't mean much anymore, not like it used to. But all I wanted to do was call her my wife. To make that promise to her, even if it only mattered to us."

We sat with the heavy air weighing us down as everyone bowed their heads out of respect for Jordan. With my eyes closed, all I could hear were sniffles and Samuel's whimpers. It felt cruel that the world stole more than just loved ones; it stole promises of love.

"Jordan would have loved that ring," I gave another attempt to console Samuel.

"Yeah," he mumbled through his tears. "She might have. But I'll never know for sure."

"Then let that be your promise, Samuel," Ava said. "With or without a ring, we could all tell your love was genuine."

He nodded as he polished the ring one more time with his thumb before closing the box on his dreams.

"Let's keep moving," he said as he stood and brushed the dirt off his jeans. "Let's keep moving for Jordan."

A glint of the silver band caught my eye as Samuel took another quick look at the ring. In a swift motion fueled by grief and anger, Samuel snatched the ring from the box and cocked his arm back. He hurled the ring upstream as far as he could before tossing the box into some brush. The ripples swallowed the ring in an instant, erasing Samuel's dream of happiness.

"I don't want anyone but Jordan," Samuel's voice cracked. His tears resumed their silent journey down his cheeks as he tried to wish Jordan back to life in the water. He turned around and snatched his shotgun. "I don't think I can do this alone, but I'll try."

Without waiting for us, he wandered off downstream. Every step took him further from his loss. I threw my backpack over my shoulders as everyone else gathered their things and followed behind Samuel.

Elu and Calian shared a look from the rear of the group, realizing they squeaked out of our recent attack unscathed. I could tell they had their own share of loss, as Calian's face dropped, and Elu wrapped her arms around him.

"We may have lucked out recently, but Calian still finds it hard to talk about our previous loss," Elu shared with everyone. "We lost Olli, my husband and Calian's dad, when this nightmare began."

My heart ceased at the thought of losing Dad. I couldn't imagine what Calian or Elu felt. In that moment, it truly felt like we were all connected because the Grim Reaper had touched each of our lives.

Unsure of how to console Calian or Elu with their loss, we trudged on. Without words, loss and the fierce need to protect what little we had left united us. Every rustle of leaves, every distant scream, reminded us of the fragility of our existence.

We followed the creek in silence. The water's soft murmur kept our movements a secret. I kept my eyes on the ground, but my mind ran through everyone we'd lost. Who would be next? Would we all be gone before stopping the monumental threat?

Elu continued her story, "Olli and I, we had just gotten home from a date night." She choked down a few tears. "Calian was home alone. We pulled up to see the living room window shattered and Calian running for his life inside."

Her recollection unfolded like a scene from a horror movie, except the people in front of me experienced it. My heart raced as I imagined the terror that must have surged through Calian.

"Olli didn't even hesitate," she continued through watery eyes. "He charged through the front door and tackled the Chipper... just in time to save Calian."

I could hear Olli's frantic footsteps throughout the house, his desperate grunts, and the thud as he fought to protect his son. The air felt thick with tension as Elu's flashback painted a picture of chaos and sacrifice.

"Calian escaped and jumped into our truck." Elu swallowed hard. Through her trembling voice, she continued. "We waited for Olli to come running out, but..." Her eyes connected with Calian's as they shared the burden of their loss. Calian's face lost all its color, and her eyes lost all their ferocity.

"Olli never returned," Elu cried through her words. The finality in her voice caused my chest to tighten. "I went looking for him and found him inside... most of him."

She struggled to find the strength to continue the story. Ava turned and hugged Calian tight as his shoulders shook. The ones I thought got lucky in the apocalypse had lost just as much as us.

"Olli's body was torn apart. I wanted to destroy the Chipper with every ounce in me, but they were still new and such a terrifying unknown. All I could do was run back to the car and drive away as fast as possible," Elu wiped the tears from her eyes as she whimpered. "The zombie... it ate him. How do you get over witnessing your loved one being torn apart and eaten?"

A shudder ran through my body. We knew exactly how she felt.

Elu's strength disappeared in a flash. "Oh... sorry. I just—I just don't know what to do. I want to survive, but sometimes I don't."

"We need to keep fighting. The ones who are gone wouldn't want us to lie down and die." Dad's strength returned to his voice, as if trying to protect the entire group. "We owe it to them. To Olli, to Jordan, to Mom, to everyone we've lost. If you don't want to do it for yourself, do it for them."

Dad's words stirred something in me. A flicker of resilience amid our deepest despair. He was right. We had to carry on for those that couldn't. We needed to survive, and we needed to be strong. I had to be strong.

Through heavy hearts, we left the creek behind, along with the misery we had endured and the stories we struggled to share.

"Martha," Ava dropped back to talk to me as we searched for a new sanctuary. "Promise me we'll stick together no matter what. I don't know what I'd do if I ever lost you or Dad."

I nodded and squeezed her hand three times. "I'm not going anywhere. And not just because I wouldn't survive on my own." We both managed a weak chuckle as we tried to move past our pain.

A genuine smile stretched across her face. "You realize these zombies will need a complete system update to catch up with us. They'll need to create a whole new zombie type. Maybe call them Slippers?"

"Slippers?" I loved the name, but wasn't sure where she was going with it.

"Slippers... because we'll walk all over them." Ava cracked up at her own joke.

"Hey back there. Leave the dad jokes to the dads," Dad called back to us with a mischievous smile. "Or the moms." Dad winked at Elu.

Elu couldn't help but smile at the shared comradery. Even Calian's mouth curved into the faintest smile I'd seen, as if trying to keep his stubborn, rough exterior, but he couldn't help himself.

Then, as if breaking from a spell, Samuel let out a laugh. He tried his hardest to halt the joy, but it emerged as an unnatural cough-laugh, which made everyone laugh even harder.

"Hey, now that it seems we're all in better spirits, maybe you guys can train us all a little to better defend ourselves against these zombies?" Dad asked in Elu's direction. "We should be more prepared for the next... Chipper encounter."

Samuel nodded, wiping his face with the back of his hand. "I can help with the training, too." He held his shotgun over his head.

Calian remained silent, his eyes fixed on his worn-out boots between occasional glances at Ava.

Elu smiled at Dad, accompanied by a flirty wink. "Of course we can. We could use a little refresher, too." Elu bumped Calian's shoulder with her elbow.

Our small band trudged along the windy creek. It felt like the water washed away our despair without us noticing, strengthening us with every step.

Dad's pace steadied, his back a little straighter than before. He paused, wiping his nose on his sleeve before breaking into a grin that predicted a ridiculous insight or dad joke was about to be released into the world. "Getting back to the 'Super Upgraded Chippers' and calling them 'Slippers' conversation... Chipper isn't a very scary name for undead, technologically advanced zombies trying to destroy the world." Dad's insight was ridiculous, but he had a point.

He took a deep breath and continued, "It's like calling them 'Happy-Go-Luckys.' What if we called them 'Meanie Greenie Weenies?' That's a little catchier. What do you guys think? Samuel?"

The absurdity of his joke, the image of monstrous beings reduced to cartoonish villains. Ava and I couldn't contain our laughter, bringing us back to when we played "tickle monster" with Dad. For a fraction of time, we had a childhood again. Even Calian cracked a full smile and everyone laughed in full form. The first time we'd all laughed since we

Martha's Notebook

began running for our lives. It felt amazing that within a day, we'd gone from uncontrollable tears to our first laughs in days. Samuel let out a laugh even with swollen, red eyes. A sight that still broke my heart.

"Meanie Greenie Weenies it is, then," Elu managed between chuckles, giving Dad a playful shove that breathed a bit of life back into him.

We carried on until the landscape split into two paths. A narrow trail, barely visible beneath the overgrowth, beckoned us away from the stream's edge. Our group set our sights on the path leading upward.

"Maybe there's a hidden sanctuary away from the creek. Somewhere we can catch our breath for a couple of days." Elu tossed her words in the air and watched a hawk soar overhead.

"Let's go, then," Samuel said, determination returned to his steps as he led the way, his shotgun an extension of his resolve.

Dad ushered everyone through the underbrush as he held a stout branch to the side. "Stay close to each other. We don't know what's up ahead."

I lingered in the back, wanting to be close to Dad. That's when I heard it. A soft rustling, like we were being followed. I halted, shifting my focus to my ears. Then it came again. A fox or a deer could cause the sound, or it could be something other-worldly. Had we been too careless in our enjoyment? My pulse rose as my lungs ceased.

"Guys, wait!" I called, not wanting to alarm them but needing to warn them.

They turned, and every ounce of joy drained from their faces. Ava and Dad were quick to display their protective stances.

"Did you hear something, Martha?" Ava whispered. Everyone's eyes scanned the area from the distant creek to the thick brush.

Nods and eye contact became our new communication, as terror halted all verbal communication.

After a few tense moments, Dad took a gamble. "It could be nothing." His hand instinctively reached for another branch on the ground, just in case he was wrong.

"Or could it be *them*?" Calian added grimly. He reached for his pistol, then remembered it was empty.

"Either way," Elu interjected, "we've got to keep moving. But let's be smart about it."

We agreed with silent nods, forming a tighter line as we ascended the trail. Each step placed the stream further behind us, hopefully pushing the stalker further in our rearview.

I turned to take a quick peek to put my fears to rest, but I spotted something in the distance. A blue glow illuminated a patch of trees on the other side of the creek. It was a distant, spectral glow we had seen once before. I squinted, trying to convince myself it could be anything other than the Chippers. For a moment, the sun even seemed to hold its breath as the glow disappeared.

"Martha?" Ava's voice softly called from further ahead.

"Look," I pointed into the forest, where the glow had disappeared, but I hoped Ava might see something I couldn't. The group halted as everyone tried to follow my hand.

"Is that…" Samuel's voice trailed off. His question went unanswered.

"Shh," Elu hushed.

We watched the trees, frozen. Then, a shadow moved between them, but it was hard to make out a green glow through the like-colored foliage. It was like witnessing a silent predator hunting its prey. The features were vague, but their intent was clear.

"Let's hurry and train," I said, more to myself than the others. "We need to know how to fight, and sooner would probably be better."

"Agreed." Dad placed his hand on my shoulder, corralling me to continue up the hill. "We can't keep running forever."

"Especially not from something like them," Samuel added.

Calian stepped forward, peering intently into the distance. "Whatever that is, it's not an animal."

"It could be the Meanie Greenie Weenies," I joked, but the severity of the situation shut down any laughter.

"Let's find the first clearing we can, and we'll begin," Elu suggested in a no-nonsense tone. "Then we'll deal with whatever is following us."

"Agreed," Samuel nodded, making his way to the front of the group.

Dad reiterated, "Stay close."

"Martha," Ava murmured as we climbed, "you know we can do this, right? We can learn together and so can Dad."

"Thanks, Ava." I couldn't hide the fear emanating from my voice. "I just wish we didn't have to learn how to fight."

"Me too," she replied, grabbing my hand and escorting me up the trail.

As I followed Ava like a puppy, I took one last look into the adjacent forest, hoping to catch a glimpse of what those shadows were.

A green illuminated face emerged from the trees, taunting me with its presence. A second green face emerged, then a third, and a fourth. Before I knew it, I made out about fifteen to twenty grotesque figures intertwined with the trees.

Training was no longer an advantage, but a necessity if we were going to survive. We couldn't just train to win the battle, we needed to train to win this war.

CHAPTER 9: TRAINING

Dusk filtered through the leaves, casting longer shadows on the forest floor, when we stumbled across a wide clearing with sparse trees. Elu stopped everyone. "This is it. This is our training ground."

The brisk air created an intimidating environment with a lingering enemy, who could appear at any moment.

"Alright, everyone," Calian called out. The leader inside him took charge. "This is suitable. We'll teach you all how to get comfortable using our guns."

"Even though we're out of ammo, it's important to know how to handle these weapons," Elu added. She scanned the group with a stern gaze. "You can also use the guns as blunt weapons, like you would need to today."

A spark of excitement grew in me at the realization that I could not only defend myself, but my family like I'd always dreamed I could.

"Okay, let's do this," I said, leaning into the confidence building inside me. My hands itched to hold a weapon and to learn what it meant to be strong.

"Martha, Ava," Calian gestured to us, "You two follow me. We'll start with the basics."

"Samuel and Peter, you're with me," Elu commanded. "And bring your shotgun, Samuel."

"Always remember..." Calian warned as he handed Ava his pistol, "These are not toys. Treat them with respect and make smart choices."

"Got it, Calian," Ava replied. A flirtatious sparkle emphasized the blue in her eyes.

"Good," Calian nodded, and he showed us the proper stance and grip. "Now, imagine there's a target ten feet in front of you. You'll want to place your feet side by side, then place your dominant foot back a little bit. Remember, the gun will kick back toward you when you pull the trigger, so prepare for the recoil and don't lock your arms. Now, focus on the target in front of you, slide your finger onto the trigger, and squeeze it."

As I mimicked Calian's instructions with my invisible gun, my muscles tensed in anticipation. The idea of protecting my family was exhilarating. But I knew it wouldn't be easy. I had to prove to myself that I could do it.

"Nice job, Martha. It probably feels weird without a gun, but we can't lose any time," Calian said. "Keep practicing that grip and stance. You'll get the hang of it and be ready for the real thing whenever the time comes."

"Thanks, Calian. You mean 'if' the time comes?" I replied. A flash of anxiety built inside me. Was it really a 'when' I need to shoot a gun, or an 'if?'

"Alright, let's keep going," Calian's eyes met Ava's, followed by an awkward smile.

I noticed Ava gaining confidence with the pistol under Calian's watchful instructions. Our eyes met and I could see her heart filled with joy. Ava found potential love in the last place I would imagine anyone finding love.

"Remember, when you're aiming, focus on your target and breathe steadily," Calian coached Ava as he wrapped his arms around hers and placed his hands over hers. "Don't jerk the trigger; squeeze it steadily. One fluid motion."

"Like this?" Ava asked, pretending to be invested in the instructions, but her eyes remained fixed on his hands as they snuggled hers.

"Exactly," Calian said with an encouraged smile. "You're doing great, Ava."

Dwindling sunlight cast eerie shadows once again. Another nightly reminder to be on guard. A cracking tree branch startled me, and I noticed Samuel picked up a stout tree branch he immediately swung with ease.

"Alright, everyone," he called out. "We're going to learn some tips and tricks on different ways to use tree branches on the Chippers."

Ava snatched a baseball bat-sized branch and instantly swung it like a ninja with a sword. She had always been the more naturally athletic one, and I felt a twinge of jealousy at her gracefulness. But I pushed those feelings aside and focused on Samuel's instructions as I searched for a lighter branch.

"First, find a branch that's strong enough to withstand the force of multiple, rough blows, but not too heavy for you to wield comfortably for a long time." Samuel demonstrated his words with his makeshift weapon as he spun it like a fan of death. "Once you've got the correct branch, you should be able to fend off any Chipper. Here are some techniques that can help."

Samuel pulled me aside. "Hey, Martha. How about you and I train one-on-one?" I noticed Elu and Dad training together while Calian and Ava continued their flirtatious training tango.

"Yeah, that should be fine, but I'm not very good at these things."

He chuckled. "Don't worry, I've actually taught dozens of self-defense classes before the world lost its mind."

Samuel taught me everything he could in the short time we had. I learned how to block, strike, and even do a "Punyo strike."

"Hey, look at you!" Samuel called out. He flashed a grin as I successfully swung my branch, spun it, then did a second fluid attack. "You're a natural, Martha."

"Thanks, Coach." My confidence grew with each imagined strike exploding microchips. Running out of breath, I took a quick moment to catch it. Everyone worked hard to hone their skills as we inched closer to surviving the apocalypse. My hope grew with every minute we learned how to defend ourselves.

While I practiced my strikes, Samuel made his way to Elu and Dad, who were having an intense discussion. Then, a gust of wind rustled the leaves watching over us as the sun tucked behind the mountaintops, creating horizontal rays of light.

"Keep your grip firm, but not too tight," Calian told Ava. His hands guided Ava's hands on the pistol. "Remember, you want to always be in control. Not afraid."

"Like this?" Ava asked, and she glanced back over her shoulder. Her eyes met Calian's for a split second before they broke into shy giggles.

I continued to watch them, and drifted toward the conversation between Elu, Samuel, and Dad. Engrossed in a discussion about Chippers, their voices hushed as they shared knowledge and tactics for combating the zombie menace.

"Remember, headshots aren't as crucial as the movies make them seem." Elu's comments were a tough realization for Dad and Samuel. "Ammo can be useful, but melee weapons should be our preferred weapons. We need to focus all our efforts on the microchips."

"True, true," Dad agreed, and Samuel nodded. "We have to save our bullets for more desperate situations, when we find more."

Curiosity commandeered my body, and I inched closer, trying to catch some ideas they were discussing.

"Hey, Martha!" Samuel noticed me eaves dropping and broke away from Elu and Dad. "Come over here. I've got something for you."

Even more curious, I approached him and saw he had picked up a branch that dwarfed mine. More sturdy and solid, he offered it to me. "I noticed you seemed bored, like your branch wasn't challenging enough. So here you go."

Dad nodded and chuckled. "She is definitely a girl that loves challenges and needs to be challenged. You've got this, Martha."

"Thanks, Dad... I guess." I wanted to overcome the challenge, but I wasn't the athletic type. It seemed like a mundane challenge for Ava, since she could conquer any athletic challenge, but it wasn't great for me.

Samuel showed me the proper way to hold and wield an oversized branch, adjusting my grip and stance until I felt comfortable and in control of the behemoth.

"There you go. It just takes some minor tweaks to adjust to smaller and larger weapons," Samuel's eyes lit up as he watched me step out of my comfort zone. "Now let's see what you can do with it."

Together, we practiced the same moves and countermoves as before, but with minor tweaks to my movements. Samuel patiently explained each step while I did my best to follow his guidance.

Between techniques, I couldn't help but sneak peeks at Ava and Calian. Their laughter and flirtation grew the hope in my heart that, even with all the loss and despair we'd endured, someone could find love in the most unlikely place imaginable.

Samuel snapped me out of my daze. "Alright, Martha," he snatched the branch from my hand. "I'm going to teach you how to use this as leverage against a Chipper."

He slammed one end of the branch into the soil and pressed it against the back of my knees. "If you plant one end in the ground like this, you can trip or even flip a Chipper if you're forced to fight."

"Whoa!" My heart raced when I grabbed the branch from Samuel and mimicked his actions. A surge of power ran through me at the idea that someone as small and weak as me had a shot at taking down a Chipper.

"Great job! Now, let's try some techniques to defend against a raging Chipper." We practiced twists and turns designed to knock an opponent's arms away as they reached for my legs or arms. His patience and encouragement reminded me of Dad when I was learning to ride a bike. Something about it seemed so fatherly.

"Martha, you're doing fantastic," Samuel praised, again.

"Thanks. I couldn't do it without your help, Uncle Samuel." I couldn't help but bow my head at the comment, hoping it wasn't too much.

I peered up to see tears flooding his eyes. "I'm sorry? Was that weird to say?"

"It… you're welcome, Martha." Samuel wiped his eyes with his shirt as he turned and sauntered into the edge of our clearing.

Without Samuel, my gaze drifted back to Ava and Calian. Their laughter echoed through the trees, and Calian leaned in and wrapped his arms around her as he continued to show her how to hold the pistol and aim properly. It was the hundredth time he'd done that, clarifying that their practice ended a while ago and they had moved to flirting practice.

A swell of warmth filled my chest at the sight of their budding connection. However, my heart slowed as my eyes connected with Samuel's figure still wiping his eyes.

"Samuel?" I called out.

One last wipe took the remaining tears from his eyes. He straightened, and a deep exhale left his chest. He spun on his heel and strutted back to me with his recent iconic, forced smile that hid so much pain.

"Sorry, Samuel," I muttered, refocusing on the task at hand. We continued to practice. My movements became smoother and more fluid as I gained control over the branch. Every twist and turn I mastered felt like power I'd never had before. A step toward becoming strong like Ava and Dad.

The Sun struggled to stay above the horizon, casting dappled shadows on Dad and Elu as they continued to discuss in hushed tones. They kept their space from one another, like they were trying to maintain a respectful distance out of remembrance for their lost loved ones. And yet, I saw how their eyes met. A spark of attraction with an unexpected, but undeniable, connection.

"Martha, did you hear me? Let's try that last move again," Samuel instructed, as he noticed my distracted attention. Perhaps his words were a distraction.

"Alright," I refocused on my training as my fingers clamped down and my muscles tensed.

I executed the attack—a downward swing, followed by a reverse block, finishing with a neck blow.

Finishing the attack, my mind reverted to Dad and Elu. Both had suffered so much. Dad lost his wife, and Elu, her husband. I wanted Dad to find true happiness, especially with how volatile things had become between him and Mom, but a part of me felt it wasn't right, either.

"Good job!" Samuel's praise snapped me back again. "You're really getting the hang of this."

"Thanks," I replied with a distracted smile. "You're a skilled teacher."

"You definitely have a competitive spirit. That can go a long way in an apocalypse... I think," Samuel chuckled.

"Did you and Jordan ever want to have kids?" The question escaped my mouth before I could stop it. The fatherly glow in Samuel's eyes had beckoned the question.

Samuel's smile faltered and his eyes swelled.

"Yeah," he answered softly, then swallowed hard. "Jordan and I talked about having three kids once we were married. Both of us were only children, so we wanted to create a big, loving family together."

"I'm sorry," I regretted my words immediately. "I didn't mean to bring up something so personal. It's just—"

"No, it's alright," he reassured me. "It's comforting to remember the dreams we once had, even if they can't come true now. If I forget about Jordan, that's when I'll truly lose her."

"Your love for Jordan... it's so pure and genuine." His vulnerability was refreshing and differed from what I had been trying to accomplish. "She must have been an incredible person."

A tear from each eye rolled down his cheeks. His conflicted face fought between true happiness and utter pain.

"She was."

A sudden, overwhelming rage hijacked Samuel. He spun and obliterated his staff against a tree trunk, and splinters shot out everywhere. The loud crack echoed throughout the forest, startling everyone.

"Samuel!" I cried out. Had I ruined his calm demeanor? "I'm so sorry. I didn't mean to upset you."

His knees buckled, and he fell against the battered tree. Wiping away rageful tears, he slowly shook his head. "It's not your fault, Martha. I shouldn't have done that. It's just... those zombies stole the only thing in this world I ever truly loved, and I have no way of ever bringing her back. It's a horrible truth I'll have to accept one day."

I clenched my fist around my branch and envisioned myself shattering it in my palms. Becoming closer to Samuel had lodged more of his pain in my heart. Even though I didn't know her very well, part of me felt like I had lost Jordan, too.

Across the clearing, Calian and Ava seemed to regain their composure after the sudden outburst. They exchanged whispers and shy glances as they resumed their lighthearted flirting mixed with gun safety.

Elu and Dad marched toward Samuel and me, concerned eyes and lowered brows locked onto our faces.

"Are you okay, Samuel?" a consoled hand followed Elu's desperate tone on his shoulder.

"Yeah." He faked a smile, but it failed to convince anyone. "It's just… it's not fair, you know? Having someone you love with every ounce of your heart snatched away like nothing."

"Life is never fair," Dad added, and his unceasing strength diminished into a shattered boy. "But that doesn't change the fact that we must keep fighting for those who aren't here to fight. Use your memories to strengthen your spirit."

I choked down the pit in my throat. Dad was right. We all had to face our despair and fight for those still here, and those who were no longer with us.

"Let's keep training," I suggested, trying to steer the conversation toward something more positive. "These Chippers are tough and 'upgrading' all the time."

Samuel perked up, drawing in a deep breath and wiping his eyes once again. "You're right, Martha. We can't be too prepared for these monsters."

The last remnants of daylight dissolved into the leaves. Samuel and I attempted to power through more training before Elu and Dad cut in with more encouraging words.

"We've all lost someone. The Chippers took my husband. Peter lost his wife. We know what you're going through. Use that pain but control it." Elu tried to assist Samuel with channeling his rage.

Dad nodded. "Our children give us a reason to keep fighting, but that doesn't mean we don't feel the pain of losing our partners. You need to find your reason to keep fighting."

Samuel's eyes filled with tears as he clutched his shotgun. "This is all I have left of my old life," his shaky voice returned. "My family growing up... they either died or walked out of my life. Jordan was the only person who ever loved me for just being... me. I never had to fake anything with her. Now I'm alone, again."

"You're not alone, though," I told Samuel and propped my branch against my shoulder, my failed attempt to act tough. "You have us now. You're part of our family, for better or worse."

Samuel's eyes locked onto mine. His eyes, red-rimmed but grateful.

"Thank you, Martha." He inhaled partial breaths between subdued tears. "You're right. All of you... you are my family now. My apocalyptic family."

The warmth of Elu and Dad's hands on Samuel's shoulders seemed to seep into his broken soul. Whether our words, or the connection through touch, light returned to Samuel's eyes. Elu and Dad stood beside him like parents comforting their heart-broken teen.

"Remember this, Samuel," Dad whispered. "We're three grown-ups and three kids who have survived the apocalypse up to this point. You're an unofficial dad, whether you like it or not. At least you didn't lose tons of sleep to be knighted as a dad."

A smile tugged at Samuel's mouth and he looked over his newly appointed "kids." Then he turned to Elu and Dad.

"Thank you, everyone," Sincerity emanated from Samuel's words.

He cleared his throat and blinked away some tears. "You know, if I'd had a child... I always wanted a daughter."

I had to exert all my strength to hold back my own tears.

My heart swelled for a stranger I'd met just days ago. As if on cue, a rustling grabbed our attention, and we turned to see two deer, a mother and a fawn, break through the trees. They turned to acknowledge our presence with alert ears. The mother seemed to have a slight limp but continued to protect her offspring.

"Wow!" Ava exclaimed, surprised by the deer because of her distraction. She tried to extinguish her excitement, not wanting to startle them. "They're so majestic."

I couldn't help but smile as I noticed Calian sneak his fingers between hers. The simple gesture spoke volumes. At that moment, it felt like the world was healing.

"Nature survives by never giving up. That's what we must do to survive." Elu reminded us, never taking her eyes off the mother. "Despite everything, we need to enjoy what brief moments we are gifted while being prepared to defend what we have."

I realized we were like the mother deer, bruised but not broken by the changing world. We could push through, one step at a time.

The moonlight cast a whimsical glow on the deer as they sauntered into the next thicket of trees. We stood, mesmerized, by the beauty of the moment.

"Last time we saw a wild animal," Dad quipped, trying to lighten the mood. "An unusual sound followed before all hell broke loose."

Everyone shot him a look of dread, but he smiled reassuringly. "Don't worry. This isn't something you can jinx."

No one spoke for several minutes, awaiting our superstitious end. Like statues, no one moved a muscle, while our eyes darted around, checking every ounce of forest for movement. But when nothing happened, Dad grinned triumphantly. "See? I told you. Dads know everything."

Laughter spilled into the forest. Everyone seemed to relax at the absurdity of it all. Elu and Samuel playfully shoved Dad over his jinx. Ava and Calian, still hand-in-hand, continued their awkward teenage flirting. All I could do was enjoy one of the best moments I'd had in years.

I let my guard down and peered up at the nearly full moon surrounded by hundreds of stars. Imagined camping trips flashed through my head, triggered by the ambiance of joy and serenity under the world's biggest nightlight.

"Wha-?" Dad stammered; his laughter cut short.

"Shh," Calian muttered, dropped Ava's hand, and caroled her behind him.

An unusual siren blared a few hundred feet from where we stood. Like a banshee's wail from some distant place, it shattered our tranquility. As it had happened before, something synthetic, man-made, stole our happiness.

"Everyone, stay close," Elu instructed. Once again, she returned to her shaky, yet strong, stance.

"Samuel, do you recognize that sound?" I asked, hoping he might provide some comfort or explanation. But his mind remained trapped in a state of confusion.

"I've never heard a siren like that," he finally admitted. His body lowered to the ground as he blindly reached for a branch to defend himself with, without taking his focus away from the trees. "But I've never heard of a "good" siren."

"Maybe it's just a malfunctioning device somewhere," Dad said to convince everyone, even himself.

"Or maybe it's a warning?" Ava whispered. "Something worse than the Chippers?"

"Let's not jump to conclusions. We know nothing yet. It could be a siren from another group of survivors." Samuel's words echoed false hope.

"Whatever it is, we can't stay here," Elu decided. "We need to head in the opposite direction of whatever that is."

Fear strangled my every breath. *Why did this always happen?* Every time we found a moment of peace, something came along to rip it away. "What if we split up?" I suggested hesitantly. "One group goes to investigate the sound, the other stays here?"

"Splitting up is never a good idea," Calian countered, still focused on the trees surrounding us. "We're stronger together."

"Calian's right," Samuel agreed. "For now, let's stick together and head west. We'll figure out our next move once we find somewhere safer."

As one, we moved through the forest in a hushed hurry. The siren continued to wail every few minutes. Eventually, I questioned if it was in my head or not. The laughter, flirtation, and connection we shared evaporated at the first ring of the electronic sound.

Would that be our life from now on? Was the sound created by a friend, a foe, or something completely new?

CHAPTER 10: SACRIFICE

After about an hour, I wondered if the siren had finally ceased blaring its doom-like song. Then the call blasted into the night sky. A bone-chilling sound that didn't signal a warning, but a threat.

"Samuel, take Martha, Ava, and Calian. You guys go on ahead and we'll slow down whatever is creating this siren," Dad instructed.

"I think we all know what's creating the siren, but I'll protect the kids," Samuel replied and nodded for us all to follow him.

Dad and Elu snuck away. Their figures blended into the trees as they headed to an overlook. From there, they seemed to stalk whatever tried to stalk us.

Curious, we walked for a bit before copying Elu and Dad's actions. We wanted reassurance of survivors attempting to locate us, or confirmation that Chippers wanted a second chance to stamp out the rest of our lives.

"Can you see anything?" I asked no one in particular, curious if anyone's eagle eyes spotted movement in the distance.

"Nothing. It's too dark and too quiet," Calian murmured back. The one person I thought would notice something, with his hunting mentality and all.

Time stretched on with nothing more than the stars above and occasional breezes parting my hair. Then, I noticed something terrifying—the sirens had stopped.

"Martha, did you notice—" Ava seemed to read my mind.

"The sirens? I know."

Samuel's confusion didn't catch on. "The sirens?"

"Do you hear them?"

"No... oh. Wait!"

A shiver made my entire body tremble.

"Stay alert," Samuel reminded, a saying that had become his catch phrase since the nightmare began.

My breath caught in my throat as movement emerged. A shadow crossed the creek with disjointed, snapping steps and the eerie green light illuminated its figure. A Chipper, unmistakable even from our distant perch. The creature meandered aimlessly, like it lacked a target or goal. It stopped every few feet and threw its grotesque head back. Its mouth opened unnaturally wide as if to produce a chilling siren, but no sound emerged. Then it erratically recoiled and stumbled directly under us.

"That's... that's a Chipper?" The words chilled me as they left my mouth. The terror remained, but we trained for the situation. A single Chipper shouldn't cause issues for our group of warriors.

Samuel gestured for us to halt with stern, silent intent. His eyes fixed on the lone figure below. Its head snapped back again as its eyes locked onto our position before it valiantly searched for a way to reach us. Its clumsy movements made it slip and stumble in the loose debris at the bottom of our perch.

"Martha, listen." Ava turned her head to lock her eyes on mine. "We've trained for this. We can handle one."

The certainty in her voice resonated inside me, even as my heart raced at the fear of confrontation.

"We take it down quietly," Calian whispered. "It's alone. And if we're fast, we won't draw any more of them here."

"If we do this, we do it right." Samuel nodded toward Calian. "It seems to know we're here. So let's creep down to it, then we'll all attack at once. Calian, you take the chip in its right hand. Ava, you take the chip in its left hand. I'll take its neck chip. Martha, you stay on guard in case any of us need help or this Chipper isn't alone."

We all nodded, and confidence and adrenaline rushed through my veins. As one, we left our overlook and crept through the forest. We tiptoed around every twig and fall-colored leaf that could announce our movements.

The zombie continued its bizarre ritual as it struggled up the hillside toward our previous spot. Its head continued to snap back for another call, but silence followed. We each prepared our makeshift weapons for the assault.

Calian's single hand in the air halted us in our scattered positions. Everyone froze as the grunting and groaning of the Chipper frantically stumbled nearby.

We descended upon the creature with vengeful rage. Ava and Calian flanked it with precise movements that relied on trust. Then Samuel directly attacked, like an arrow shot from a hate-filled bow.

With each silent stride, we drew closer as I followed Samuel. I followed so close I saw his vengeful tears fall onto dead leaves.

My fingers curled around the rough bark of an old maple branch and I peered through the dense foliage. The heavy air wrapped around my chest, squeezing the air from my lungs. Like a spider, we waited for the lone Chipper to enter our web.

Hours passed between heartbeats. Then, a silence shattering siren erupted. Shrill and close, it shattered our confidence in the trap. The crunch of dead leaves followed the noise underfoot as the Chipper entered a perfect opening for our attack.

I made eye contact with Samuel before he tucked behind a protruding jagged rock. Ava and Calian shared their hiding spot behind a forked tree as they glanced at me, then at Samuel. We shared acknowledgement that our time neared, despite the terrifying Chipper scream.

I held my breath when Calian climbed around the tree with an assassin's expertise. He closed in on the zombie, ducking from tree to tree and motioning for Ava to stay in her hiding spot.

The Chipper paused mid-stumble. Its head jerked to the side as if sensing something amiss, but it was too late. Calian launched at it and struck a leaping blow on the Chipper's neck. The strength of his strike surprised the Chipper, and it stumbled against a tree, like a newborn deer learning to walk.

Seizing the moment, Calian swung at its right hand, but he missed. His determined demeanor shattered with the branch as it slammed against the tree trunk and steely confidence disappeared with the branch as he became an unarmed child. We remained frozen in fear.

As Ava turned away from the impending end of her crush, two shadows darted from nowhere and landed two coordinated blows on the Chipper's left and right hand.

A guttural groan escaped the creature as it faltered. All its jerking movements ceased as its limp body crumbled. The two figures stood over the Chipper as the green luminescence faded into the white glow of moonlight. The features of the two heroes slowly became more visible, and Calian wrapped his arms around one of them. Elu and Dad stepped into the moonlight, seizing the moment none of us were strong enough to do.

"Ava! Calian is safe. We did it!" I shouted to Ava, who continued to cover her face. After she peeked through her hands, she sprinted toward Calian and reached him just as he turned to embrace her. They shared a deep sigh of relief. We emerged from our hideouts to revel in a rare moment of victory. The stillness of the Chipper's fallen form gave us a sense of security. We were safe, for the moment.

"Dad," I said, swaying as the adrenaline leaving my body. My body couldn't muster more words to express my excitement at seeing Dad safe.

Our hope was short-lived. Another siren wailed, a chilling echo that raced through the valley and made my skin crawl. Did the defeated Chipper announce our location and did its last signal call for the others to attack its last location? Were the upgraded Chippers already that advanced?

Silence fell over us as we awaited another siren. On cue, a second wail followed, more distinctive than the first. Before we knew it, the Chipper calls echoed from varying locations. Each siren seemed subtly different, like voices calling out to each other... or wolves howling to alert the rest of the pack.

"Positions!" Elu barked, breaking the spell the ominous chorus had cast upon us. Instinctively, we formed a circle facing outward, backs pressed together. My heart hammered against my ribcage. We had struggled against a lone Chipper. Were they the howls of the dozen earlier across the creek?

"Stay close," Ava whispered to me, her motherly instincts taking over even in the face of overwhelming odds.

I nodded, swallowing the lump in my throat. I gripped my branch like it was the only thing standing between me and the Grim Reaper.

The forest oozed with movement. Shadows morphed and twisted into macabre silhouettes. The dozen Chippers I had noticed before caught up to us, a finality to a terrifying, deadly game of cat-and-mouse. The green glow reflected off their dead eyes, vacant and milky, fixed on us with relentless determination to end our lives. Fresh mountain air carried by the breeze became stale and wreaked of death. And the wind ceased, scared off by the monsters.

Ava snatched my hand, and Calian grasped her other. "Martha, whatever happens, don't give up."

Terror kidnapped my voice along with my breath. Words felt meaningless when a massacre could begin at any moment. But I clung to her hand like it was the only thing keeping me anchored to survival, and perhaps it was.

The open area teemed with technological zombies. With darting eyes, I tried to count the endless Chippers encircling us.

Calian's whisper alarmed us all. "Seventeen."

"Seventeen?" Elu tossed the question into the air in disbelief.

"There's seventeen Chippers. That means we need to defeat roughly three Chippers each to survive."

A chill rushed up my back so violently my body shook. Up to then, we'd struggled to defeat a single Chipper alone.

I descended further into the heart of our group, holding onto Ava's hand, and the adults and Calian stepped into the threat. Determined not to let it be our last moment.

As our self-appointed warriors stepped closer into a lopsided battle, the Chippers didn't move an inch, aside from their typical twitches and spasms. Their tactics had changed from our last battle.

Without warning, all seventeen zombies charged at once. Like a dam breaking, a flood of decaying flesh and green lights roared at us. Crunching twigs and guttural groans filled the fall air.

"Look out!" Ava screamed, and she shoved me sideways. I slid with the movement and sidestepped the creature. Its loose flesh brushed against my forearm, a disgusting reminder of who we were fighting. Its rancid breath lingered in the air near me.

"Keep moving! Don't stand still!" Calian shouted, followed by a duck under a swipe and a shove to knock the Chipper off balance.

Elu quietly drew her hatchet. Her eyes glossed over and she became a woman on a mission, possessed by the soul of a samurai as she danced around the Chippers. She sliced and gutted creature after creature in fluid spins and dances, trying to reach her "three Chipper" goal as fast as possible.

"Got one—no, two!" she shouted.

Her triumph was short-lived as she realized her mistake. The Chippers kept attacking, unfazed by the loss of a couple of them, and Elu quickly lost some stamina.

"More of them!" I pointed to the tree line, where another three Chippers stumbled from the shadows. Our combined effort ended six of the seventeen Chippers, before the new ones joined the assault.

"Stay together and keep fighting!" Dad's voice reminded me to trust the process and use my training. I tightened my grip on the branch and inhaled, breathing strength into my muscles and heart.

A single step forward with renewed power propelled me into Dad's battle as I assisted him. His movements had improved, parrying side to side as he struck the Chippers's neck.

Not wanting to distract Dad, I scurried through the chaos back to Ava's spot.

"Martha, watch out!" Ava's shout ricocheted through the bodies.

I spun to face a lone zombie that had singled me out. It staggered toward me, desperate lust in its milky eyes. Eyes void of life yet fixed on my presence. Perhaps it sensed my innocence, my doubt in my abilities. But underneath my hesitation, a fire of survival had awakened.

A voice in my head reminded me I could do it, but those words slammed against a brick wall of fear. I shifted my weight and gripped the sturdy branch as I settled into the training I had become comfortable with.

The Chipper closed in and lunged at my chest. Its lunge stirred feelings of dread with its unnatural gait and distorted limbs. I ushered the mangled body past me with the branch like a matador dancing with a raging bull.

"Nice move, Martha!" Samuel cheered for me as he took a moment from his battle while his Chipper struggled to rise from the dirt.

The zombie prepared for another attack; I planted my feet firmly, imagining them rooting into the dirt to become immoveable. The Chipped barreled toward me with continued resolve. I jammed the branch into the earth and twisted it sharply. The makeshift lever caught the Chipper by surprise and sent its feet high into the air as its momentum threw it several feet from me.

Nausea hit me as I battled between my "fight or flight" response, seeing the moment as an opening to flee. But there was no room for weakness, not then. Its hand, embedded with one of those cursed microchips, shone like a lighthouse, calling to me. Hesitation kidnapped my muscles, though. The thought of crushing flesh, even zombie flesh, made the acid in my stomach rise into my throat.

"Come on, Martha. Do it!" the voice in my head screamed at me.

With a muffled battle cry, partly asking for forgiveness and partly wanting vengeance, I swung the branch down with everything I had. The microchip shattered and tiny crystal-like fragments glistened in the moonlight. I officially progressed in gaining the strength I'd yearned for, but the battle was far from over.

Curious if anyone had witnessed my takedown, I scanned the battlefield. Bodies, blood, and green luminescence glittered around the scene. The Chipper I took down stood as upright as it could and prepared for another assault. Its slumping body tightened like a spring about to launch.

I prepared, too, and hoisted my branch over my shoulder into a striking position. The twitching Chipper lunged, and I met it with all the strength I could place behind my swing and closed my eyes. The strike felt unusual, and I opened my eyes to a terrifying sight. My dedicated Chipper, with its one bloody eye and missing chunk of skin that reached from the corner of its mouth up to its ear, clutched the end of my branch with a haunting, calm demeanor. Terror radiated from my hands into my body and I locked eyes with the Chipper. In a confusing twist, it seemed to plead for forgiveness. A small tear rolled from the bloody eye, but its mouth curled into a demonic, threatening smile that forced every muscle in my body to go limp. The instant I slackened, the Chipper hurled my branch far into the woods and returned to its unnatural twitching, meeting my every retreating with an advancing one.

I scurried back and all I could do was stare into the Chippers's eyes. It stopped advancing on me when my back slammed into something. I spun around to find Ava in an identical situation.

The snarling, flailing limbs and branches transformed into an almost silent forest as we realized the Chippers slowly encircled and cornered us against a cliff. My breath came in ragged gasps and I peeked over the ledge at the sheer drop none of us could survive.

The eight remaining Chippers slowly closed in on us in synchronized movements. Dad and Elu shared a loving and longing stare accompanied by tearful smiles.

With her eyes still locked on Dad's, Elu called to Samuel with a calm finality in her tone. "Hey, Samuel…"

"Kinda busy here!" Samuel barked back, making wild swings at the Chippers closest to him.

"Look after Calian!" Elu said through a continued, tearful smile. A sense of calm washed over her as the words left her mouth.

Calian's gaze snapped to Elu and his puzzled look couldn't understand what to do next. But there wasn't enough time to react with the monsters closing in on us.

"Dad?" I yelled, terrified that his facial features matched Elu's. "What's going on?"

"Samuel, please, take care of Martha and Ava for me, too!" Dad's tone included the same finality, unfazed by the impending technological terror.

A dread settled in my stomach that almost knocked the breath from my lungs. No. They couldn't be thinking… I refused to let that thought finish. We were supposed to survive the apocalypse together and keep what family we had left, all three of us.

"Martha, stay strong!" Dad called to me as he turned with a smile. Tears flooded his eyes. "Ava, make smart choices and watch after your sister." Dad's eyes met mine before he turned back to Elu. "I love you two very much. Always remember that."

Before Ava or I could react, a blur of motion caught my eye. Elu sprinted toward the Chipper closest to the cliff, directly across from her, and slid into its feet. The attack launched the creature to its demise on the unforgiving rocks below. She hopped back up to her feet and lunged for a fallen tree trunk in desperation. We couldn't move a muscle, our feet rooted in place, refusing to shuffle. As she reached the trunk, Elu struggled to lift the bulbous potential weapon.

"Go!" Dad's command struggled to pierce through the growing snarls and groans emanating from the hungry Chippers, curious about Elu's actions. But Dad understood Elu's goal, and he took off as soon as the Chippers attention changed to spectating Elu.

He sprinted past the creatures and headed for the same tree trunk. Dad slid up to Elu and grabbed the opposite end of the trunk. Together they lifted the stout piece just as the Chippers launched toward them with their jerky, unnatural movements. I assumed they figured out Elu and Dad's plan.

"Stay strong, all of you." Dad shouted as his demeanor flipped to a dedicated warrior. "Watch over one another!" Elu added, her features constricted into an unbeatable protector.

Their words reached my ears, but it was like they were in an unknown language. My brain still struggled to process their strategy. Then hit me that every Chipper left our position to stop Elu and Dad.

"Stay focused!" Samuel shouted. He stood in front of us with his arms outstretched to create a protective wall. "We're not done yet!"

I nodded and clenched my jaw. We weren't done. Not by a long shot. Dad and Elu had a plan, but we still needed to cover them. Whatever it took, we fought together until the end.

Wrestling the stout trunk between them, Dad and Elu hoisted the heavy piece to their chests. Their muscles bulged under the weight. The fallen tree, thick and unwieldy, demanded the strength of both to maneuver it. Slow with their movements, the moonlight emphasized the menacing figure they became as the Chippers closed in on them.

"Samuel, thank you for everything," Elu struggled to shout as she and Dad corralled the Chippers between the tree trunk and the cliff. "Look after them and keep them safe."

"Stay safe, too, Samuel," Dad shouted, a finality in his voice, a tone of thank you and goodbye.

Their words hung in the air, and my heart twisted. A lump formed in my throat, making it hard to speak or breathe. Was our family about to be down to Ava and me? Were we about to become apocalyptic orphans? The thought engulfed my brain, making any other thoughts impossible.

Dad and Elu shared glances. They weren't just saying goodbye to us; they were saying goodbye to each other. I rebelled against the thought, refusing to believe what was unfolding before us.

The zombies, reinvigorated by their sinister AI, fought back against the trunk. They pushed back as one, creating a stalemate against Dad and Elu. Dad noticed a nearby tree, locked his end of the trunk against it, and rushed to help Elu on her side so as not to lose any ground against the hellish nightmare.

"Keep pushing!" Dad let out a battle cry that expressed the unbearable pain of losing.

Standing between us and death, Elu and Dad pushed with every ounce of resolve in their bodies. I swallowed hard, fighting back tears. Winning meant losing Dad. But maybe we didn't have to lose Dad and Elu if the rest of us helped them push the Chippers off the cliff.

I sprinted toward Dad to help rid the world of these Chippers. "We need to help!"

"Back! Stay back!" Dad's voice cut through the chaos, ending any chance of aid.

The Chippers clawed at their faces and arms, desperately trying to stop their own end. Blood stained the tree trunk as Chipper claws tore into Dad and Elu's flesh. Blood smeared across their arms and droplets splashed onto twigs and leaves strewn across the forest floor, painting a grim portrait of their battle.

Putting their heads down, Elu and Dad attempted to finish the battle immediately. Their added strength, as little as it was, forced the Chipper's backward, inching ever closer to the cliff's edge. In a last, desperate attempt, the relentless zombies clung to Dad's and Elu's arms and torsos as they attacked around the tree trunk. Red streaks adorned their faces, contorted with effort and pain, yet they pushed on, driven by a love for us that knew no bounds.

"Please, stop," Calian's voice broke, raw with disbelief. "Don't do this."

But it was too late. In an ultimate act of love, Dad and Elu leaped from the cliff, sending themselves, the tree trunk, and the seven remaining Chippers to their brutal resting place. For a moment, it seemed as if time itself had stopped, hanging suspended by their sacrifice.

"NO!" The scream tore from my throat, a futile plea against our reality. Ava and Calian collapsed to their knees in unison. Both struck by the same pain of losing their remaining parent.

Samuel dropped to his knees. He didn't need to say anything. His eyes spoke volumes of the love and camaraderie we'd all lost. Torn away in an instant.

The uncomfortable silence proved the cliff had swallowed them whole. Something inside me wanted to do something, to rewind time and change what had happened, but my legs wouldn't move. My world narrowed to the spot they had disappeared, and something inside me broke.

"Samuel, why?" Ava's broken whisper followed the wind that swept through the trees, carrying away the echoes of our parents' final screams.

I stood there, numb with disbelief. The silence enveloped me. No more snarls, no more groans, just the void they left behind. Our bodies crumbled feet from each other, yet it felt like we were light-years apart. Dad and Elu had given us a chance to live, and we needed to honor them by surviving and remembering every lesson they'd taught.

Tears blurred my vision, and the ground beneath me trembled. My knees hit the dirt with a deep thud, but I barely felt it. The searing pain in my chest eclipsed everything else.

"No, no, no!" I screamed in my head. The surrounding forest absorbed our cries, offering no comfort, only an eerie silence in return.

"Martha," Samuel's voice strained as he crawled closer to where Calian, Ava, and I crumpled on the ground. He reached out, his hands trembled as he pulled me in close, his attempt to shield us from the reality we couldn't escape.

"Stop them! Please, someone stop them!" Ava's powerless plea drifted to the stars above.

Like the last remnants of an innocent pre-teen childhood flew over the cliff with everyone else, it shattered me. Dad and Elu… they were gone forever. And there we were, alive, but so very lost.

"Samuel, what are we going to do?" Calian's weak whisper was nothing like his typical confidence. A heavy sorrow that handcuffed his strength.

Samuel emphasized the need to stick together and leave before other Chippers could swarm the area. Samuel choked down his emotions, trying to put us first like a stand-in parent.

A chill swept through the forest, stirring from the spot of our loved ones and the creatures that had gone with them had left the world. Ava was all I had left. The cruel new world had ripped both my parents from my life in mere days. But I couldn't let it consume me. I needed to find my strength, and fast.

"Samuel's right. We need to go." My voice startled everyone. I was the last person they expected to speak up. "Let's not let their sacrifice be in vain."

Samuel looked at me, then squinted and something shifted in his expression. A flicker of determination that mirrored the same resolve hardening within me.

"Martha's right." Ava wiped away tears with the back of her hand. "We need to keep fighting for them."

We clung to our sobs, the only testament of the battle we'd endured. I knew one thing with chilling clarity; the Martha who had laughed and played at school while enjoying her childhood, was dead. In her place, I needed to build a new Martha. Someone who could grow in a hellish world, just like our nemesis did. With Ava, Calian, and Samuel by my side, I couldn't let the darkness consume me.

CHAPTER 11: ALONE

The world beyond the cliff blurred through my tears. I clutched Ava's hand. Her weak grip was the only thing that kept me tethered to reality. Calian stood beside us, his eyes hollow. The last remnants of childhood innocence swept away with the chilly wind drifting into the valley.

"Come on, kids." Samuel's words fell on deaf ears and he choked back his own tears. "We can't stay here."

I didn't want to move, didn't want to leave the place where Dad… where his form became a permanent memory. Samuel broke my bubble of grief when he crouched in front of me.

His gaze met mine, and I noticed his swollen, red eyes, tired of shedding tears for the fallen. "Martha, listen to me," he breathed. "You showed me there's still something to fight for in this hellish land. Let me return the favor."

Ava's breath hitched next to me. A sob struggled to break from her lips. She was always the strong one, always holding me up. But, as she battled her pain, I saw the little girl who used to steal cookies from the jar, or tried to convince Dad we needed pizza every night.

"Samuel's right," Ava whispered through broken sobs. "Dad... he wouldn't want us to give up."

"Everything's gone," Calian muttered. His voice filled with rage. He was alone, truly alone. Where Ava and I had each other, Samuel and Calian were orphans with no family left.

"Not everything," Samuel said, rose, and sauntered toward Calian. "You have us. And we're going to survive this together. All of us." He placed his hand on Calian's shoulder and glanced at Ava, then at me. His palm seemed to quell the rage in Calian's heart.

"Let's take it one step at a time," he continued, pulling us close. "If you need an outlet, let's aim that anger toward defeating these demons."

The words were a vow, a silent oath that bound the four of us together amid our destroyed lives. Ava removed her hand from my grasp and retreated to Calian's protection.

"Okay," I said, the warmth of Ava's hand leaving mine adding to my pain. "Let's keep going."

"Good." Samuel nodded. His eyes briefly closed, and he took a few breaths. "And we start now."

We agreed, knowing we'd need to turn our backs to the cliff and to the void below. With Samuel, our stand-in parent, leading the way, we'd need to follow his leadership and guidance to descend the mountains.

The dirt felt cold and unwelcoming, and Samuel gently lifted me to my feet. "Focus on your next step, nothing more," he urged, positioning his sturdy frame between us and the edge of loss. I only nodded weakly, biting my lip hard to keep the sobs at bay.

"Martha, Ava." Samuel gazed into our vacant eyes. "This is our time to move forward with the remaining family we share. Our apocalyptic family." A single tear escaped his eye.

Calian remained on the ground, his eyes locked on the jagged ledge where his mother's life had ended. "I want to see her." His icy whisper chilled my body, but my heart warmed at the thought of closure. "One last farewell."

"Calian…" Samuel's voice trailed off, thick with empathy. He kneeled beside him. "That's not a memory you'll want."

Calian shook his head in denial, adamant to see Elu one last time. His eyes sparkled with desperate, pleading tears. "I need to."

Ava nodded, and she glanced between Samuel, Calian, and the ledge. "I want to see Dad, too," she murmured. "One last time."

My heart shattered all over again with continued, unyielding pain. My grief ushered me to join as I added, "Me too, I guess." It wasn't just about seeing Dad, but a chance to get closure with one last goodbye. Something we hadn't had the chance to do amid the chaos.

Outnumbered by our collective need for closure, Samuel exhaled slowly and gave a resigned nod. "Okay," he agreed solemnly. "Let's make this quick, though. Who knows how long we have before more Chippers appear."

Together, we tentatively approached the cliff. Samuel guarded our backs. He positioned himself so he could remove us from the sights below if any of us became overwhelmed.

"Watch your step near the edge." Samuel's stern tone left no room for argument.

We peered over, and the vertigo-inducing drop stretched into oblivion. When we inched closer to the edge, rocks and debris tumbled from our perch.

Calian's voice cracked as he leaned over the edge. "Mom?" The word, laced with grief, resonated through the still air, mixing with continued debris leaping from the ledge.

Ava and I carefully leaned over the ledge, hoping for a glimpse of Dad. Ava gasped as her delicate voice whispered, "Goodbye, Dad." She clutched my hand, and together, we faced the reality of our loss.

I leaned a little farther to make up for my height when the gut-wrenching vision came into view. "Goodbye," was all I could muster as a lump formed in my throat. My eyes stung as I swallowed hard, imagining our father's contagious smile, his arms always ready to envelop us in safety. Safety that etched itself into my memories.

"Let's get going," Samuel said as he watched the despair constrict us. He attempted to guide us away from the ledge with a sweeping motion.

We wanted one last glance at the jagged rocks that ended our old lives and shuffled closer. Dirt and rocks crunched under our death-defying steps. I hesitated, and so did my breathing, as we peered at the full scene below.

The view twisted my insides. Among the wreckage, bodies lay strewn like discarded dolls against the unforgiving rocks. Mangled bodies intertwined with shattered limbs. My sight snagged on pieces of the hefty, splintered tree trunk, dissected like the Chippers. A singular figure pinned beneath the largest section.

"Watch out!" Calian's urgent tone pulled me back from the precarious edge.

There, beneath the broken trunk, a trapped zombie thrashed. One leg grotesquely twisted beneath the weight, with one of its arms dangling by tendons. Its movements were frantic in a futile struggle against the unmovable wood. As if sensing our presence, it unnaturally snapped its head upward at us, revealing the green glint of a hand microchip.

Without a word, Calian drew his gun and fired. His revenge echoed down the valley as he murmured, "My last bullet was for you, Mom." The creature's body ceased. One less monster to destroy lives. A combined hush followed the gunshot as the echo bounced off the mountains. The finality of the shot marked an end to the last of our known pursuers.

"Down there," Ava pointed to a mangled mess of bloody bodies.

I leaned forward and my heart pounded against my ribs like a jackhammer. There they were, Elu and Dad. Their forms connected enough to suggest one last embrace amid the horror. Their hands clasped in an eternal moment, an ultimate gesture to reach out for one another in their budding romance. Around them laid the embodiments of death, a selfless reminder of their sacrifice to save others over themselves.

"Dad… I love you." The words leaped from my mouth to his resting body. Sobs handcuffed my throat, refusing to release additional words. Among the bloody monsters, they looked peaceful, covered in a blanket of blood that tucked them in for the last time.

"Let's remember them as they were." Samuel bowed his head, followed by a mumbled prayer.

"Heroes," Calian added. His eyes never retreated from his mother's figure.

"Dad… found love in the end," Ava murmured, reaching for light in the darkness.

"Forever together," I added.

A chilly gust bit my cheeks and I leaned into Ava, both of us wincing away from the ledge. Calian's breaths turned to ragged gasps and his eyes squeezed shut in pain. He pulled a cross from underneath his shirt and breathed a prayer.

"I love you, Mom," he concluded his prayer. "I'll miss you." His voice changed, and it was like he was a little boy again, the one who desperately needed his mother. After his prayer, he tucked the cross back into his shirt.

Ava closed her eyes, and I knew she pictured Dad, not as the weary fighter he'd become but as the man who'd playfully tossed us into the air, played "Tickle Chicken" with us, or kissed our boo-boos. "Goodbye, Daddy."

Samuel stood silently behind us and I caught him crossing his heart before he kissed his hand and pointed to the sky. Whatever words he offered to Elu and Dad flew off with his skyward gesture, meant only for them and the heavens above.

As we finally stepped away from our greatest loss, the sun peaked over the horizon to usher us into a fresh day. A future without our loved ones to guide us.

"Focus on the now." Samuel offered a half-eaten bag of trail mix to us from his pocket. The grief occupied our minds, but it couldn't silence our growling stomachs.

"We can't keep losing like this. I'm tired of saying goodbye," I mumbled through the handful of trail mix I tossed into my mouth. "We can't keep up with their 'upgrades,' so we need to find another way to beat them."

"I'm tired of losing people, too," Ava responded through a haze, still lost beyond our conversation. "There must be a way to stop their 'upgrades.' "

"Easier said than done," Calian interjected. The flicker of anger in his tone emphasized the challenge looming over us. "Every day we create new tactics, they evolve, making those tactics worthless."

"Dad and Elu gave their lives to find a solution. To give us a chance," I shot back as the sun's rays charged my soul. "They had faith in us discovering a way to defeat them."

"Martha's right," Samuel chimed in. "With each person we've lost, we've learned more about how they strengthen. There must be a pattern, something we're not understanding yet."

"But what are we not understanding? We don't even know what's controlling these things." The confusion in Ava's voice proved we understood little about the creatures that continued to destroy our world piece by piece.

"Today," I declared, "we begin. We need to learn and grow as fast as they do so we can end this nightmare, no matter the cost. We've all paid a heavy price already."

"Did you notice? The Chippers... they've changed their tactics every time we've encountered them," Calian pointed out and hurled a rock over the trees. I watched it disappear into the bright sunrise. "The first day, their attacks were sporadic. Then they hunted in packs. Then, they changed to fighting us on-on-one. When that failed, they tried calculated attacks. Now that they've failed again, it's almost certain there will be another 'upgrade' coming."

Calian's insight caused the muscles in his jaw to tighten. "They're adapting with every fight. Learning and changing to our defenses, figuring out how to eradicate us more effectively."

I unconsciously wrapped my arms around myself to smother the anxiety rising in me. The heat from the sun did little to thaw the dread that had frozen my joints. His words painted a grim picture of the growing horrors we struggled to contain.

"Plus, they ignored the deer... and the fox," Calian continued. The flicker in his eyes connected the traces of a pattern. "They knew we were there... They're not mindless zombies. They think. Their actions have an apparent purpose to them, even if it's as simple as wiping out humanity."

Samuel caressed a smooth, flat rock between his fingers as we descended the mountain. "Their upgrades," he murmured, almost to himself, "they're getting more sophisticated. Smarter. Stronger. More complex."

"Can we keep up?" I asked, hoping to hear the answer that screamed in my mind.

"Truth is, Martha," Samuel sighed, throwing me a glance that carried the weight of unspoken fears, "I don't know how much longer we can fight them if they continue to evolve at this pace."

His admission hung in the air. Calian's catatonic silence supported Samuel's fears.

"We need to learn more about them, understand them. They must have weaknesses." Ava's words cut into the conversation.

"Exactly!" Calian erupted. "We can't outpace them, so we need a different tactic altogether."

A rush of adrenaline shot through my veins and my mind dove deep into thought. It screamed at me it was a perfect time to write. I sat slightly apart from the group and slid down a tree trunk for a brief break. Everyone else took a moment to rest as Calian and Ava enjoyed the sunrise and Samuel drew in the dirt with a stick.

I gripped the pen and pulled the notebook from my teal backpack. My eyes hovered over the worn pages that mirrored me. Each word I etched was an attempt to anchor myself, to keep from being swept away by the tide of loss that threatened to drown me. I hoped that through the flood of words that leaped onto the page, or even from a past page, I could discover our next step toward understanding the Chippers.

Ava's dirty blonde hair reflected the orange sunrise, and the clear skies highlighted her blue streak. She perched on a fallen log, her eyes attached to Calian's silhouette. She hung on every syllable as he spoke to Samuel. A look into her soft eyes gave away her secrets. The way she leaned closer whenever he spoke, the hand holding, their shared grief and constant time together, had woven a thread between them that resembled more than just a fling.

"Calian's right." Samuel's words yanked me from my writing. "We can't just react anymore. It's about anticipating their moves. We need to do more than just try to beat them when in a fight."

"More than beating them in a fight?" Ava reiterated under her breath. Her confusion fed her fear.

I scribbled what I'd heard of their conversation, not wanting to forget any of it. Not wanting to lose the moment if it became the turning point for our survival. As a quick side note, so I wouldn't forget anything, I wrote *Mom and Dad are gone*. As each letter appeared, my vision blurred. *How do we move forward with our hearts torn in two?*

"Martha, you okay over there?" Samuel called out, noticing my seclusion.

"Fine." My typical answer emerged without thinking. I couldn't let them see the cracks. Couldn't let them know it was taking every ounce of me to not bawl my eyes out at the absence of Dad.

"Focus on the now, Martha," I whispered, echoing Samuel's advice. "One step at a time."

The conversation continued, theories and strategies bouncing like a game of apocalyptic tennis, but I didn't want to play. I wanted answers instead of more questions. I wanted to break down the walls of fear from ignorance.

Calian caught my attention when he dropped his head in defeat. "We need to stay one step ahead of the Chippers. There must be a pattern or something we're missing… but what is it?"

"Those microchips seem to connect them all together. Could something control them? Something 'upgrading' them?" I thought aloud, not realizing I'd spoken until three pairs of eyes turned to me.

"Possible… very possible," Samuel admitted, stroking his stubble. "If there is a main controller for those things, we could try to disable it?"

"Then maybe we could get back to a normal life?" Ava's eyes doubled in size at the hope of a normal life once again. But it wouldn't be a normal life without Mom or Dad.

Martha's Notebook

"Maybe." I couldn't bring myself to burst Ava's bubble. "We need to find whatever is controlling the Chippers first."

"That's easier said than done," Calian added grimly.

"It is," I repeated softly, closing my notebook with a thud. The action held a finality, the end of one chapter and the beginning of another. I would charge toward the future, no matter how bleak it seemed. I would charge without looking back.

The dark thoughts crept in just as I promised I wouldn't look back. Dad's laughter would never again echo through the trees. No more dad jokes. No more reassuring words of wisdom. No more hearing his voice call out to me. No more Dad.

"Martha?" Ava's voice cut through my torment, but I couldn't look at her. My hand trembled as I wiggled my notebook into my backpack. Our once sizeable group had dwindled to just the four of us, Ava, Calian, Samuel, and I.

"Are you okay?" she pressed again.

"I'm fine." My lies tasted like metal, burning the trust between us.

The truth gnawed at me. The Chippers were evolving, learning. They'd grown from mindless zombies to calculated monsters, able to wipe out humanity with ease. They had become the alpha predators, and we were without our strongest and wisest assets to guide us through the hellish landscape. I swore under my breath. The reality of the Chippers' invincibility ignited something deep inside me. With each thought, my anger flared, searing away the numbness that had enveloped me since the cliff.

"Martha," Calian's voice replaced Ava's. Concern grew between them as Calian crouched beside me. His eyes searched for what hid behind my stare.

"Those things took everything from us," I hissed, throwing my backpack over my shoulder. "They keep coming, relentlessly, and for what? To destroy us all? What did we do?"

"You're not alone in this," Calian attempted to console me. He placed his hand on my shoulder before immediately removing it, sensing the space I needed.

I shook my head as my rage bubbled to the surface. "But we are alone, every one of us. Orphaned by this apocalypse."

"Martha," Samuel interjected, his voice steady despite the pain in his eyes. "This is the second round of darkness we've faced. We'll probably face more, but we will push through each one."

"How many more rounds will we face until it's our last round?" I retorted, the image of Dad's lifeless body intertwined with Elu, or of Mom's body, lifeless and severed. The relentless monsters transformed our loved one's faces, once so full of life, into bloody, hollow shells.

Samuel's face contorted into pure despair before he pushed away the swelling tears and his body straightened. "Then let's make sure that doesn't happen. Let's find their control center."

Energy surged through me. I stood, feeling the weight of my parents' absence like a kick in the stomach, yet also feeling their presence lift me as though they were still guiding me. We wouldn't let their sacrifices be in vain. I would remember them, even if Mom wasn't herself toward the end. She was still my mom. The pain became fuel.

"Whatever it takes," I declared, the sun's warmth charging my words. "I'll end this apocalypse. For Mom. For Dad. For all of them and for all of us."

Ava nodded with a clenched fist. Her grief shone through her rage-filled eyes, while Calian and Samuel exchanged a look that spoke of silent agreement. It would take all of us to do it, but maybe that was enough.

The strength I searched for, to be like Dad and Ava, roared into an inferno. Its flames consumed every corner of my being. The remnants of the child I was had burned away.

"Listen. We—"

A chilling scream halted everyone. It wasn't the electronic ambush sounds we'd heard before; it was another survivor meeting their gruesome end. "If we keep trying to run, that could be us."

"Agreed," Samuel conceded.

"Where do we go then?" Calian's eagerness grew, even through his weariness.

"The government facility!" Ava shouted. "Didn't you and your mom hear about a government facility near here, Calian? Could that hide some answers?"

Calian lowered his head, followed by a deep sigh. "I completely forgot about that. They were working on... something, something that terrified the Survivalist."

"Then that's where we should start," Ava announced, her sisterly strength on full display.

"Are you sure about this?" Samuel questioned, though his stance suggested he was ready to follow wherever the path might lead.

"More than anything," I replied, meeting his glance with all the ferocity that had consumed my sorrow. "They've taken everything from me. They've taken everything from us. How many other lives have they ruined? They need to pay."

Samuel's hands attempted to smother the fire that grew inside us. "Look, I'm sure we can all assume there are Chippers nearby, and who knows how many. I think we should hunker down for now, quietly, and get some rest before we head out. It'll give us time for whatever Chippers are nearby to leave the area."

His words held a lot of truth. Our goal was to find answers, but none of us knew what those answers hid. More Chippers? Something worse than Chippers? The search for answers to end the nightmare had no limits.

Silently, we each settled under separate trees as the sun tucked us in for a brief nap. Just like I had done after extra-long school days, I let the warmth of the day lull me to sleep. Samuel mumbled something that included the words, "I love you, Jordan." Then, I glimpsed Calian kissing Ava on the cheek as they huddled close, but settled in for their quick nap.

Once we woke, we would learn what the government's involvement was with the end of the world.

CHAPTER 12: UPS & DOWNS

A robin's call startled me awake, and the sun warmed my face. It must've been afternoon, or late afternoon, based on where the sun perched. Once I sat up, I realized the soothing sound wasn't electronic or distorted and immediately, my blood settled. I glanced around and noticed Calian sitting next to a still sleeping Ava, as if on duty to watch over her and us.

He stared into the trees with a distant look, as if waiting for rustling. He noticed me and his expression flipped to one of eagerness.

"Martha, remember our discussion earlier about the Survivalist and everything?" he asked. Samuel rolled over to interact with me, too. He wasn't asleep, but laid in the sun to soak up every ounce of serenity before our journey.

I nodded, recalling the rugged stranger Elu and Calian had mentioned.

"That government outpost he mentioned…" Calian continued and glanced around as though the government would emerge and arrest him for conspiracy theories. "If Samuel and I are right, it could be close."

My heart pounded at the thought. An outpost, a beacon of hope that could be close by. I had convinced myself the journey would take months, traveling the world, searching for a chance at hope. "Could either of you guide us there?" I pressed, leaning forward, eager for added hope.

"If it's where I think it is." Calian's words felt like he was forging a weapon to fight the Chippers right in front of me. "It's only a half day or less in that direction." He pointed into the trees, exactly where he had been searching when I awoke.

The gesture sent chills through my body, both of excitement and terror. We had a direction to chase the chance to turn the tables on the zombies who had taken so much from us. We could claim vengeance for those we lost.

"Let's go find it." My determination burned as bright as the sun surfing through the clouds. "Let's find this outpost and make these things pay."

The sun's rays illuminated the land, making us feel like heroes as lights from above bestowed blessings upon us. A new, shaky confidence grew like a seedling breaking through the dirt, but I wasn't sure how surefooted its roots were.

Even as the sun's rays and my confidence tried to warm the chilly landscape, I couldn't help but retreat inward with my knees against my chest before a few icy gusts blew through our clearing. Samuel shuffled through a pocket in his jeans and produced a thin pair of small gloves. He offered them to me with a gentle smile. "You look a little chilled there. They were Jordan's…"

"Thanks, Samuel," I replied.

He wiped away the tears flooding his eyes. Samuel stepped into Dad's shoes, for us, for his desire to always be a dad. But his attempt at parenting was more than about survival. There was a tenderness in his actions, a silent promise not to let another child slip through the cracks of the broken world.

"Martha..." Samuel's softened voice reminded me of a loving dad speaking to their child. "You remind me so much of the child Jordan and I hoped for. You're stronger and braver than you know." There was a battle in his eyes between dreams of a perfect family with someone he truly loved and the nightmares of once thought to be fictional creatures, tearing away every chance of his dreams becoming reality.

I stood and gave Samuel a hug, wanting to quell his demons. Ava and Calian were on their feet across the way. They leaned into one another as they shared laughs, a rare melody that differed from the sirens that pursued us. They were like two pieces completing a heart-shaped puzzle.

"Keep your weight balanced. Aim for the center mass," Calian instructed Ava, mimicking a stance with an imaginary rifle in his hands. Ava mirrored him, nodding with absolute attentiveness. It was more than a lesson in survival, it was a dance of love. Each movement brought them closer.

"Remember when Uncle Chris took us hunting that one time?" I called to Ava as Samuel wiped additional tears from his eyes. Calian's expression softened as his loving eyes glanced at Ava's shy demeanor as she tried to play the coy girl.

"My dad would have loved you," Calian said, staring into Ava's eyes with pure affection. "You have the same spark my mom had."

"Dad and Elu..." My voice trailed off, and an ache pulsed through my heart. Calian seemed to notice the unspoken bond our parents held for one another, just like Ava and Calian had.

"Maybe they could've had something special if they had more time, just like—" Calian's gaze drifted back to Ava, and I saw it. How his eyes lingered, his careful touch when he corrected her posture.

"Like us," Ava finished with a growing smile that yearned for a forever love. Her eyes met his, and their attention became consumed by each other. Their hands met, fingers intertwined naturally. Among the decay and despair, they'd found a glimmer of something beautiful. Perhaps Ava could have some semblance of a normal family life, like she'd always dreamed of. Samuel and I may have had our dreams shattered, but perhaps someone still had a shot at theirs.

"Maybe we should give them some alone time." Samuel chuckled and ushered me toward my backpack. "We can head out whenever they're done." Another chuckle escaped Samuel and there was a twinkle in his eyes, either caused by more tears of what he'd lost or joy over the realization that others could build what he lost.

Over the next few hours, we enjoyed the sounds of the forest. Multiple birds sang their songs, and the leaves rustled. We enjoyed every second without green lights in the distance or distorted sirens tracking our movements.

Ava and Calian continued their flirtatious "training" and I dove back into my notebook. The recent events jumped from my pen onto the pages and I poured the rest of my thoughts and feelings into more blank pages.

Eventually, Samuel sat beside me, and he glanced over my shoulder and noticed the notebook. "I've been meaning to ask. Is that a diary or something?"

"Not exactly. A diary is full of secret confessions, and that's not me. This is my notebook. It's full of my thoughts and notes about life. Sometimes I feel like I'm about to explode with all the words running through my mind. And this… this helps me get my thoughts organized and stops them from fogging my brain." I chuckled, realizing how crazy I must sound. I wasn't a typical girly girl or a tomboy like Ava. I was something different.

"Wow. That's one of the most mature things I've heard. You understand a fault of your own and you've learned how to not only deal with it but twist it into a strength. You are much stronger than I thought you were."

The words hit me like an insult at first, even though I knew he never meant it that way. "I'm not strong. Ava is strong. My dad is—was strong."

We chattered about our past lives, music we liked, foods we missed, and our favorite subjects in school. It only felt like a few minutes before I noticed we'd talked away what remained of the day as the sun set. We watched what we could of the sunset as its broken light bounced between the trees. Samuel opened his mouth to speak, but before a single word emerged, a woman's scream vibrated through the mountains.

Samuel's eyes widened as he placed his finger to his lips slowly. There was a heaviness in his movement as he peeked at Ava and Calian. His voice was steady but tinged with an urgency I recognized. "We need to leave."

I nodded. My nerves hardened like the cold ground beneath us. "Maybe it's time to search for the outpost," I whispered. "We can't keep running forever."

He reached out and squeezed my shoulder, a gesture that felt paternal. "We'll get answers." His fatherly tone emerged as a promise.

As the sun tucked itself in for the night, the darkness surrounding us grew thick and suffocating again. The crease of the moon created a more eerie night than usual.

"Over here, guys," Ava called softly. Red and orange colors flickered near them as a fresh campfire burst into the dark night, its embers reflected in everyone's eyes.

I tucked my notebook away, and we wandered over to the campfire. "Do you think it's safe to light a fire when there could be Chippers heading this way?" I asked Calian.

Calian broke some twigs off a branch and tossed them into the fire. "Those screams were far away. Even if the Chippers knew exactly

Martha's Notebook

where we were, it would take them a while to reach us and they're probably busy with whomever they attacked."

As we settled by the fire, Calian's words brought comfort, despite my partial skepticism. Ava wrapped her arms around me. Her embrace quelled my fears more. "We need to get some rest, sis," she whispered, her breath warm against my ear. "Tomorrow, we can search for the outpost. Tonight, we can get some extra rest. Who knows when we'll have another chance to have a full night's sleep."

Calian and Ava snuck off to a quiet spot under a tree where they cuddled and drifted off to sleep.

With unfinished words on my mind and a stoked fire lighting the night, I carefully retrieved my notebook. The silence, punctuated by the crackling wood, created a perfect environment to complete my thoughts.

"Tonight, the fire grows inside me, a flame kindled by loss and fueled by the need to protect what's left of my world. Tomorrow, everyone promises we'll find this outpost."

I finished my sentence, then closed the notebook before returning it to my backpack. Nestling up to the fire, I fluffed my backpack to use as a pillow. My last thoughts before I surrendered to sleep were of the coming day. I could almost imagine the relief that understanding the monsters would give me, knowing we would be that much closer to ending the nightmare. The scream lingered in my mind as I shut my eyes.

Leaves crunched and my eyelids flipped open. Samuel smothered the flames with handfuls of dirt, plunging us into darkness.

Samuel's voice broke through the shadows. "Sorry, the flames were keeping me awake."

I smiled at Samuel, nestled into my backpack, and shut my eyes. But it wasn't the dark that frightened me anymore, it was the possibility of never enjoying the light again. My eyelids grew heavy. Even with our naps, I couldn't fight the exhaustion the apocalypse created in our bodies. A restless sleep welcomed me, haunted by nightmares of what awaited us at the outpost.

The shrill cry of a distant siren tore through the stillness of the encroaching morning light. It wrenched me from my wearying sleep and felt like I'd just closed my eyes. My muscles froze and my heart dropped, trying to escape my body's torment from the memories connected to the sound.

Calian's voice cut through the surrounding creeping fog. "It's coming from the east and we're heading west. We should probably leave now."

I scrambled to my feet and shook Samuel awake. He struggled to his feet like a town drunk after a night of drinking. We snatched up our backpacks and our weapons. The backpack's weight no longer felt like a nuisance, but a comforting familiarity. Without a word, we set off in a synchronized march.

As we moved through the forest, the trees loomed above like silent sentinels that hid our location. Calian took the lead, and Ava trailed close behind. "The outpost should be near the edge of the mountains ahead." He gestured at the horizon in front of us.

"It's weird they'd place something like a government facility near the base of some mountains with nothing around them," Samuel yawned and rubbed the sleep from his eyes.

I clutched my backpack straps tighter, realizing every step took me further from what remained of our past lives and deeper into an uncertain future. The sirens of death rang again, intermittent and closer, accompanied by electronic voices pleading for help. Each sound sent electricity through my body.

My mind raced with questions of how many demons were following us. We were being followed and with more intent than previously. Could they have seen the fire before Samuel extinguished it? Why didn't they attack while we slept? Or did they wait for us to wake?

Without a word or glance, Ava stuck her hand behind her. I noticed and reached for it. Her hand closed around mine with a loving squeeze and I squeezed back, grateful for the silent promise between us. Mom and Dad may be gone, but even if Ava was all I had, she was enough.

We zig-zagged through the trees, increasing our speed. The sounds behind us propelled us. Calian would occasionally stop and inspect the ground or a broken branch to make sure we weren't falling into a trap. The undergrowth became denser as we discovered no creatures or survivors had ventured down the path to flee.

"Don't get too distracted. We need to keep on track and stay ahead of however many Chippers are following," Samuel instructed. His protective instincts had grown stronger as he did his best to be a stand-in parent, filling the void left by Dad and Elu.

"Stay close," Calian reminded us, casting a glance over his shoulder. His hand found Ava's. Their fingers intertwined naturally. I glanced back and put my hand behind me. After a moment, Samuel grasped my hand, and we became a connected apocalyptic family.

Adrenaline flowed through my veins, thrusting me forward. With every crunch of foliage underfoot, I imagined the technological horrors that awaited us beyond our line of sight and behind us. But we couldn't afford the luxury of fear. Whatever awaited us, we needed to vanquish it to remain survivors.

The forest thinned, signaling our approach to the end of the mountains. Vast fields peeked through the trees, along with increasing sunlight.

"Almost there," Calian announced. His words carried a mix of hope and caution. Our pace quickened, driven by the possibility of uncovering the truth to the monstrous plague that had ravaged civilization. Hope was within our grasp.

The world opened as we emerged from the tree line to the expanse of the valley before us and the weight of the unknown. But within me, the fire that had ignited the night before night simmered to a timid glow. Confronting the unknown rekindled my fears, extinguishing my enthusiasm.

"Look." Calian's voice, low and urgent, cut through the silent awe as we inhaled the mountain air. We halted, following his finger to the few remaining trees in front of us. Shotgun rounds had violently kissed the bark of several trees just feet away. Splintered wood stood as proof of a recent struggle. At their base lay the twisted forms of Chippers, torn apart by bullets. Their menacing microchips reduced to cold, useless technology.

"We must be close. Only the government has enough firepower to do this much damage in such a strategic way." Calian's words seemed to ooze with terror, even as he did his best to cover it.

We treaded carefully past the remnants of a slaughter, but was the government the good guys, or another foe? We stepped over the debris of shredded trees. I examined each Chipper as we passed. It gave me hope that someone fought back and won, but it added a fresh terror, too.

I became too invested in the Chipper bodies, then the all-too-familiar blare of sirens sliced through the air, sending shivers down my spine. The electronic cries for help followed. The sounds were eerily human and yet so hauntingly fake. We knew better than to respond. We all knew of the tricks the Chippers played. Traps designed to prey on the compassion only humans had.

"Stay quiet, move fast," Samuel whispered as he took the lead. A paternal fire to protect burned in his eyes. A desire to end this nightmarish existence and uphold his promise must have become his driving force.

Our pace quickened, a silent sprint through the underbrush, or as silent as we could be. A disabled Chipper dragging itself along the ground caught my eye. Its missing leg emphasized its grotesque figure, its other leg shredded and barely recognizable as a limb. The microchips on its hands sparked as it reached out for us. An overwhelming sadness shot through my heart as I looked into the

Chipper's eyes and the soul of the human trapped behind the microchips.

Calian was upon it in seconds with ruthless aggression. In a swift motion, he stomped out one microchip beneath his boot and bashed the other with his branch, ending the pain within the relentless creature.

"Let's keep moving," he said, offering his hand to Ava again. She took it without hesitation and stepped over the lifeless body. I followed close behind.

"Look!" Ava hurried. She pointed at a silhouette of a dilapidated structure illuminated by the peeking sun. Weathered wood and broken window frames hid behind overgrown sunflowers and daffodils scattered about. Shattered glass glinted in the growing light. The eerie sight created confusion. Was it really a government facility? It seemed as no one had occupied the building in decades and it wasn't big or secure enough for the four of us to call home.

We approached the building, and our hope shattered in another way. Rustling leaves sounded from the underbrush. Electronic voices, synthetic and cold, sliced through the silence again. "Help me," they pleaded in a loop of empty cries, followed by a mechanical "hello" that sent shivers down my spine.

"Hide," Samuel commanded. His hand pressed against my back, pushing me against the rough wooden planks of the building. Calian and Ava followed suit as Calian wrap his arm around her, keeping her body protected and flush against the building.

Samuel and Calian's eyes darted around, assessing the situation like eagles searching for movement. We knew the sounds were traps, cleverly set by Chippers to entice us. We had grown wise to these deceptions, yet the familiarity created terror in even the most hardened.

"Shh," Samuel mouthed, pressing his finger to his lips. I nodded, the grit of the building's facade rubbing against my cheek. Its icy touch seeped through my skin.

The commotion grew louder; disembodied voices multiplied and surrounded us. Before we knew it, the entire forest seemed to plead for help, with a wide-open field behind us. Each breath became sharp and shallow. Feeling trapped and with no way out, I questioned whether the Survivalist had made up the rumors or if there was another hidden building. Had the Chippers "upgraded" to the level of fabricating rumors? Was the Survivalist an advanced Chipper?

A door slamming open and shut on its rusted hinges drew our attention. The repetitive banging cut through the distorted voices. With no other options, Samuel searched for the source. Through a window, he noticed a door that swung wildly in the fall breeze.

He crept forward with silent determination and nodded for us to follow. Remaining one with the siding, we shuffled quietly around the decrepit house. The door beckoned us to its possible salvation.

As we approached, Samuel's hand cautiously guided the door open long enough for us to slip through. I held my breath, praying that whatever welcomed us wouldn't end us.

Samuel found the deadbolt with practiced ease. As long as the Chippers couldn't crawl through the windows, the click secured our temporary haven. The deadbolt clunked like a gunshot in the quiet house. We held our breath as the rustling and electronic voices transformed into an eerie serenade outside our barricade.

The door handle jangled, a metallic rattle that kept my body on the verge of a heart attack. Ava's eyes met mine, wide and filled with the same fear that clawed at my insides. Ava wrapped her hands around Calian's arm, her knuckles pale with locked fingers. Samuel stood with his back pressed against the door, his posture rigid, as if bracing for impact.

"Keep away from the door," he mouthed, and we backed further into the house and into the void.

Minutes stretched into an eternity. Each second added weight to my chest. Then, as abruptly as it started, the noises ceased. A heavy stillness blanketed the house, thick and terrifying. The thought of dozens of Chippers waiting outside created a fear unlike anything I'd ever felt before.

I located a light switch as I sunk deeper into the house, tucked into a dark hallway with no windows. Flicking it released a pathetic, flickering light that struggled to remain lit but revealed a tapestry of destruction. Bullet holes decorated the interior walls. Splashes and streaks of dried blood painted a gruesome picture. I could almost hear the echoes of violence that occupied the space.

My throat tightened, hoping we accidentally stumbled upon the outpost we'd searched for.

"This—this is what the outpost offers?" I whispered, feeling the color drain from my face.

Tucked behind a doorway to another room was confirmation that we were in the government facility. A dark green sleeve sat in a puddle of blood. Samuel nudged the door open to reveal a body garnished with ranks and a badge. It was the room, the one the Survivalist had described in hushed, haunted tones. The government's dirty secret, where they had tried to erase their mistakes and test subjects that had become more than they could handle.

"Is this where the government tried to destroy the evidence?" I whispered, a shiver running through me. The air suffocated us with the scent of death and the weight of answers we longed to hear.

Calian, Ava, and Samuel stood motionless, absorbing the scene. We all silently reached the same conclusion: it was no ordinary room, and the violence that had occurred there was not random.

"Martha, don't," Calian warned, his voice low as he watched me inch toward the corner of a hallway. But I couldn't help myself; I needed to see more, to understand what had led to that moment. My curiosity took control of me.

"Stay back," Samuel added, his protective instinct as strong as ever. He might not have been my father, but in that instant, I felt the parental care behind his words.

I ignored them both. My feet carried me forward until I rounded the corner. Stopping dead in my tracks, my heart pounded so fiercely it threatened to burst from my chest. Hundreds of empty shell casings and more blood littered the floor. Ava, Calian, and Samuel followed tentatively.

A haunting question nagged at me and finally sprung from my mouth. "If they were getting rid of test subjects, and there's all this blood… where are the test subjects?"

Samuel ran his hand over his short hair. His face dropped, emphasized by blank eyes. "We came for answers, and now we have more questions. But, obviously, we're not safe here."

"Could they have turned into…" Calian couldn't finish his sentence, but he didn't need to. We all knew what he was implying. The Chippers, the relentless creatures hunting us since the world fell apart. Were they the missing test subjects?

The question hung in the air, and more questions nagged in my ear. These zombies weren't like the ones in movies, as they could not multiply. There was a finite number of them. But it only raised more questions, such as how many test subjects were deceived into enduring this torture?

The only thing I knew was we were searching for answers to more than just an apocalypse. We needed exact answers to who, or what, we were truly fighting.

CHAPTER 13: THE OUTPOST

The iron scent of drying blood filled the air, coating my nostrils as we peered into the dark stairwell past the hallway of mysterious deaths. The hall highlighted a violence we couldn't comprehend, save for the bullet holes that littered the walls, floor, and ceiling holes. Calian's eyes mirrored my terror as he ran his fingers across the jagged edges of the splintered wood.

"Look at the size of these holes," Calian conversed with himself. "These are from an assault rifle, an M4, most likely."

Ava followed Calian, invested in every word he muttered as the bullet wounds in the house entranced him further with each hole he examined. I shuffled ahead, my eyes absorbing the dark stains marring the floor. The blood covered the walls and floor so much it painted a grotesque picture, hiding how many subjects there were. Once again, the missing bodies chilled me more than any amount of blood could. Like a crime scene, we tried our best to piece together what had happened, but it was near impossible without bodies to examine.

"Martha?" Calian's voice interrupted my thoughts, and I realized he'd recognized my catatonic stare into the dark abyss beyond our location.

"Calian," my voice trembled despite my desperate attempt to sound composed. "If they lined up a few or a dozen people right where we're standing... how did they just... disappear?"

I wasn't sure if the question or the answer was more terrifying. As the silence stretched on, the scent of death wrapped around me. We stood in what was essentially a grave without bodies. A mystery I wasn't sure I wanted to solve. But worse yet, we needed to push on into the darkness, where either the murderers or the murdered awaited us.

Cautiously, we tip-toed through across the sections of floor not covered in thick blood. Our steps echoed through the corridors. The dead lights above flickered like a morse code, warning us to turn back. I glanced down the stairwell and flicked a nearby light switch, which illuminated another pathetic light that tried its best to brighten our path as it hummed. As we descended deeper into the cabin, we found a landing that appeared oddly out of place. The building didn't have a typical basement, but the wooden stairs that transformed into concrete walls and floors halfway down. Concerning cleanliness guided us down, and our presence triggered powerful lights that illuminated our path.

A quick glance at each other gave us the courage to continue. Uncomfortable was an understatement, as mixed feelings stirred inside me like a cauldron. The dilapidated outpost was obviously a front for a facility hidden deep inside the earth. It seemed cliché, but maybe that was the point.

When we finally reached the bottom of the staircase, we met an intimidating metal door meant to keep things in, or out.

"Careful," Samuel cautioned as he stepped in front.

He turned the doorknob and dropped his shoulder into the heavy metal door that groaned as it opened gradually. An expansive office filled with deserted cubicles lit up with a semblance of normality. The scene at our feet was of abrupt abandonment. Desks littered with papers, chairs upended, and a stale smell of printer ink and dust stirred in the air.

"Look at this place," Ava said as she scanned the room, trying to make sense of the disarray. Everything felt surreal, like we'd walked onto the set of a movie.

Calian furred his brows in deep concentration. He sauntered over to the closest desk and shuffled through some papers. "We need to find something on the Chippers. Unusual schedules, reports, anything that can give us some insight. And I feel like this is the place to find answers."

"Got it," Samuel replied, diving into a stack of folders on an adjacent desk. Ava hustled to another one in the center of the room and followed suit.

I wandered past the desks, drawn to a dark corner with white laboratories just beyond the shattered windows separating the rooms. Laboratories in a place like that had to hold secrets like a treasure chest held riches. My hands trembled as I imagined the work conducted in them. The demonic microchips invented. Test subjects tortured. I neared the window and a wave of evil passed through my chest.

"Martha, don't go too far," Samuel called out, but curiosity muffled his words. I peered through the broken glass. The lights sensed my presence and lit its secrets for me. Desperation and fear covered the bright environment. Broken vials and needles littered the countertops, with one hospital bed shoved against the wall and another against the door. Every inch of the room sent shivers down my spine.

"Anything yet?" Calian's voice echoed from his cubicle.

"Nothing yet. Just printed memes and emails," Ava responded in frustration and annoyance. Every document someone mentioned sounded like another piece of mundane corporate life. More reminders of the world we left behind. How many of the workers planned to get through their day and then head home to their loved ones? Loved ones that could have passed. Many of those workers may have succumbed to the creatures they created.

"Keep searching," Samuel urged, his head still buried in the hundreds of folders. He understood the stakes just as well as any of us, maybe better. We were all acutely aware that every second we spent in the graveyard of a facility brought us closer to being discovered or facing the monsters we wanted to destroy.

Noticing everyone deep in their research, I crept into the nearby hallway. Trying to shove the laboratory door open, I could barely get it to budge with the hospital bed, acting as a last line of defense. After several shoves, the door cracked open just enough for me to slip through the narrow gap.

I stepped into the white room that reeked of blood and chemicals. My gaze landed on an overturned desk in the shadows. The papers scattered around it had blood splattered on them, long since turned brown. The harsh reality of the forsaken place clawed at my resolve, but I pushed the fear aside because I needed answers.

I approached the desk, noticing the overhead light hanging off-kilter, casting eerie shadows in half the room. The shadow of a boot protruded from under the desk, the leather stained dark-red. The scene strangled my voice as I edged around the desk and discovered a leg, gnawed and abandoned. Nausea surged within me, but my determination kept it settled. I nudged the grotesque remnant aside with my foot, careful not to fixate on the cause of the violence. "Just another day in the apocalypse," I mumbled under my breath, trying to laugh it off.

The papers were a mess, but among the clutter, a sheet with bold block letters caught my attention. "WARNING" the page screamed. My fingers trembled as I smoothed the crumpled paper, squinting to make out the words beneath the dire heading. The test subjects were nearly indestructible. With the microchips installed, the subjects could withstand horrors that would spell the end for any normal person.

"Dr. Marbh." The name radiated fear and pity. The doctor had seen the danger of what they created, realizing the microchips implanted in those poor people had made them too powerful and erratic. As I read on, I learned Dr. Marbh wanted to reverse course and return to the drawing board, but it was too late. His warning left abandoned, just like the remnants of what could have been him.

Martha's Notebook

"Hey Martha! Where did you go?" Samuel's voice pierced the chilling silence, pulling me back from the edge of despair.

"I'm over here," I replied. I clutched the papers and everyone needed to see this information. Whether they found anything, it could give us insight into what drove the creatures and caused them to overrun the facility. I wondered if I found something that big. What else might we find deeper in the facility?

I exited the room, clutching the damning paperwork close, and nearly collided with Samuel. "Guys!" My voice echoed through the hollow corridors of the facility. "These test subjects... they're almost invincible according to these papers I found. The microchips implanted in them, they're—"

"AI controlled." Calian held up a crumpled sheet of his own. "The bastards turned them into AI controlled zombie soldiers."

"Exactly." Anger and helplessness surged inside me. "But there must be a way to stop them. We can't just shatter microchip after microchip, hoping they never find a way around that."

"Martha's right." Ava cut in, popping up from behind a filing cabinet. "We're learning about who and what they are. Now we need to find paperwork describing their weaknesses."

Calian stepped forward, his face lit by sporadic lights overhead. Only one out of every five lights functioned.

"That's not all," he said, glancing at the paper in his hands before locking eyes with me. "The test subjects, they thought they were part of a high-tech, advanced gaming system. A virtual reality system controlled by military-grade AI. This says it would 'make all other gaming systems obsolete. The most advanced gaming system the world has ever seen.' "

"Video games?" I gasped. "They destroyed the world over video games?"

"Looks like that's what the test subjects were led to believe," Calian nodded. "But it was a trick to gain enthusiastic test subjects for government experimentation of a top-secret project."

"An AI gaming system..." The words blew me away, realizing all those lost over a gaming system. "If it's AI, doesn't that mean we could try to—"

"Control it or shut it down?" Ava suggested. Our sisterly bond made it easy for her to follow my thoughts.

"Either. Both." I squeezed the papers. The word *WARNING* seared into my mind. "We must keep moving, though. There's got to be more answers here."

"Let's not waste time," Samuel said as he held clutched a handful of papers he'd found.

"Stay sharp, everyone," Calian said.

The stale air of the abandoned facility mingled with dust as we ventured deeper, setting my senses on edge. We navigated down the hallway with cubicles on our left, locked doors on our right, and overturned trash cans with their waste scattered everywhere. Classified papers and empty soda bottles laid against the walls.

Ava had wandered off, disappearing into some cubicles, and called us over. "Martha, Calian, Samuel!" She beckoned to where she stood behind a cluster of monitors on a desk.

Their screens were lifeless, with only a blue screen and a single logo fading in and out. The flickering lights above morphed Ava's face into a menacing scowl. "This place... it's military. Check out these logos, and..." She held up a binder thick with schematics and official ink stamps. "This says the government was working with an entertainment company, using it as a front for this AI gaming system."

"An entertainment company? Which one?" I asked. My mind raced to connect the dots. What facade could hide such horrors?

"Can't find a name." Ava's brows dipped in frustration. The binder trembled in her grasp, breaking through her usually calm demeanor.

"Keep searching," I urged. "That name could be our ticket out of this nightmare."

We split up among the cubicles, each diving into a section. We scavenged every desk for clues through the vast chaos. I held my breath as I checked every paper and every drawer that squealed open under my desperate search.

"Guys!" It was Samuel. He emerged from behind a cubicle wall, holding a thin packet. "I've found the test subjects' names."

"Let me see," I said as I jogged to his cubicle. The list was a spreadsheet of identities doomed by their involvement in the twisted experiment.

"Look at this." He tapped on a separate paper that sat on the desk. "It says all test subjects were to be exterminated, effective immediately. Removing the microchips would fry their brains because of the cerebral pathways."

"Exterminated…" The word hit me like a bullet. The words dripped with the finality of countless lives, reduced to mere trash that needed to be disposed of. "So, they treated people like faulty machines that needed to be *recycled*," I murmured, disgust welling in my eyes.

"Better than letting them turn into those… things," Calian said grimly. The choices were two terrible outcomes that should have never happened. "Still, no one should play God like that."

"Or play games with human lives," I said, recalling the cruel virtual reality lie we'd learned of moments earlier. "We need to end this for all of them, to spare their lives of any more pain."

"Agreed, but is there a way to save them? We can't remove those microchips." Samuel rolled up his papers and shoved them into my backpack. "But to save these test subjects, we need to save ourselves first."

"Then let's keep going," I said. "Every second we stand here, we risk—"

A low growl echoed down the hollow walls, making it hard to pinpoint where it emanated from. It was a reminder that death lurked in every corner, and we needed to be prepared.

"Let's move," I whispered. We couldn't afford to linger. With one last survey of the room, we left behind the eerie silence.

A second growl, followed by pounding metal. shook the room. Before leaving my desk, I snatched some papers covered with warnings and protocols, and shoved them into my backpack.

My hands trembled. I couldn't hide the fear of knowing what was most likely creating those noises. No matter the precautions we took, the Chippers seemed to be everywhere.

"Martha, hurry!" Ava yelled, zipping her backpack shut and slinging it over her shoulder.

Samuel stood firmly in front of a door, with Calian by his side as they waited for us. Calian scanned every inch behind us for movement, and Samuel watched the hallway.

We ran over, and Samuel peeked behind a nearby door. "Alright, we have another staircase leading deeper into this place, so let's be extra careful." We cautiously slipped through the door, but just as we shut it, distorted growls and moans echoed behind us.

We sprinted down the stairs. I glanced back and witnessed the metal door bow outward as snarls continued from the other side. My body shivered at the sight.

After we'd run down five flights, it happened. The squealing and tearing of metal split the air as distorted growls filled the stairwell. A surge of adrenaline propelled me forward as we finished our sixth flight.

Martha's Notebook

"Keep going." Samuel barked, taking the stairs two at a time.

"Can we make it in time?" I asked, my voice trembling.

"What choice do we have?" Calian shot back. His hand gripped Ava's tightly as they continued in front of me.

"Martha, keep close!" Ava shouted over her shoulder.

The staircase seemed endless as we finished flight after flight, a coiled serpent winding deeper into darkness. My legs burned with each step, but I pushed through, driven by the terror of what chased us and the slim hope of salvation below.

"Almost there," Calian panted.

I wondered what would meet us at the bottom, though I wasn't sure I wanted the answer.

"Keep moving," Ava said, her words punctuated by the stampede and the guttural roar of the Chippers on our tail.

"Keep moving!" Samuel repeated, somewhere in the shadowy depths.

"Let's go, Martha," Ava said as she reached for my hand, a reassured comfort I was right behind her.

When the world falls apart, you cling to family, you cling to hope, and you run until you can't run anymore.

The staircase ended abruptly after what felt like a million flights. We opened a more secured metal door that weighed as much as a car into a dimly lit corridor marked by a sign that read: "Underground Bridge." I couldn't decipher if my heart pounded from exertion or the anxiety of what the Underground Bridge led to.

"Everybody in?" Samuel asked as he scanned behind him for everyone.

The corridor stretched endlessly, lined with pipes on the right, cables on the left, and dim lights down the center of the ceiling. The continuous concrete instilled so much fear I questioned whether we should take our chances with the Chippers.

"Samuel, the door!" Ava called while pointing at a locking spin-dial with two handles. We couldn't let those things follow us, not when we might be on the cusp of something vital, something that could change everything.

Samuel's gaze snapped to the door, and he grabbed the handles. Even with all his might, he couldn't get the handles to turn.

"Help me with this," he grunted, motioning us over.

My hands shook as I gripped a cold handle and threw what little weight I had behind it. Ava and Calian joined us and we forced the deadbolts into place with a thud that echoed down the bridge. The four of us took a few steps back as our chests rose and fell with exhaustion, but we had a promise of safety.

"Let's keep moving," Calian said, exhaling the biggest breath I'd ever heard.

With the door secured, we had only one way to go. We left behind the safety of the lock to deal with the danger of the Underground Bridge.

The Underground Bridge created a new chapter for us and we moved further from the door. A loud bang alerted us that the Chippers had reached the door. Just on the other side of that locked door stood a dozen or more Chippers, waiting to tear us apart. The hairs on my arm stood straight up, but nothing followed the single bang, which created more questions about what the door hid. Was it even a Chipper? We all stared at the door intensely before a bone chilling sound followed.

"Hello? Let us in," a distorted female voice called in a pathetic, gentle tone like a frozen child locked outside in a blizzard.

The words chilled my soul, but I didn't know what frightened me more. Was it the fact that they could speak more, or was it the singular word "us?"

Another chilling voice called out, a deeper, distorted male. "I'm all alone out here. Let me in."

I couldn't stop a laugh from escaping my mouth. Very misplaced in the dire situation. Calian, Ava, and Samuel stared at me as if I lost my mind.

"Sorry," I said, stifling another giggle. "It's just—Dad would have some ridiculous dad joke of a reply to bloodthirsty Chippers if he were here."

"Martha? Martha?" Ava's voice mixed dread with cynical joy as she tried to suppress a smile. "Remember how he always made light of scary situations?" she continued. I envisioned Dad standing smug, his eyes twinkling with that mischievous glint as he prepared to deliver one of his classic dad jokes.

Ava's lips twitched into a growing smile, despite the situation. "A lock is better than a B lock," she said, followed by a soft chuckle.

The memory came alive, and I couldn't resist. I mimicked Dad's deep, playful tone. "Lock, lock. Who's there? No one because the door is locked."

The absurdity of laughter in such dire straits overtook us, and we all succumbed to it. Calian chuckled low and warmly, Ava laughed bright and light, while Samuel suppressed his laughter. It appeared his own ability to find humor amid our desperate circumstances took him aback.

Maybe the stress of the world had finally made our minds snap, but it chased away the darkness that threatened to settle in our hearts. It seemed to do the same outside our hearts as the voices ceased.

"Okay, okay," Calian managed between laughs, wiping a tear from his eye. "We needed that, but let's not forget why we came all this way."

"Right." I nodded, feeling a small surge of courage. The laughter had bridged the gap between the scared kid I used to be and the strong woman I needed to become. We ventured further from the door and prepared to face whatever awaited us in the depths of the facility.

The echoes of our laughter had barely faded when a chilling sound reverberated from high in the stairwell. Electricity shot through my body as the unmistakable clank and scrape of Chippers entering the office cubicle area echoed through the stairwell. We exchanged glances. Had all the Chippers left us in peace, knowing they couldn't break down the locked door, or did they know something we didn't?

"We should continue," Samuel said as he took the lead, guiding us further away from the door.

We shuffled forward with a sense of release. The concrete walls and metal beams of the corridor surrounded us like the ribs of an enormous beast. The air was cold and thick. Each breath chilled my lungs as it became clear that whoever abandoned the place didn't plan on returning.

Before we found an end to the Underground Bridge, a clatter echoed further down the hallway, freezing us in place. It was as if the darkness itself had come alive. We halted immediately and listened intently as the silence that followed seemed to do little to soothe our fears.

"What was that?" Ava whispered.

"I don't know," Calian replied. My eyes did their best to pierce into the dark corners, but I couldn't spot anything.

"We can't go back, no matter what it is." Samuel said.

With that acknowledgment hanging, we forced ourselves to continue. The distant sound confirmed something awaited us deeper into the Underground Bridge. Yet, the sound solidified answers awaited us, too.

Our journey into the heart of darkness had begun.

CHAPTER 14: THE SEARCH

I trailed behind the others, my sneakers shuffled against the cold tile. Ahead, Ava's hand found Calian's in the dim light, a silent pact of reassurance. It was a slight gesture I'd seen before, but each time it tugged at something deep within me. I wanted the same certainty that I wasn't alone.

"Keep close," Ava called back to me. Her voice cut through the eerie silence that cloaked us.

I nodded, though she couldn't see it, and quickened my pace enough to tighten the gap between us. The intermittent pools of light from overhead did little to comfort me. Something about the occasional dancing shadows, caused by broken fixtures, portrayed the same jerky movements of the Chippers.

A sudden slam echoed from behind, reverberating off the metal door we'd locked moments ago. My heart seized again, which I knew would become a common occurrence down there. Samuel inhaled sharply as he turned his head slightly toward the sound. We all froze, a collective breath held in suspense. We waited, like statues, for dozens of Chippers to burst through the door.

"Martha, stay alert," Ava whispered, squeezing Calian's hand tighter. A mantra for herself but also for me. It served as a reminder of the role she attempted to assume.

"Will the door hold?" I asked, unable to subdue the shakiness in my voice.

"Of course," Calian replied with more confidence than I felt he truly possessed. His feigned confidence wavered as the silence crept back in.

Samuel grunted as he squinted his eyes. A futile attempt to peer into the darkness enveloping the door. "I don't think that was the Chippers. That almost sounded like someone unlocked the door... from the inside."

Another word that felt like it wanted to pull my heart from my chest. "Inside," the word propelled us further from the door as the lights played tricks on our vision. In every flicker I saw movement, imagined twisted forms clawing after us. Each time the illumination returned, it revealed a post, or an abandoned briefcase. The terror of the shadows gnawed at my sanity.

"Stay sharp. We don't know what that sound was or if someone, or something, is in here with us." Samuel's eyes darted from shadow to shadow as if he could will the creatures out of existence. "They're bound to be—"

Another slam, louder, closer, so it seemed. I flinched, realizing the determination of whatever undead monstrosity attempted to reach our location. They were relentlessly driven by their desire to eradicate humanity and devour every one of us.

"We need to go," Ava said, yanking Calian along as they navigated the patchwork of light and dark. Calian was undoubtedly strong, but Ava could be just as strong in the right mindset. Her determination became our beacon, and we couldn't help but follow Calian a little more so.

"I think I see something," Ava said as she continued our pursuit of safety through the possibility of death behind every shadow.

"Stay close," Samuel added, another protector making sure I was safe.

I clutched the straps of my backpack like a life vest and kept my gaze on Ava's form.

Another metal bang reverberated through the corridor, followed by a subtle squeak of a door opening. We spun in unison, a choreographed swirl of fear and anticipation. The shadows danced along the walls, mocking our fragile safety. I pressed my back against the cold concrete, and the vibrations through the wall synchronized with the squeaking.

"That's it. They're in here." I whispered, possibly my last words before an onslaught.

Across from me, Samuel had settled into a crouch, his shotgun aimed steadily at the steel barrier that separated us from them. I wondered how many bullets he had. Would it be enough to fight, or enough for us?

"Shh," Ava hushed as I turned to see her locked on the opposite end of the corridor. "Do you hear that?"

"No," I answered.

"Exactly."

Seconds dragged into minutes as we waited for something to appear. The dim light flickered overhead. An otherworldly glow shone on Calian's face as he clutched his pistol with grim desperation. He had always been the brave one, the first to step into danger, but the lines on his face and brows told a different story where he mimicked a frightened boy who wanted his dad to step in and protect him.

"Martha, stay down," Ava instructed softly, her motherly instincts never faltering, even as the world crumbled around us. There was comfort in her presence, a silent promise she would shield me from the horrors that lurked beyond our sight.

I tucked my legs closer to my chest as I hunkered down to make myself as small as possible. I wanted to become invisible to the nightmare that preyed on us. Samuel's grip on his weapon never wavered as each muscle remained coiled like a spring. He sat, ready to unleash death if challenged.

Then, as if the cosmos themselves commanded it, the silence became eternal. The metal bangs ceased, the squeaks ceased, and no additional sounds followed for what felt like an hour. The only sounds left were our ragged breaths and the sweat dripping from our faces. It was an eerie quiet that reassured and terrified us. If something was in the darkness, which there had to be something, it wouldn't attack us, at least not yet.

"Should we continue?" I dared to ask, knowing my voice could trigger their assault.

"Just a bit longer," Samuel said, his eyes never leaving the far end of the corridor.

Time hung suspended, a delicate line between relief and dread. For those few minutes, we existed in a limbo created by our terror and hope.

"Let's not waste any more time," Calian finally said, breaking the spell anchoring us to the spot.

With caution, we rose to our feet, limbs stiff from the tension. As one, we moved away from the walls and continued down the corridor. The haunting sounds that held us in terror propelled us forward for an eternity, but we were determined for answers, and we were close to getting them.

With each step, the weight of the situation bore down on me. Every creak of the foundation or clank of a pipe sent the entire group into defensive positions.

My eyes leaped from wall to wall when we encountered several doors. Their oversized metal frames and hefty locks expressed their unwillingness to let us enter.

"Do we even try any of these doors? Not sure if I want to know what's behind them," Ava said, and a chill creeped down my arms. Her words launched my imagination into a frenzy and giant versions of Chippers and Chippers mixed with radioactive slime stirred in my head.

I studied the labels affixed to each door, focusing my mind on something other than more horrible versions of our monsters. I searched for clues to the answers we wanted, like a life-or-death version of a TV game show where every door contained either a wealth of information or a creature wanting to end our existence.

"The Situation Room"; bold letters left an ominous impression in my mind, and one of dad's jokes popped into my head: "We definitely have a situation here." I reached out tentatively and, against logic, hoped for an unlocked entry, but the door remained firm.

Samuel grunted in frustration as he rattled the handle of an adjacent door marked "Military Testing." "Locked tight," he announced, confirming the futility of our efforts.

A shiver trailed up my spine when we halted before the most foreboding door yet. With a separate key-card entry and a security camera above, the words "Onakele Enterprises Headquarters" emblazoned the door. The title and added security seemed out of place in such a top-secret environment, which deepened my questions and fears. Why would a company have their headquarters in a top-secret underground facility?

Calian stepped forward, one hand resting on the grip of his pistol tucked into his belt. He pointed to a red horizontal light shining from the top of the card-reader.

"We're definitely not getting in there," Calian said, confirming our suspicions. "There's no breaking into there without making more noise than we'd like."

"Plus, who knows if someone is watching this door, too," Samuel added, and he tightened the grip on his shotgun. "Supplies, answers... or more you-know-whos."

"Let's not stick around to find out if someone is watching us right now," Ava insisted. "We should move on."

Despite our disappointment, a part of me relaxed. Locked doors meant we could pass without disturbing whatever horrors hid on the other side. Yet, the chaotic and ruined state of the underground labyrinth embraced a fear greater than the threat of the zombies. Hidden under the chaos was a well-maintained, clean environment, a secret society of elites had used for who knew what. What caused them to abandon such a seemingly impenetrable fortress? Were the Chippers that bad, or was there more to them?

"Come on, Martha," Ava urged, noticing my hesitation. "We'll find a door we can pass through."

More locked doors built our unease. Were there that many secrets hiding around us, or was it rooms of nothingness?

"Wait." Samuel cut through the silence. He stood, frozen, in front of a door with a sliver of darkness emanating from it. The door remained ajar. Its lock was in pieces, destroyed by a desperate stranger.

"Upgrade Testing Lab," the sign read ominously. The word "upgrade" sent a chill down my spine and I prepared for battle and raised my branch.

"Stand back," Samuel said, pushing the door open wider with the barrel of his shotgun. The void beyond the door swallowed every ounce of courage I'd had.

"Anyone got a problem with me taking point?" Samuel whispered. No one objected, and he crept forward. His stoic demeanor never faltered despite the palpable tension in the air.

When he crossed the threshold, a symphony of metallic rustles and low growls cut through the darkness, stirring the stale air. Samuel's hand found a switch just inside and flipped it. Fluorescent lights flickered to life above groaning figures. Some wore a green, ominous glow.

"God…" The word escaped Calian's lips in a mumble. The rest of us were too stunned to move or speak.

Before us stood six large cages, each containing an intimidating figure. Their human bodies had morphed into grotesque parodies of the human form. But it wasn't just their looks that unnerved us, it was their differences. One thing they all had in common was their iconic, twitchy, jerking movements.

"These aren't the Chippers we've seen," Ava said in a calm tone laced with fright. "None of them have chips on their hands."

The creatures, like Samuel, never lowered their relentless stares. Like a starving caged animal, the monsters waited patiently. Their eyes revealed a hunger that couldn't be satisfied. Those true monsters made the Chippers we fought seem like bunnies. They were true alpha predators, only separated from us by metal bars.

The first Chipper, labeled "1.0" on a grimy placard above its cage, seemed the most typical. A man over six feet that peered at us with three green microchips in the typical spots. It seemed like a typical Chipper, but something was different. It appeared calm, its stare locked on us like it knew us.

"Be careful," Samuel warned, but the creature's lunge created a rowdy clang against the bars that smothered all other noise. Its hand clawed the air inches from Ava, halted only by the sturdy bars. She stumbled back into Calian, who steadied her with a hand on her shoulder, his own face pale with shock.

"God, we've seen these before," Ava said. Her gaze fixed on "1.0" that returned to its calm demeanor and comfortable stare.

"Let's keep going," Samuel urged and pressed on. The next cage housed "1.5," with a single green microchip lodged in its forehead. It sat eerily still, aside from an occasional twitch, until we got within a short range of it. Then it emitted short bursts of a bizarre and shrill sound, like a distorted woman's scream, but the creature was a man. It raised the hair on the back of my neck as each squeal seemed to mock our humanity, reminding us of how far the creatures had strayed from their origins.

Creature "2.0" was even more unusual. It watched us approach with what appeared to be calculated interest. The female's lowered head spoke to its eerily calm demeanor. Its narrowed eyes watched Samuel level his shotgun at the being before it spoke with unsettling clarity. "You need to let me out, friend." The smooth words didn't match her intimidating stance. "I assure you, locking me away was a grave mistake." Every word felt calculated and fluent, but its tone remained distorted and forced like the other rare times they'd spoke.

"Like hell," Samuel said, then aimed his gun right at her chest.

"That's not terrifying at all," Calian joked, gripping his pistol tighter.

"Hey, wait. This '2.0' Chipper... where are its microchips?" I asked.

Everyone studied the Chipper, trying to spot a microchip.

Samuel took a step back in horror. "It has none. I don't even see a glow or anything on her."

No visible microchips meant it couldn't "upgrade" since that would mean removing the devices or implanting them further. Could they do that now?

"Let's continue," Calian said, eager to put distance between us and the talking nightmare.

As we proceeded down the line, my heartbeat quickened. "3.0," "4.0," and "5.0: Diabhall" labels hung over empty cages. Their doors swung slightly ajar, the surrounding silence more menacing than any growl or plea for help.

"Think they're down here still?" Ava asked as we scanned the room.

"Or maybe they weren't created yet?" I offered, half-joking to mask the dread boiling in my stomach. The thought of encountering something even more advanced than what we'd seen in the cages was too horrific to believe.

"Let's hope that's the case," Ava said, her eyes enlarged with fear.

We stared at the empty cages one last time, each lost in our own fears and imaginations.

"Whatever's missing… let's just pray we don't run into it," I said.

Our retreating footsteps shuffled against the tile in a defeated chorus. We'd gotten some answers to our questions, but those answers provided proof we were further from surviving the apocalypse than we'd thought.

"Let's shut this door and make sure it locks," I said, wanting to wipe my memory of ever being in the presence of those Chippers.

Ava clutched my hand tightly as if to siphon strength from our bond. We backed out of the room slowly. The Chippers' gazes followed every step we took with intense attention. Samuel, the last one out, shut the lights off and gave some final words, "Please don't escape." He gingerly shut the door, as if he'd just put a baby to bed.

"Martha, you okay?" Ava asked. Her eyes searched mine for reassurance to calm her nerves.

"Let's just check a few more rooms for answers, then get out of here," I said. "I just realized… if this place is the 'Underground Bridge,' bridges connect things, right? So, where does this corridor lead?"

Everyone's eyes grew, but no one spoke. Instead, we turned and continued down the hall, leaving the upgraded horrors behind us. The echo of their growls haunted us and questions lingered in my head.

The corridor was longer than we could've ever imagined, but it felt like we were nearing the end. Back in the flickering lights, shadows danced ominously. A hiss from an overhead vent sent shivers down my spine, and Ava flinched, too.

"Shh," Calian hushed, though no one had spoken.

Then I saw something. "Look." I pointed at droplets that stretched ahead of us.

A short way from the door, hidden by the shadows, crimson stains spotted the floor. Droplets of blood, fresh and glistening against the sterile gray floor, formed a trail to horrors we thought we'd left behind.

Calian and Samuel, weapons poised, led the way with calculated steps. We followed the sinister trail as the droplets grew in size and frequency, merging into a morbid stream tainting our path.

We attempted to move like the surrounding shadows, silent except for the faint shuffle of our footsteps on the cold concrete. My gaze never strayed far from the bloodied path we tracked. It became thicker and more persistent, a silent testament to an unseen violence.

"Something bad happened here," Samuel grunted, his voice low and tense.

"Keep your eyes peeled," Calian added, his pistol scanning the darkness ahead of us.

I clutched my backpack strap for comfort, my branch in the other hand. The weight of the backpack pressed into my shoulders. Ava's presence was a minor comfort, yet the fear gripping me was unrelenting. Every instinct screamed to run, to hide, but where could we go? The underground maze offered no sanctuary without added threats.

Martha's Notebook

We turned a corner and the trail of blood swelled into a river, ominous and heavy. My heart thudded painfully against my ribcage. What horrors awaited us at the end of the gruesome path? Would it be one of the missing upgraded subjects?

"Hello?" Samuel's voice boomed down the hallway, hopeful for a human response yet dreading what might answer. No sound responded, only our anxious breaths.

Samuel continued, his shotgun raised but shaky. Calian followed close behind, his pistol at the ready. Ava gripped my hand tightly and laced her fingers with mine. We followed at the back. The earlier sounds had lodged an intense fear in me of getting attacked from behind, so I constantly checked our backs. My eyes darted between the pooling blood and the solid shadow ahead.

We drew closer and a flicker of the lights cast a ghostly spotlight over the scene. The body leaned in a fetal position against the wall. Ava tensed beside me. Her protective instincts fled her even as Samuel lowered his gun, a clear signal of the lifelessness before us.

Calian moved first. He dropped to a knee beside the corpse. His movements were cautious, respectful even, while investigating. His examination thorough without touching the body. The body held a grizzled face with a bushy beard, dirt filling the lines of his skin were partially hidden beneath a worn cowboy hat.

Death was no longer a stranger to us, but each encounter took a variable chunk of me with it. Calian glanced at Ava before he dropped his head. The man had been someone until the apocalypse claimed him as it had so many others. *Whoever he was,* I thought, *he deserved better than this.* But I realized maybe death was an escape from the world, possibly even a gift.

Calian's face scanned every inch of the body. His eyes narrowed on the gruesome details of the man's last moments leading to his death. A bloody stump of muscle and bone poked out from his arm where his right hand should've been, with his left hand grasping just below the cut. Dark, dried blood painted the flesh around the wound, while two ragged incisions marred his abdomen. Calian's eyes narrowed again as he tipped the cowboy hat up a few inches with the barrel of his pistol, revealing a large burn across the man's cheek.

"Did you know him?" Ava's voice broke through the silence. Her compassion and true feelings for Calian were hard to hide in the horrific scene.

Calian didn't look up from where he crouched next to the body. "Yeah," he said in a sorrowful tone. "This was the Survivalist. The one who told us about this place."

I turned cold, like every drop of blood inside me froze, remembering the tales of the lone wanderer who moved like a ghost through the apocalypse. *The guy with no name, just a purpose,* I thought.

"Wasn't he an elite survivalist? A trained master at this stuff?" Ava's words hung heavy in the stale, pungent air.

"I watched him once," Calian said from his catatonic state. "He took down three Chippers without a scratch or wasting a bullet. Swordsman, marksman—didn't matter. He was unstoppable—was…"

Unstoppable, and yet here he lay lifeless. Another victim in a world that had become a graveyard of fallen heroes. The revelation left a cold pit in my stomach. If this man couldn't survive, what chance did we have?

I glanced at the others, their faces ghostly under the flickering lights, each lost in their thoughts. My thoughts raced as questions flooded my mind. *Which of the three missing Chippers could have done this? Or was it a horde or Chippers? Or maybe something entirely new that we hadn't even seen yet?*

Calian finally raised his head and scanned our defeated group. For a moment, fear flashed within him, but he quickly buried it. "Is there something out there more terrifying than what we've already faced?" he asked through uncertainty as his fear bubbled to the surface.

A silent chill silenced the group. Until then, we'd survived through sheer will and desperate actions. Each interaction with the creatures still tore loved ones from our group. But Calian's question painted a nightmare so intensely dark my brain couldn't fathom a monster capable of that.

Another terrifying question hit me, one I grew too scared to voice. *Why was his hand the only thing missing?* The Chippers killed then devoured, either getting rid of the evidence or for sustenance. It appeared someone has brutally murdered the Survivalist simply to remove him as a threat, then left him in the lonely, dark grave.

Kneeling beside the Survivalist's lifeless form, Calian rifled through the man's worn leather satchel. Respectfully, he searched the body, removing things he deemed useful. Gingerly tugging something, Calian removed one, then two revolvers from the bag. He created a small pile comprising the two revolvers, a few granola bars, a couple bottles of water, a few boxes of bullets, and a fire starter kit.

We distributed the weapons and loot between us. The weight of a revolver in my hand was comforting and terrifying. Reaching deeper into the satchel, Calian removed dry goods—cans, some packaged food—and we divided those amongst us, too. Calian paused, the revealed unexpected; a pack of gum. With a swift motion, he unwrapped a piece and popped it into his mouth, offering one to Ava, who accepted it immediately.

"Here's hoping minty fresh breath counts for something in the apocalypse," Ava said. Her attempt at humor did little to lessen our predicament.

Samuel appeared confused as he added, "What if the rest of us would like a piece of gum, hm?"

As if snapping out of a deep thought, Calian shook his head then offered a piece of gum to Samuel and me, which we both took eagerly.

After shoving the gum into his pocket, Calian took a moment. He bowed his head and removed his cross from his shirt and clutched it tight. His lips moved in a silent prayer for the man who'd once been a master of survival. We all shared a moment of reverence for the

Survivalist. Though only Calian knew him, he'd served as a beacon of hope and strength. In the end, the world proved that even the mightiest could fall.

"Let's go," Calian finally said and rose to his feet with a more determined posture, different from the somber one he'd had since we discovered the Survivalist. We followed Calian and Samuel stayed behind for his own silent prayer for the fallen, before leaving the Survivalist in the shadows.

We continued and opened a dividing door into a new section of the hallway. The oppressive flickering of the lights ceased, yielding to a steady glow that let us see every inch of the new section. Polished floors and unmarred walls welcomed us to the area's warm presence. How pristine the corridor appeared compared to the horror we ventured through was unsettling. I wondered if the Chippers had somehow left the area alone, or if someone, or multiple survivors, still occupied it? Was it the Survivalist's doing?

"This makes little sense," Samuel said as everyone squinted into the light in confusion.

"Nothing does anymore," Calian replied, his pistol never leaving his grip.

"Keep your guard up," Samuel added, his tone as stern as a dad. "Clean doesn't mean safe."

I nodded, gripping my new revolver, though I didn't have the confidence to wield it.

A door loomed at the end of the hallway, a carbon copy of the one we'd passed through to enter the subterranean limbo. To our left, a sign marked "Storage Closet" hung slightly askew next to another sign that read "Women's" in chipped paint. To our right, hung signs that read "Men's" and "Executives Offices." Ava's eyes locked onto the door on the left and her muscles dropped in relief.

"Before we go any further…" she said, pointing to the door labeled "Women's."

"Agreed," I replied, acknowledging my own feeling of relief. I hated to admit it, but nature was calling with an urgency that seemed indifferent to the apocalypse.

Ava chuckled, a sound like a balm against the harsh backdrop of our reality. "Let's go, Martha."

Calian and Samuel planted themselves against a wall as Ava and I entered the restroom. We pushed open the bathroom door, and a familiar echo of Dad's voice filled my head, prompting a snicker to escape me. "Dad always said, 'if you find a restroom…' " I mimicked his deep, often sarcastic tone.

"You should always try to go," Ava finished the quote. Her smile was weary, but warm as we shared a moment we'd never hear again. It was a joke that would've earned an eye roll under normal circumstances, but it served as a fragile thread tethering us to a past that felt more and more distant.

We checked every stall with cautious movements before we did what we needed to do, and quickly. It felt like our bladders knew there wasn't time to waste. As we washed our hands, my thoughts raced. Were we about to delve into the Executive area? What secrets lurked behind those unassuming doors? And how much longer could we survive in the horror-filled labyrinth?

"Ready?" Ava asked as she chucked her paper towel into a trash can with exaggerated force.

"Ready," I said and snatched my revolver off the counter. We stepped out and rejoined the boys, who awaited us with nods of understanding.

"Let's find out what's behind executive door number one," Calian quipped, though his attempt at humor didn't quite reach his eyes.

Together, we turned away from the promise of escape the exit offered and toward the unknown of the Executives' sanctuary. The distant answers felt closer than ever as an intense gut feeling that we would find the answers we wanted, good or bad, filled me.

"Let's do this," Ava said.

My fingers tightened around the grip of the revolver, and every step toward the door weighed on me.

We reached the threshold of the Executives Offices. Samuel nudged the door open and the pitch black of nothingness greeted us. Samuel stepped into the darkness and it burst into a blinding light that caused all of us to flinch and raise our guns at empty, oversized mahogany desks. The half-closed doors of the offices seemed to whisper, inviting us into their secrets. Secrets it knew we were desperate to uncover.

"Clear," Samuel grunted after a tense moment, lowering his weapon slightly but never fully relaxing.

"Looks untouched," Calian said as he entered the room, gesturing at the layer of dust on the desks. The vast differences between the previous corridor and the new one gave me chills. Why did the area have so much dust on the furniture, like no one had visited it in months?

"Let's be quick," Ava said, her body quivering.

The thought of what might hide in the offices made my heart beat erratically, but we needed answers. Could the offices be just as vacant and dusty as the rest of the room?

We began our reconnaissance of the room. We checked corners, searched desks, and I realized the main area was more for receptionists of the bigwigs who hid in their offices.

I tried not to think of the Chippers or the pools of blood that led us there. Instead, I focused on the faint hope that maybe, just maybe, we'd find something that could help us turn the tide.

Calian and Samuel's footsteps echoed dully as they crossed to the first office, their silhouettes framed by the doorway. I kept my ears tuned to their movements. Meanwhile, Ava rifled through the papers on a desk with an intensity that made her seem older than her fourteen years.

Martha's Notebook

"Martha, come here." Ava cut through the stillness in a mix of excitement and urgency. I ran to her side, her fingers hovering over a set of plaques mounted on the wall. The brass shimmered under the artificial light, contrasting against the dark wood.

"Look at this," she said, pointing to a central plaque with bold letters. "Members of the Board—Onakele Enterprises." We scanned each plaque, "Executives—Military Branch of Control," and "Executive Branch—Mion-Lach Republic." Her fingers traced the engraved names, each one etched with precision that spoke of importance and power.

"Any names we'd recognize?" I asked as I squinted to read the dozens of names listed on each plaque. They felt like ghosts. Each person listed was most likely gone. All for power over what? Us? The Chippers?

"None so far," Ava replied, her brow furrowed. "But these are the people who were in charge. If anyone knows how to stop this, it might be them. Or at least they may have left clues."

"Or they're the ones responsible for this," I shouted, something twisting in my gut. Every name might match with one of the offices surrounding us, but if they were too selfish and sold out the world for money, what hope did we have?

"Let's try to memorize these names," Ava suggested, her eyes scanning the list with determination. "We don't know when this information might come in handy."

"Got it," I said, committing the names to memory. With each name that settled in my mind, I felt a little more empowered. Knowledge could be a weapon in the world, especially against an increasingly intelligent force of zombies.

A creak froze us in place. We exchanged a look, hearts pounding, then relaxed as Calian emerged, nodding to indicate the room was clear. Samuel appeared soon after, giving a similar signal.

"Anything important?" Calian asked, his gaze flickering to the plaques.

"Names," Ava answered. "Lots of them. Could be important."

"Alright," Calian acknowledged with a tight nod. "Keep looking. We need every piece of the puzzle we can find."

I glanced back at the plaques, their significance weighing heavily on me. These names could have been the decision-makers on the screwup that led to the Chippers being released.

My fingers traced the cold brass edges of the plaques when Ava's voice pulled me back from my thoughts. "Martha, look here," she beckoned, her eyes flitting across the engraved names. "It says 'Ms. M. Noirytz' on the Onakele Enterprises board."

"Could it be Aunt Megan or Aunt Madeline?" I asked, a flicker of hope kindling within me. The idea that someone we knew could be involved in everything was unsettling and oddly reassuring.

Ava shook her head, her brows knitting. "No, Aunt Madeline is Mom's sister; she wouldn't have our last name. But Megan…" Her voice trailed off as she pondered the possibility. "Wasn't she a lawyer?"

"Yeah, but…" I hesitated, trying to reconcile the image of my aunt in such a grim place. "Do you think she could be part of this company? Of all this?" I gestured vaguely around, encompassing the shadow of suspicion that tainted everything.

"Maybe." Ava's lips pressed into a thin line. Her gaze locked on the name like it might yield answers.

"Hey!" Calian jolted us. His tone rang urgently. We spun, instinctively bracing for danger.

"Found something," he called, waving a sheet of paper like a flag of discovery. I noticed an official seal and a signature blazoning it.

"Is it about the Chippers?" I asked. Every piece of information felt like a step closer to unraveling the tangle of horrors outside these walls.

"Could be. I saw the words 'DHIA AI System Trials,' " Calian said, turning the paper over to verify the wealth of information it held. "Figured this could be big."

We huddled around the document. The dim light cast shadows that seemed to lean in to overhear the revelations inked on the page.

Calian's fingers trembled slightly as he flipped through the several papers in the pile. His eyes scanned the contents with intensity. I leaned closer over the back of a desk chair.

"DHIA AI System has become compromised and must be shut down immediately," he read. The words startled me, but seemed obvious. "The Mion-Lach Government has lost control—"

"Lost control?" Samuel cut in with eyes almost popping from his skull. "Of the AI? Are we not fighting zombies? We're fighting against some AI system?"

"Sounds like they lost control of everything," Calian said grimly. "It says all microchips installed in the test subjects were to be eradicated. However, they can't remove the microchips without... without killing them."

Silence descended on us like a shroud. The room felt colder as darkness creeped in to claim victory.

"So, all those Chippers out there..." Ava's quiet, calm voice struck me harder than any scream could have. "They're just government test subjects. They're trapped in some government technology plan or something?"

I bit my lip hard, fighting the swell of pity and horror that threatened to overtake me. They were people, not monsters. People with families, dreams, lives before the chips turned them into blood-thirsty zombies.

"And we can't save them," Calian added quietly, lowering the paper as if it weighed more than the desk. "We can't remove the chips. We can't bring them back. They're gone for good."

My hands clenched into fists at my sides, a mix of anger and helplessness bubbling within. We stood in the heart of a catastrophe, one far greater and more insidious than we could've imagined.

"Then what do we do?" Samuel's question floated in the silence without an answer to anchor it.

"Survive," I said. "We survive and win, because that's what we've done since day one." My answer was blunt, but it was the only thing we could do, and I didn't even know if we could continue to do it.

"Martha's right," Ava agreed, the blue streak in her hair catching the light. "Let's find the trick to stopping these things and put these poor test subjects out of their misery."

"Let's help these poor people and get our lives back to normal," Samuel said, followed by a small prayer.

We gathered the strength to continue our search for more answers, and a cold realization settled in my bones. Innocent people were turned into monsters, all for some sick game played by those who considered themselves gods. My fists shook and a fiery rage ignited within me. "We have to shut this AI system down," I said with all the rage building inside. "No matter what it takes."

"I want to help these people as much as you do, but even the government couldn't shut down the AI." Samuel interjected. "How do you suppose we—"

"By staying alive!" I shot back, more forcefully than I intended. My heart raced, but not from fear. It was revenge fueling me. "All we've done for days is survive. We've lost loved ones because we didn't know what we were up against or how to fight them. Once we learn more information, we'll have the edge we need to win permanently."

The room fell silent. The weight of our future and our mission weighed on everyone. Was I asking too much, or was the world asking too much?

"Then let's find the answers and end this AI mayhem," Ava said with growing conviction.

"Right," Samuel agreed, leaning his shotgun against his shoulder. "I plan to live through this, and getting rid of these Chippers seems like the best way to do that."

"And then?" Ava asked, looking at me expectantly.

Determination flared in the eyes of my apocalypse family over a few answers to our nightmare. Despite having gone through hell and back, we had more left to accomplish.

I swung my backpack over my shoulder and gripped the straps tightly. "I thought I saw a door at the end of the hall before we entered this office." I pushed past the others to the door. My heart pounded and something deep within wanted me to take the lead, to show my strength. "If this is an Underground Bridge, it's got to connect on two sides. The other side may hold more answers."

Ava saddled up beside me with her pistol at the ready. The pride in her eyes supported my strength to take the lead, even if it was false. "Let's go find out, sis."

Behind us, with approving smiles on their faces, Samuel and Calian followed with weapons drawn and created a protective barrier. We exited the Executives Offices and reentered the hall. It stretched out in front of us, lighting the way to a distant, secured door.

"Keep your eyes peeled. We still don't know if we're alone down here," Samuel warned with eagle eyes scanning our surroundings. "We don't know what's waiting for us beyond the door."

"Or down there," Calian pointed back at the dividing door and the previous end of the corridor.

The thought shook my strength, but I squashed it quickly. Fear had no place, not anymore. It was anger that drove me, anger at the faceless 'elites' who thought they could play god with people's lives and ultimately stole most of my family.

We approached the end of the Underground Bridge, where a similar door sat ajar. I could only hope we'd find another set of stairs, like how we descended into the perceived sanctuary. "Here's to hoping this is our way out of here." I said in a jovial tone, despite the twisting in my stomach.

"Daylight, here we come!" Ava shouted with childlike joy. She was ready to be rid of the creepy place with little escape, and so was I.

"Let's just get out of here," Calian whispered, and I shoved the door open with my shoulder. The hinges groaned like the door's at the opposite end.

"Agreed." I tried to sound braver than I felt. Taking a deep breath, I stepped into the stairwell.

"Back!" I shouted, raising my revolver. But it wasn't a Chipper, it was worse. The figure was human or had been once. Its jerky movements were iconic, but a bright green glow shone directly in my eyes. It took a moment for my eyes to adjust, but when I did, I realized I was face to face with a demon. No visible microchips, but the demon's eyes weren't human. Blinding green eyes replaced them.

"Upgraded Chipper," Ava yelled, stepping back into Calian as everyone froze. We were not prepared like we'd thought.

The creature turned with a calm, jerky twist. It seemed to have been waiting for us and possibly knew we had no place to run.

"What do we do?" Ava asked, fear tightened around her voice.

"Fight!" I shouted as anger and rage boiled over. "I'm not dying!"

I aimed my revolver at the demon's chest as my adrenaline pulled the trigger. *Bang.*

CHAPTER 15: TRUE VILLAINS

Training without a gun hadn't prepared me for the kickback a gun would create. The force of the shot threw my body backwards as I stumbled to the ground.

My face pressed against the chilled floor as empty shells from the shots firing above rained down around me. The air grew thick with the scent of gunpowder and blood as the zombie stumbled before collapsing, inches from where I lay. My chest heaved against the unforgiving concrete.

Wasting no time, Calian dashed toward the Chipper's motionless form. He steadied his pistol at its head, and two more shots rang out, loud and final. He stood for a moment, his breath came in shallow gasps as he waited for any reason to fire another shot.

"I almost had my first kill!" I shouted, picking my shaky body off the floor. Even though I wasn't successful, I drew strength from the fact that I pulled the trigger. If I could muster the strength to do that, maybe I could find the courage to survive.

The Chipper's burning green eyes dulled into a black hole where no life remained. Calian's brow furrowed as he scrutinized the fallen enemy. A puzzled expression slowly contorted his features.

"Calian?" Ava called out while she stared at his stony face with concern.

"Does anyone see any microchips on this thing?" His question sliced through our brief victory.

We all knew microchips meant someone was a Chipper. Its eyes were a dead giveaway that he wasn't a person. But was it a Chipper? Or was it one of the missing upgraded versions, and if so, which one? If it didn't have a chip we could see, then what were we really up against? The question hung heavy in the air, unanswered but undeniably terrifying.

We huddled around the body, our breaths ragged as we searched for the telltale glint of metal among the torn flesh and ragged clothing. Hands sweaty and trembling, I reached out tentatively. I probed the cold skin on his right arm, half-expecting it to spring back to life under my warm touch. But there was nothing, no sign of the microchips anywhere on its arm or hands. All I could find were our bullet holes in its shoulder and two in its forearm.

"Look," Samuel said, trying to keep his voice level, "I think it's still a Chipper." He pointed out an old bullet wound nestled in its matted hair, a dark, missing chunk on the back of its head covered by the male's long black hair. "Our bullets have fresh blood oozing from them. This hidden exit wound has none. If this wasn't a Chipper, it would be dead already," he affirmed, though the hollow note in his voice betrayed his unease. Our relief was short-lived.

Calian, ever the thinker, kneeled beside the creature, his eyes sharp with a sudden idea. "Hold on," he said and his hand disappeared into a gruesome cavity Ava's shots had created. With a sickening squelch, his fingers closed around something solid amid the carnage. He drew back, revealing a metallic object caked with blood and tissue. A microchip lodged deep within the zombie's body, where no casual search would find it.

A wave of horror crashed over me. Ava paled, her youthful exuberance extinguished like a snuffed candle. "How are we supposed to manage against 'Upgrades' and other types of Chippers now?" Her voice shook like a leaf blowing in the wind. "If they've hidden microchips inside them, how will we ever know who's who before it's too late? Some of them can talk now, they can ambush us... How do we stand a chance?"

Her question echoed in the silence, amplifying our fear. We'd moved further and further down the predator list as the predators evolved, learning faster than we could and existing in varieties that we weren't even aware of. The hunt had just become a lot more dangerous.

"Could've been one of the escaped ones from the lab," Samuel said, staring down at the corpse.

My mind whirled with the what-ifs. "Maybe it's the 3.0? Or 4.0? Or 5.0? But what if it's none of those and it's something completely different?"

Samuel's eyes met mine, crestfallen in defeat. "What if it's just one of the lower ones?" he pondered. "There might be more advanced ones than that, and that one took all of us with our guns to take it out."

The silence of the underground compound grew heavier, as if it anticipated the unseen threats lurking in its shadows. We crept around the fallen zombie, our bated breaths held until we were clear of its grasp.

"Let's get out of here," Samuel whispered, leading the way up the stairs. Each step echoed ominously, amplifying our fears. Guns drawn, we stayed vigilant, our pessimistic thoughts weighing us down.

We ascended two flights. The light from our flashlights bounced off the concrete walls like jittery specters fleeing our approach. Then I saw it, another bloody puddle. There was no body, no bones, nothing. It was evidence of someone, or something, being devoured entirely.

"Keep moving," Calian said, his voice urgent. We couldn't afford to dwell on the gruesome scene when every moment standing still meant Chippers could find us.

Another two flights and two more signs of chaos. Deep scratches marred the wall, telling a tale of desperate struggle. Bullet holes pockmarked its surface, silent witnesses to a fight that had raged right where we stood. I imagined screams echoing through the stairwell as someone frantically sprinted for the Underground Bridge, not knowing their last minutes would be right there.

"I bet this fight ended at that puddle." Ava's grim tone reminded me of scary stories. The evidence was undeniable that a battle for life had occurred, and by the looks of it, life had lost.

"Let's hope whatever did this is long gone," Calian added, tightening the grip on his gun.

"Or lying dead downstairs," I said, trying to convince myself as much as my companions. But the pit in my stomach knew better. Fear clung to me, a shadow I could neither shake nor escape.

We approached every new flight of stairs like an impending battle. Climbing another flight of stairs, our breaths echoed in the emptiness.

Ava's voice cut through the silence, her attempt at humor clouded by the gravity of our situation. "You know, lots of zombie movies have people die in malls. At least we're not in a mall," she said, the corners of her mouth lifting in a forced smile.

"Great," I said. "Then let's avoid malls and clichés."

We ascended the last set of stairs when we reached a more typical door, instead of the hulking security doors from before. Samuel, once again, opened the door with his shotgun before disappearing behind it. After a tense few seconds, we heard the relieving words, "Clear."

We entered what seemed like a basement of a building. It felt like we'd returned to normal, aside from the creepy basement and the

Chippers that could be right above our heads. There were two doors, one marked "Housing Wing," and the other "Cafeteria." Despite the chill that ran down my spine, Ava stepped confidently toward the housing door, leading us away from the stereotypical death trap of the cafeteria.

We finally found a heavy door that didn't squeal, and it welcomed us with more darkness. As we crossed the threshold, motion sensors detected our presence, and the room blinked to life with artificial light. A barracks-style dormitory, with rows upon rows of bunk beds, each meticulously made, created a military tone to the room.

"Looks like no one's slept here in a while." Samuel's words floated across the eerie stillness.

"Keep your voices down," Calian hissed, and checked under the first bed, gun poised.

Ava and I trailed in the back, our guns raised as we focused on every inch of the shadows for movement. We were the last line of defense, and the weight of that responsibility settled on my twelve-year-old shoulders. With every rustle or imagined movement, my finger twitched for the trigger.

"Clear," Calian called, moving systematically from bed to bed. Samuel followed suit on the opposite side, his tall frame stretched awkwardly as he inspected each top bunk.

"Nothing but dust bunnies here," Samuel said, trying to lighten the mood. But even his joke couldn't penetrate the oppressive atmosphere of the Housing Wing.

"Looks clear," Ava confirmed.

"Let's hope it stays that way," I replied. My eyes never left the empty bunks stretched out before us.

Our cautious footsteps whispered against the concrete floor as we progressed. The room, once dark, was alive with our wary movements. It wasn't until we reached the far end of the bunkhouse that something caught our attention. A bed unlike the others, its covers thrown about in disarray.

"Look," Ava called out at the same moment I noticed. A chaotic nest of possessions surrounded the last bed on the right.

Samuel and Calian moved in like trained military, their guns ready, eyes darting for any sign of danger. I held my breath, half-expecting a ghastly figure to rise from the tangled blankets.

Calian approached and nudged the blankets with his gun. Noticing no movement, he yanked the blanket off. "Clear," his voice rang out, even though we were right next to him. It was just an unmade bed. A rare glimpse into someone's life.

Ava and I approached the mess of personal items while Samuel kept watch. My fingers trembled as they brushed crumpled papers and scattered photos on the floor. A worn backpack laid tossed against the wall, its contents spilled out like memories.

"Martha, ammo," Ava said, kicking a box toward me with the edge of her boot.

I pocketed the cartridges, grateful for the find, when a photograph caught my eye. It showed a family smiling, whole, untouched by the horrors that defined our existence. The father bore a long brown beard, his arm wrapped protectively around a woman with laughter in her eyes, and the two boys stared lovingly at their parents.

A lump formed in my throat, the image mirrored what I had lost, what we all had lost. The mother in the picture transformed into Mom. The boys, carefree and innocent, were a painful reminder of our former lives. And the dad in the picture, who had zero resemblance to ours, still reminded me of Dad and how he always seemed to protect the family between jokes.

"Martha?" Ava's voice laced with soft concern.

Tears pricked the corners of my eyes, blurring the joyful faces in the photo before I wiped them away. I let out a shuddering breath and folded my legs beneath me as I sank onto the bed with the weight of loss I couldn't outrun forever.

"Are you okay?" Ava plopped onto the bed next to me as she'd done so many times in our room.

"I—it's just…" Words failed me. How could I explain the ache for a past that would never return? The longing for a father's guidance, that would never ring in my ears again. I couldn't remind Ava of our loss and the toll it continued to press upon me.

"Hey, it's okay to miss them," Ava said.

I looked up in surprise, then noticed her fingers caress the photo.

"I'd do anything to bring them back, faults and all. But you know Dad would want us to live the best lives we could, whether he was here or not."

Her presence, warm and real, anchored me amid the storm of emotions. She was all that remained of my family. If we continued fighting and joking, that's all Dad would ask of us.

"Wait a minute…" Ava whispered, extending a trembling finger toward the photograph in my hands. "Guys!" Ava's voice rose, urgent. "I think the dad in this photo is that survivalist guy."

Calian sprinted over. His eyes narrowed on the image. "He did mention something about a family once," he said. "But he never gave details. Couldn't tell if the apocalypse took them… or something else. I guess that's a story lost to the apocalypse now."

The unspoken fear that we might be treading on the ghosts of another's sorrow filled us.

We turned our attention to the backpack, its contents spilled like the chaotic remnants of a life interrupted. I rifled through papers, some stained with time or faded by water. Among them, notes scrawled in hurried handwriting, maps with routes marked in desperate red lines, and scientific jargon I couldn't hope to understand.

Ava snagged one of the pages. "Any idea what this is about?" she asked.

"Survival stats, maybe?" Calian suggested, peering over her shoulder. "Or research?"

"Could be anything," Samuel said. The dread of not knowing clawed at my mind.

That's when we heard it, the unmistakable thud of a door closing from the other end of the wing. Our heads snapped up in unison, waiting for a figure to emerge through the door. We dropped the papers and photos and raised our guns. The seconds ticked by as my tense finger sat on the trigger.

"Easy," Calian breathed.

I scanned every molecule of the door as my mind attempted to convince me it moved. Adrenaline surged through me, a bitter cocktail of fear and readiness. My fingers curled tighter around the grip of my gun. The images poured into my mind again. Was the sound another survivor, or was it another creepy upgraded Chipper? Was it the horde that had followed us down the stairs and they found their way to this side of the bridge?

"Whatever comes through that door," Ava's voice halted my rambling mind, "we do what we must."

"Always," I replied.

Together, we waited, shrouded in the thick anticipation of a battle yet to come. With our guns still raised, we swept the room with vigilant eyes, but no further sounds disturbed the quiet. I glanced around, heart hammering, and then I realized Samuel was missing.

"Where's Samuel?" My words scared me. What monsters were we facing that could make someone disappear?

"Sam?" Ava called out softly, pivoting on her heel to scan behind us.

"Shh," Calian hissed, his gaze darting from wall to wall. But it was clear Samuel wasn't in the room with us.

I turned, my breath catching, as I noticed a handle on the wall with a sign next to it that read, "Executive Housing." The door completely matched the wall, with only a smooth vertical handle revealing its presence. A shiver ran down my spine. "Could Samuel be in there?"

"Let's check it out, but stay close," Ava said, her pistol at the ready as she moved toward the door. Each step felt heavier than the last, and my mind raced with possibilities of what hid beyond.

Calian reached the door first and pressed his ear against it. He paused for a few seconds before he nodded and creaked the door open. We stepped into the "Executive Housing," keeping our guns aimed at any signs of movement, muscles tensed for whatever horror might greet us. Then, the lights illuminated at our presence, forcing us to aim at every corner of the room in panic.

"Clear left," Calian announced, weaving between plush, king-sized beds and elegant furniture. He checked every nook and cranny methodically, his movements precise. I admired his strength, the certainty in his actions, and wished I could emulate it.

"Right's clear, too," Ava confirmed, her voice carrying a hint of relief mixed with the ever-present anxiety clinging to us.

"Samuel?" I called out louder. The name echoed off the walls, unanswered. My grip on my gun tightened, the weight both a burden and a comfort.

"Stay sharp," Calian reminded us, though his words were unnecessary. We knew better than to let our guard down.

We moved further into the Executive Housing, the luxury a mocking reminder of those who thrust us into the world. Every lavish detail stood as a safe contrast to the chaos outside the walls.

"Where are you, Samuel?" I called out again and hoped for some sign. I prayed we weren't walking into a trap. The absence of our friend weighed heavily on me. A smug reminder I truly couldn't save anyone from this world. We had to find him.

"Samuel?" I tried again, and hoped for a response. My heart ached more and more each time I called out and received nothingness.

Then, a strong grip seized my shoulder. Adrenaline surged through me and fear clawed at my senses. I screamed and spun, finger tight on the trigger of my revolver. But instead of the blast of a gunshot, there was just a hollow click.

"Martha!" Ava shouted, her weapon swinging in my direction. Calian pivoted on his heel, his gun at the ready.

There stood Samuel, his eyes staring at my gun with utter death written on his face. He held a frozen pizza box. For a moment, time stood still, our panting the only sound in the luxurious silence.

"Samuel?" I managed, my voice shaking, both from the scare and the realization that my gun had failed me at a crucial moment.

"Did you just shoot at me?" His eyes remained locked on my gun and he held up the pizza like a peace offering. "I found this. Figured we could use a good meal."

"Could've gotten yourself shot!" Calian shouted, annoyance in his tone and across his face.

"Or worse, given us a heart attack," Ava added, her brows knitting in her own annoyance and concern. But despite the sharpness in her voice, her eyes softened.

"Sorry, Martha," Samuel said. His eyes searched mine, checking if I was alright.

"I'm sorry. I promise I didn't mean to shoot… well, I did, but not at you." My hand shook like a dog drying itself.

"Let's just find somewhere to settle down for the night," Ava suggested, eager to move past the scare and regain some semblance of peace. Samuel's idea, albeit delivered in a startling manner, wasn't bad. We needed to stop and eat, and we needed rest.

"Next time I'll announce myself with a trumpet or something," Samuel said, wearing a smirk reminiscent of one Dad would have. He gestured to my revolver, still gripped tightly in my hand. "Have you reloaded your gun lately?"

Embarrassment filled me. "How do I reload it?"

Everyone chuckled and Samuel announced, "Family pizza night. Who's up for some culinary experimentation with our stovetop pizza oven?"

"Absolutely," Ava chuckled, shaking her head. Her blue eyes sparkled with joy. "Can't be worse than those canned beans."

"Speak for yourself. I'm starving," Calian said through his amusement, and he gave me a reassured pat on the back. "I'll take my chances with Chef Samuel's famous cafeteria cuisine."

While Samuel headed off with his cardboard treasure, presumably toward the cafeteria to wrestle with the frozen pizza, I followed Ava and Calian into the makeshift bedroom of the Executive Housing. If we were going to spend the night there, might as well live like kings and queens. Choosing a bed to rest on felt like an ordinary decision in an extraordinary world, a luxury almost forgotten.

Ava and Calian gravitated toward the two beds he'd placed side by side. They continued to be respectful while not denying their romance. Their adorable fling soothed my heart, remembering that some things could still happen in the world that I thought the Chippers had stolen.

Finding solace at the back of the room, I picked a solitary bed tucked in a corner. It provided a view of the entire area, and the solitude offered a momentary escape from the constant vigilance required of us. As I settled onto the mattress, the springs creaked under my body. I took a deep, relaxing breath, attempting to forget the horrors I'd seen.

"Marth, are you good back there?" Ava called as she and Calian snuggled up on one of the beds.

"Yeah," I replied. My fingers traced the edge of the comforter. "Just… thinking."

"Try not to do that too much," Calian joked, a rare action from him. "We've got tonight to rest up. Tomorrow, we search the rest of this building."

Tomorrow would come soon enough, bringing with it all the uncertainty and danger we'd grown accustomed to. But for the moment, we had a frozen pizza and luxurious beds.

The thought brought an unexpected smile to my face as I laid down, hearing Samuel rummaging in the kitchen in the distance. The soft whispers and flirty giggles between Calian and Ava helped my heart finally relax.

Calian and Ava pulled me into their conversation without warning. "Hey Martha, what about you? If the world went back to normal, what would you do?"

I propped myself up on the plush pillows. It felt strange to entertain the idea of the world returning to normal when we didn't know if we'd see the next morning, but I indulged for my sanity.

"I don't really know. What would you do?" I asked, curious about what Ava desired without Mom and Dad around.

Ava's gaze leaped to Calian, then back to me. A coy smile engulfed her mouth. "I'd find a big house, somewhere safe and warm, with someone special." She connected with Calian's with an intensity that spoke volumes. Winks and giggles followed as Ava continued. "Two kids, maybe. And I'd live out every single day with my family until it's my time, dying peacefully in the arms of my husband."

Calian's face softened at her words. He glanced at her with the unspoken promise they shared—a silent communication that I sometimes felt left out of.

"Sounds nice," Calian smiled with a twinkle in his eyes. His hand reached out for Ava's and they squeezed before Calian kissed her hand.

My heart ached with happiness for them. If only they had a chance for their dreams to come true. Their dreams were beautiful, but they felt so distant from our current situation. My turn to answer the question came back around, and I hesitated, feeling the weight of our predicament more heavily than the idea of a comfortable dream life.

"Martha? There must be something you'd want," Ava prodded as her hand remained in Calian's, with a permanent smile on her face.

"I don't know," I admitted, honestly unsure of my future and unable to see through the fog to what could be. "Maybe… find love? Live high in the mountains like at Scoite's Peak. Find a place like what Dad loved. Get married and have Dad walk me down…" I paused, grappling with the truth that gnawed at me relentlessly. "Never mind, it doesn't matter anymore. All I can think about are the Chippers. My dream future is one without those monsters in it." I swallowed hard. "Even if it means giving my life to rid the world of them."

The room fell into a dark silence, punctuated only by the distant echo of Samuel clanging around in the kitchen. I could feel their gazes on me, heavy with their shattered dreams. The world had become nothing but shattered dreams and we clung to shreds of hope.

"Hey," Ava attempted to dull our dark thoughts. "We'll figure this out together. None of us are giving up on a life after this nightmare.

And you know I'd do anything to give you a better life. That's what big sisters do."

"Agreed," Calian chimed in. "Ava isn't the only one who has your back. I know we're not family, but now we're an apocalypse family, bonded together until our last days." Their words wrapped around me like a warm embrace, strengthening my resolve.

The clatter of something metallic and the smell of charred dough wafted into the room. Samuel confidently entered the room like a server at a Michelin Star restaurant, balancing a large, circular object in his hands that looked like a pizza, if you squinted and didn't mind the sparse patches of black and missing cheese.

"Feast your eyes on my culinary masterpiece," he announced with a confidence that almost made me excited about the lackluster meal. "I've confirmed it tonight. My talents definitely do *not* translate to the culinary world."

"Hey, at this point, anything edible is gourmet to me," I said, trying to lighten the mood and reached for a slice. The cheese that wasn't missing had melted slightly, and my stomach rumbled with approval.

"Jordan would have done a much better job," Samuel muttered, and his smile faded. The jovial joy in his voice fell, replaced by an ache so tangible it seemed to dim the flickering lights above.

His pain felt like my pain. "Samuel, your pizza is perfect." Watching his struggle felt like watching Ava or Dad struggle, and I couldn't take it. Whether we were a true family, an apocalypse family, or a strange mixture, I couldn't allow him to get swallowed by the jagged teeth of loneliness.

Ava and Calian hesitated, then joined in, each taking a slice. Ava tore off a bite and her eyes betrayed her surprise at finding the taste acceptable. Calian chewed thoughtfully, nodding his approval before reaching for another piece. Our collective hunger turned the pizza into a feast, and for a time, we savored the taste of normalcy. Our version of a shared family meal.

"Really, it's not bad," Ava said with a smile as she dusted crumbs off her purple penguin shirt and then off the bed. "I mean, it's not five-star dining, but it's got a certain… apocalyptic charm."

"Apocalyptic charm," Calian echoed with a laugh. "That's one way to put it. But seriously, it's good."

We ate in silence for a while, the sound of our chewing filled the space. It felt incredible to relax and enjoy a meal rather than constantly rummaging through cans and eating dry granola bars. Each mouthful of the subpar meal brought joy to my stomach and my soul. Within minutes, the pizza was nothing but oil spots on the cardboard circle. Not even crumbs remained.

The remnants of our makeshift dinner lay scattered across a bench. Calian's eyelids fluttered, then he took deep, relaxing breaths. I couldn't help but mirror his tranquility as the food settled in my stomach. I crawled into my temporary bed as I felt the covers warm snuggle envelope me.

"Martha?" Samuel whispered as he quietly shoved one of the beds against the door. An added precaution for our safety. He then crawled across the bed before locking the door. "Thanks for saying you liked the pizza."

"Of course, Samuel," I replied, sincerity emphasizing my words. "It reminded me of… before. You know, when things were normal."

"I can't believe it's only been a few days since everything went to hell. It hasn't been that long since things were normal, but at the same time, I can't remember what normal feels like anymore." Samuel added before he sighed, the sound heavy with memories and loss. "I just feel so lost without Jordan." His voice broke on her name. The silence that followed filled with unspoken grief.

My heart ached. "I understand," I said. "Since Dad's been gone… I've been missing a piece of me no one can replace. He protected me, made me laugh, was my biggest cheerleader, and that's all gone."

Samuel nodded through his own darkness that he couldn't hide.

I continued as if some of the weight of losing Dad floated away. "I want to learn how to stand up for myself. Dad never really got to teach me. I don't want to need protecting, I want to protect like Dad always did for me, and like you, Calian, and Ava do for me now."

"Your dad would be proud of you. You pulled the trigger on a Chipper Upgrade," Samuel said and a fatherly smile grew at the corners of his mouth. "You're stronger than you know, Martha Noirytz. For what it's worth, I'm proud of you."

"Thank you." I clung to Samuel's words. They may not have been Dad's, but they were the words I longed to hear. I wiggled into my covers as Samuel prepared the room for us all to sleep.

Samuel cut the lights before he slid off the bed, slammed against the door, and sauntered over to my bed. "I can't fill your dad's shoes," he whispered with the pure respect for Dad he'd fostered in the short time they spent together. "But I'd be honored to be your stand-in dad, Martha. I promise to teach and guide you as much as possible until my final days.... or until I tell one too many dad jokes and you tell me to get lost."

I nodded and extended my hand, which he took, creating a deeper connection between Samuel and me. His fingers were rough, calloused from hard work, yet his grip was gentle and reassuring.

"Goodnight, Martha," Samuel whispered as I rolled over, trying to cocoon myself in the sheets. He rustled into bed before I heard a deep exhale. I realized I hadn't heard a peep from Calian or Ava for a while, but I peeked over at their bed and noticed they were lost in their dreams. Between the pitch black, the silence, and the dash of light peeking out from underneath the bed that blocked the door, acting as a night light, it was the perfect ambiance to sleep.

I tried to fall asleep, but past events raced through my mind, begging to be cataloged into my notebook. I had only one option. So, I pulled my backpack close, unzipped it, and slid out the worn notebook. The cover felt softer under my fingertips. The wear and tear took its toll on objects as much as us. Flipping it open, I realized how much had transpired since I last scribbled down my thoughts and fears. With each page, memories flooded in. Echoes of laughter, glimpses of home, and fragments of answers laid scattered about the pages.

I yanked out some of the papers I'd gathered earlier and used the faint light under the door to read what I could from each page. Maps, notes, sketches, all pieces of a puzzle we blindly tried to complete. I spread them out around me and threw the covers further away. The king-sized bed became my workstation with plenty of room for my small body and my scattered papers.

I brushed over the photo of the Survivalist, imagining his past life compared to his apocalyptic one that was cut short. So many pieces to fit together, so many lives ruined, so many thoughts racing through my head. Could we be the ones to end something we didn't understand?

I tucked the photo between the pages of my notebook, a silent reminder and a promise to win this war for everyone we had lost. Looking back, I realized I'd shared a meal, and shared living quarters with two people who were complete strangers just a couple of weeks ago. It hit me how quickly people could connect and unite with a common enemy trying to destroy them.

"Peter Noirytz," I whispered into the silent, dark room. "Everything I do from today on is for you. I really hope I can make you proud, from wherever you're watching me from. I love you, Dad."

I wiped a tear from my eye before I transferred the information into my notebook, determined to keep our story alive through ink and paper. It was the least I could do to document, to remember, and perhaps, one day, to guide others with the knowledge we'd gained from the darkness.

The heaters kicked on and the soft hum of the Executive Housing's air system serenaded me as I hunched over my collection of salvaged papers. My ballpoint pen glided across my notebook with the finesse of a figure skater. My hand moved with a frantic yet deliberate pace, capturing every detail, every theory, and every tiny victory we'd scraped together in our mangled world.

"I must keep going," I whispered to myself as my eyes protested the long hours, blurring the crisp lines of ink into lullaby notes. As sleep took control of my brain, my thoughts turned to Dad. His laughter booming through the halls, followed by some ridiculous joke about zombies or the end of the world not being as bad as he thought. His strength mixed with his calm had always been a prized trophy I aspired to claim.

I woke from my hunched position, my hand still clutching the pen, having fallen asleep on my notebook. I blinked hard, shaking my head to dispel the looming sleep. Just one more line, one more tribute to the man who'd taught me that fear was only scary when you didn't understand it.

"Dad, I miss you more than I ever told you. I wish you were here. You always seemed to know what to do. You've always been my rock, and as long as I keep you alive within me, I'll always have your strength." I fought back tears as I worried about smudging the wet ink and ruining the respect I laid out on paper. "I will always love you more than your dad jokes. Keep smiling down on me."

My fingers trembled as they traced the final words, and a period that felt like a dam holding in the flood of emotions and words I'd spewed. The notebook, ever heavier with our journey, continued to be my anchor. Clutching it close, I collapsed onto the bed, the musty fabric mingling with the remnants of the pizza.

As I allowed sleep to claim me, my heart clung to the hope that somewhere, somehow, Dad was truly watching over us. With the notebook pressed against my heart, I drifted into dreams where zombies feared us, and the world bloomed anew under a watchful, loving gaze.

CHAPTER 16: NOT ALONE

I woke with a jolt, my mind snapping awake faster than it had in months. For the first time in too long, I'd slept on something softer than a concrete floor or the unforgiving ground. I noticed Calian, Ava, and Samuel sprawled across their plush beds. I let myself enjoy the luxury of waking up slowly as the comfort warmed my bones.

My fingers brushed the soft leather of my notebook as I slid it into my backpack. Flashing back to the words I'd scribed the night before. A glimmer of hope lingered in the air. My gaze wandered to Ava, her chest rising and falling in the steady rhythm of deep sleep, with Calian doing the same in a synchronized slumber.

As the initial haze of waking wore off, something felt off. The bed we'd pushed against the door, our makeshift barricade, was no longer snug against it. There was just enough space for something to slip through. I squinted, noticing a sliver of darkness beckoning from the gap. The door was cracked open.

"Samuel," I whispered urgently. No response. Louder, I repeated, "Samuel!" Still nothing.

I crept toward him, my pulse quickening. Shaking his shoulder, I braced myself for any movement, any sign that danger had entered the room. A snore erupted from Samuel like a cannon blast before he finally stirred awake.

His eyes blinked open in confusion as they studied me. "Martha?" he mumbled, his voice rough with sleep. "You okay? Nightmare?"

Fear squeezed my throat, words desperately trying to escape my mouth. "No, look." I pointed to the door, willing him to understand without speaking the fear. The safety we thought we'd secured, the sanctuary we thought we'd created in the nightmarish world, might have become compromised while we dreamed of better days. And whatever was out there, whatever horrors lurked in the shadows, they could be monsters under our beds.

"Something's wrong." I could barely speak before terror shook my vocal cords.

Samuel's eyes followed the direction of my trembling finger. With a flurry, he flung off his blankets and seized the shotgun at his side. He moved like he was awake all night. Not an ounce of morning fog showed. He leveled the barrel at the door, his body coiled like a sprung trap as he sat propped against the headboard.

"Calian! Up now!" Samuel barked across the room. The command shattered the peaceful sleep of the other two. A soft rustle came from Calian's bed as he awoke, disoriented but quick to grasp the gravity of Samuel's tone.

"Door," Samuel said urgently, nodding in its direction and Ava and Calian's gazes snapped toward the ominous gap in its frame.

Calian reached under his pillow and snatched his pistol as he aimed at the door in one smooth movement, like he'd practiced it a million times. The sharp click of him checking his bullets, then slamming the magazine back, punctuated the severity of the scene. Ava, meanwhile, fumbled beneath her pillow, her fingers seeking her pistol. Her movements became more deliberate. The act of someone who knew hesitation could mean death.

I stood frozen, the icy fingers of fear clenched my heart. I did my best to race to my bed and retrieve the revolver from my backpack before aiming at the door.

Creeping toward the door, each step became a struggle, like I wore weighted shoes of terror. My ears became muffled, and my senses narrowed to tunnel vision as Samuel's muffled voice called out.

"Hurry Martha." The words refocused my sense on the issue at hand. I took cover behind Samuel's bed, next to him, and we pointed our guns at the door. Ava and Calian did the same in an adjacent bed.

Feeling Dad's voice in my ear, I became overcome with confidence and left the safety of the bed to scope out the terrifying door. "You've got this kid. Believe in yourself like I do." It was like he was standing behind me, guiding me to find my internal strength.

"Martha, where are you going?" Samuel reached out to stop me, then grasped the shotgun with both hands to keep his aim on the door.

Approaching in a crouch, I kept my unsteady revolver focused on the door as much as I could. I extended the unforgiving metal and nudged the door. It creaked open with an ominous squeal, revealing nothing but the rows of abandoned bunk beds. The room sprang to life under the motion sensor, which highlighted the empty room.

"Clear," I said, followed by the biggest exhale of my life. Then, just as my heartbeat slowed, the air itself came to life with the sound of death.

A distorted, electronic screech we'd become familiar with tore through the facility, reverberating off the walls and making it impossible to determine its location. Somehow the sound felt like it came from the stairwell, but hauntingly could have originated just outside the rooms.

My feet became one with the floor, unable to retreat into the room or move further into the barracks. I couldn't move, couldn't think, couldn't even scream. The echo of that ungodly cry seemed to rattle within my skull, a taunting reminder that Chippers lurked behind every corner.

The aftershock left us petrified, but it wasn't silence that followed. Gunfire erupted as human voices called out in terror and pain. The most bone-chilling symphony swept through the building. The overwhelming sounds rang out faster than the gunfire. Shotgun blasts, pistols, distorted screams, family members calling for loved ones. It all became too much for me to handle.

I fought my urge to crumble to the ground and wobbled back to safety. With hands I could no longer feel, I fumbled for the door, then eased it shut. Locking the deadbolt again, I stumbled back, further from the death outside our doors. Samuel heaved the bed back, our makeshift barricade, before turning to bearhug me.

"You're safe," he said, a muffled voice reaching me through the screams and gunfire.

We scrambled back to our beds and a cold sweat trickled down my back. My fingers desperately wrapped around my revolver once more. The grip dug into my white-knuckled hands. We sat, shivering under the weight of our destiny. Our guns pointed at the door as if they'd scare off anything that stepped inside.

Then, as abruptly as it had begun, a final shot rang out before complete silence washed over everything. It was a quiet that echoed in my ears. No more shots followed, no more screams tore through the stillness. The absence of noise brought its own fears. Who won? Were there survivors left, or Chippers? Were they friendly survivors?

In that silence, every rustle of fabric tempted fate. Should we stay barricaded in the room that had become a temporary refuge? Or should we brave the building, where death had just claimed its share for the moment?

Determination filled Samuel's eyes, and he pushed himself off the bed. He steadied the shotgun, continuing to aim at the door. "We can't stay here like sitting ducks," he said with contagious confidence. "Let's go see what's waiting for us out there." He flashed a grim smile mixed with suicidal eyes. "Worst case, we'll all get a family reunion with the ones we love."

The idea was morbid, but it contained a depressing truth. Even more so, every minute was borrowed time when any one of us could have been wiped off the planet in the first days of the apocalypse.

Calian's chuckle broke the tension, light but tinged with the same darkness that covered us all. "I'm all for family reunions," he quipped, standing and slinging his pistol in the air, "but how about we push that particular gathering further into the future?" His eyes locked on Ava, and the corner of his mouth twitched upward.

"Agreed. I'm in for pushing that meeting a little further out." My jaw tensed as I stuffed the last of our scavenged supplies into my bag. Ava meticulously checked her pistol before tossing her backpack onto her shoulders. She caught my gaze and shot me a comforting wink. The moment terrified me, and I wondered if we truly were entering the last minutes of our lives. Would we soon mirror the Survivalist, left and forgotten in the nightmare creating building?

I shouldered my backpack, the weight a little lighter from the adrenaline coursing through my veins. The thoughts pulled at me. *Did I pack all our items just to leave them scattered on the other side of these rooms? Will I take my last breath in these rooms?*

Dad's voice popped into my head again, washing away all the negative thoughts, still jovial and oozing with love, "Marthy Martha, are you really giving up? You've always conquered whatever you set your mind to. You can be brave for this moment and conquer whatever is on the other side of that door, even beyond that. I know you've got this and I'm still so proud of you."

I returned to reality with tears streaming down my face and noticed everyone lined up by the door. They all had their weapons in hand and ready for the nightmares that surely prowled beyond our makeshift sanctuary.

With one synchronized breath, we stepped into the unknown. Unsure of who or what awaited us and if we could handle it.

My hand trembled, the heavy revolver bouncing in my hand. The chill in the air was a grave contrast to the warmth of my newfound determination. Samuel dragged the heavy bed away from the door with a grunt, his muscles strained.

"Ready, Ava? Ready, Martha?" Calian asked, peeking into the next room. I nodded, not trusting my voice, and together we crossed the threshold. My grip tightened on the revolver, my aim wavering as adrenaline surged through me. The room chirped with soft creaks of the bunk beds. We moved in unison toward our next obstacle, one last shield between us and the apocalypse.

"Let me take point," Samuel said, his voice low but firm as we approached the stairwell. His shotgun was a familiar extension of his will to protect us, to lead us through this hellish landscape. He flung the door open, and the cafeteria door loomed ominously. Its frame marred with deep gashes and smatterings of fresh blood, another trail leading into darkness.

"Remember what I said about cafeterias being death traps?" Ava's whisper tickled my ear, her eyes gleamed with a mixture of fear and excitement.

"I know, I know…" I replied, trying to muster a smile, but it felt hollow. We were living the horror she'd joked about, and the punchline was lost to the silence of the room we were about to enter.

Samuel crept forward, and I followed close behind. I scanned every nook and cranny for bodies, more blood, or worse. Calian brought up the rear, his sharp gaze leaping back and forth. There wasn't much to search in the petite cafeteria and open kitchen, which meant only one thing: it was time to take the stairs.

After exiting the cafeteria, we paused. Without a word, we each nodded, then turned to the stairs. In silent agreement, I took a calming inhale before we continued our search. We ascended the last set of stairs, listening for any sign of the chaos that had erupted prior.

With each step, the tension wound tighter within me, a rubber band ready to snap. The silence that followed us up the stairwell was a living thing, oppressive and thick, suffocating the hope that had blossomed in my chest. I tried to focus on the rhythm of our steps, a futile attempt to drown out the memory of the screams and the screeches that had filled the air only moments ago.

"Stay alert," Samuel said, soft, but urgent, as we turned the corner at of the landing. My foot hovered over the next step, slick with dark, coagulated blood. A severed arm lay discarded on the edge, its flesh torn and ragged. An acknowledgement of the horror that had unfolded. The sight sent a shiver through me, and I swallowed back the bile that rose in my throat.

We moved with excruciating slowness, each mindful of the treacherous footing. Ava's hand found mine, as it had so many times before. Her firm grip reassured me, despite the tremor in her fingers. It was a comfort, but also a reminder that no matter how much she tried to protect me, we were both walking through the same nightmare.

The gruesome trail of blood, bits of clothing, and other pieces I didn't want to identify led us higher. The sheer volume of blood painted a picture far grimmer than any of us wanted to admit. I couldn't help but wonder whose life had been so violently spilled across the steps, and whether they had fought bravely or succumbed to fear in their last moments.

Finally, the crimson path ended, giving way to a clear expanse and a wooden door attached with heavy locks that stood between us and the champion of the recent battle. Samuel reached the door first, always taking the lead when it mattered most. He took his oath to protect the three of us very seriously. With his shotgun, he steadily creaked the door open.

A welcoming from hell shattered our silence. An electronic screech tore through the stillness. The sound originated from behind us, somewhere in the stairwell, echoing off the walls with a bone-chilling resonance. Two more followed, identical in their menacing pitch, and my entire body shut down. Had the original pack of Chippers waited for us to move before continuing their pursuit?

"Move! Move! Move!" Samuel's command pushed us through the door and he raced across last.

As we crossed the threshold, I snuck a peek into the darkness behind us, expecting to see many creatures following us. But there was nothing, only shadows that concealed the unknown behind us.

Samuel's fingers found the lock just as another round of hellish screams echoed up the stairs. He slammed the door shut with a force that spoke volumes of the terror trailing us closely, and his hand wrestled with the old lock. The thud of heavy bolts connecting with the thick door frame gave me reassurance that we should be safe for the moment.

"Stand back!" Samuel said and jumped from the door like someone igniting fireworks.

The pounding began just after Samuel left the door. A relentless rhythm that vibrated through the walls and air. After several beats, an earth-shaking crunch slammed against the door, causing subtle cracks to form. Something monstrous hurled itself against our only barrier, each strike a promise of violence and death. I clutched my revolver tucked into my belt, my sweaty palms rubbing against the wooden grip. I wondered if five bullets would be enough to keep me safe, and how long we could continue to survive.

"Whatever's on the other side won't get through." I tried to sound confident, but my voice betrayed me.

Before I could draw another breath, a new sound entered the chaos. A heavy set of steps, deliberate and ominous, approached the door. My heart dropped in unison with each footfall, a countdown to an end I wasn't ready to meet.

The next thud against the door nearly toppled me. The metal buckled, ever so slightly, from the impact. A gasp escaped my lips, and Ava's oversized eyes mirrored my same fear.

"Martha," she whispered. "Is this it for us? Is this how our lives end?"

Everything ceased within a second; a single screech sliced through the air. Scratches, slow and deliberate, turned into twisted claws, raking against the door, emerging from bulbous arms attached to a deformed monster with the same burning green eyes. They were truly hunting us, trying every tactic and using other Chippers more suited for the task of annihilating us.

"This can't be happening," Calian mumbled. "That door should withstand gunfire and explosions."

"How?" I asked, confused by the wooden appearance of the common-looking door.

Calian's eyes snapped to me. "You didn't notice, did you? This is the same metal door we've dealt with before. It just has a faux wooden exterior to trick people into thinking it's a basic door."

I glanced at Samuel, who nodded with his eyes closed, a subtle acknowledgment in the face of our demise. No one dared lower their weapon or move their eyes from the door that could give way at any moment.

Every eerily slow scratch taunted us that, at any moment, a technologically advanced horde could wipe us out in the blink of an eye. Shotguns, revolvers, pistols. We didn't have enough power to fight off the combined force of the Chipper horde and whatever other Chippers or monsters waited with them.

A bone-jarring thud, echoing through the hollow space like a knell, punctuated the fifth and final scratch. My hands re-gripped the revolver that slipped in my sweaty palms. The cold metal couldn't ease my nervous hands. A lone screech that had haunted our every step peeled into the distance, taking with it the heavy, relentless footsteps that left the door but remained in my nightmares.

"Are they—are they gone?" I asked, my quiet voice boomed in the silence.

"Seems like it, for now," Samuel's reply reassured me, but none of us lowered our guns.

In the aftermath, the silence became overwhelming. My heart pounded as I realized I was still alive, and a single door had saved our lives again. Like snapping out of a coma, everyone shook off their catatonic state before lowering their guns and expelling all the carbon dioxide in their lungs.

"Every time I think these zombies can't get any worse or more terrifying, they do," I said, trying to inject some levity into our shared dread. A nervous chuckle slipped from my lips, but it died as quickly as it came, disappearing into the thick, musty air.

"Martha," Ava said in a stern tone, reminiscent of Mom. Her eyes narrowed into a scowl. "Stop jinxing us, will you? Maybe if you quit saying things like that, they'd stop chasing us."

I managed a sheepish grin, unsure if it was an honest scolding or a joke. The corner of my mouth twitched upward despite the nightmarish footsteps echoing in my brain. Ava's face didn't change. I felt the sincere love in her words, but the stress of defying death every waking minute pushed her closer to a breaking point.

"Right, because the zombies have a lookout that waits for me to jinx us before they attack," I replied, half of me hurt by her tone, and the other half nearing my own breaking point.

"Let's just hope they don't have good hearing." Calian attempted to break up the impending fight. His pistol hit his thigh as he collapsed against a wall.

We lingered in that awkward silence as I tried to regroup my thoughts and emotions. Our weapons remained near our knees, our shoulders and arms weary from holding the "ready" position for so long. From our exhausted bodies to our exhausted minds, we needed a break from our persistent enemy.

I spun around and surveyed the room we found ourselves backed into, taking in the chaos of overturned furniture and shattered glass everywhere. The lab was an obvious downgrade from the lavish, underground chambers we'd left behind. The secrets of this floor had been laid out for us to find, either from lives flipped upside down like the desks, or from Chippers hunting down their next snack.

"Look at this mess." Ava bent over to snatch up some papers lying at her feet with an annoyed swiftness. A golden crest caught the light and my attention. Its bold design commanded attention amid the disarray. I moved in closer to read the contents with Ava, regardless of if she was unhappy with me or not.

"Does that logo mean something?" I asked, peering over her shoulder.

"It's a government seal. It means this must be the actual government outpost the Survivalist mentioned," she said, keeping her tone low to hide the contents we may find. She flipped the paper and scanned it over before tossing it to the side.

When the floating paper reached the floor, it signaled the rest of us to sift through the contents surrounding us. Each paper bore the same crest, some an official gold crest, others inked in black from a printer. The possibility sent a shiver of excitement through me, tinged with fear I couldn't shake. Then another nagging question entered my mind. Were we being pursued so relentlessly because the Chippers wanted to prevent us from reaching this area? Why didn't they try harder in the Underground Bridge?

"Can you imagine what we might find here?" I could barely contain the excitement in my voice. "Answers, Ava. Real answers."

"Or more questions," she replied, still teetering on the edge of anger.

"Either way," I attempted to quell the tension between us. "let's agree to leave any doors with heavy locks alone, okay? We don't need a repeat of what we just locked away." My attempt at humor fell flat and Ava's eyes shot at me with a burning rage she didn't need words to convey.

"Agreed," Samuel cut in before literally stepping between us to block us from each other. "No more surprises if we can help it."

We continued our search, the quiet only interrupted by the rustle of papers and the occasional thud of boots hitting chair legs or crunching on shattered glass. Answers were there, somewhere among the documents. The story of how our world had turned into a nightmare. And I was determined to uncover every ounce of it, piece by fragmented piece.

With determination pulsing through my veins, I followed Samuel and Calian through the dim lab lights. Shuffling papers turned into occasion gasps, then defeated exhales.

"We'll find something, just keep looking," Samuel broke the continued silence, then laid his shotgun on the only upright desk. He took a moment to stretch and scan the room, not wanting to get caught off-guard by any surprises.

"Let's just hope our biggest enemy in here is paper cuts." I peeked up from my papers to a smile that forced a smile on my face. Samuel's warm eyes healed my soul.

We checked every paper around every desk meticulously, peeking into shadowed corners and under everything. Next, we exited the lab and entered a nearby bathroom. We found nothing but broken mirrors and drips of water that sounded like ghostly whispers. In the adjacent break rooms, more upturned chairs, discarded meals, and scattered remnants indicated hurried escapes. Every room told a ghostly story of lives uprooted in the middle of an ordinary day.

We cautiously entered the hallway, Samuel and I from the break room, Ava and Calian from the janitor's closet. "This place looks empty," Ava said as her pistol fell against her thigh.

"Too empty," I couldn't help but added. My eyes lingered on a slanted picture frame hanging on the wall. One of the lucky ones compared to the six or seven others shattered on the floor. The smiling co-workers in their lab coats seemed to mock our grim situation, while my mind twisted the faces into the terrified form they may have become, if not worse.

Calian straightened the picture, taking extra time to get it perfect, a futile effort in this world. "I wonder how many of them are dead."

Samuel's face took on a disgusted and confused look before he snapped back. "Who knows? Maybe none of them are. Maybe they're hiding in a different bunker with their families, safe and sound."

Still staring at the picture, Calian replied with a patronizing chuckle, "Unlikely. Think about the odds of how many of us survived. Fifty percent? Less? Maybe more like twenty-five or thirty? And some of us knew how to fight. Do you really think scientists knew how to fight or survive in this environment?"

Calian and Ava linked hands as Samuel and I shared disgusted looks of disbelief. What had happened to Ava and Calian? It was like their minds had snapped from optimistic teens in love to stone-cold souls only out for themselves. Maybe it was a fork in the road that the apocalypse gave survivors. Either you keep your sanity and your past self, or you take a right and transform into your corrupted twin.

Things felt different, like a thick fog of evil settled over us. We stopped checking rooms, and everyone seemed to just want out of the facility. We reached the front lobby and finally enjoyed the shining sun again. The wall of floor to ceiling glass separated by thin metal borders bore several shattered pieces along with both glass doors. The reception desk sat vacant, scattered papers danced in the draft like the wings of injured doves.

As we continued into the lobby, something caught my eye. A solitary Chipper, its head unnaturally tilted upward as if searching the ceiling for survivors. Its stillness felt unnatural too, after the relentless onslaughts we'd faced over and over. We took a chance and closed in on the lone foe.

"Blue," Calian hissed sharply, gaining our attention. "Its microchips are blue."

I quietly peeked at the Chipper and verified a pale blue glow illuminated both hands and its neck. We all knew what the terrifying color meant. The creature was "upgrading" right in front of our eyes, learning something new to destroy us.

Samuel and Calian didn't hesitate. They snuck up on the creature before bashing the microchips embedded in its hands. I flinched at the crunching of metal, flesh, and technology.

In desperation, the Chipper released a shrill shriek. Ava darted behind the spasming figure before it could react. She raised her pistol and slammed the handle onto the Chipper's neck. The last microchip erupted into sparks, silencing the creature's wails and sending it to the ground in a slumped mess.

"Good shot, Ava," I whispered.

We stood in the uncomfortable silence, waiting for any further sounds or Chipper calls to echo through the building. After a few moments, we considered the area safe enough to continue.

With the blue microchips reduced to nothing more than fragmented circuits and lifeless metal, Calian crouched beside the Chipper's body. He prodded at the remnants, ensuring not a flicker of the unnatural light remained. "All clear," he confirmed, and I exhaled a breath I didn't realize I'd held.

"Brace yourselves." Samuel's words sent chills through my body, drawing our attention from the fallen Chipper. He stood by the window, shotgun still in hand, staring in the distance with wide eyes and a tight grip.

We crowded behind him, peering into an outside world we hadn't seen in days. My eyes enlarged at the devastating sight. Seven Chippers stood like eerie security guards in the parking lot. Their postures rigidly aimed skyward, stuck in their own "upgrades." A haunting blue glow painted the asphalt below them, sending me into an uncontrollable shake. They looked like some sort of grotesque garden gnomes, receiving new information on how to erase us from the world.

Before we could contemplate our next move, a rustling in the distance stole our focus. Four more Chippers sprinted across the barren landscape, their limbs jerking with unnatural speed. Another group of five followed close behind, forming a world-ending horde we had no chance of defeating.

"Samuel, look—" I began, but he raised his trembling hand to silence my words.

"Do not let them know we're here," he whispered so quietly I could barely make out his words.

To our left, three solitary Chippers prowled the building, their heads swiveling as they hunted for any sign of life. They acted like lookouts, trying to alert the rest of any intruders.

"Scavengers," Calian whispered, disgust in his voice. "They're getting too smart." The longer the nightmare dragged on, the more dangerous our enemies became.

As much as part of me wanted to confront the threat head-on, to show we weren't afraid, another part knew that they vastly outnumbered us, and hiding was our best chance of survival.

I retreated from the window, along with everyone else. Would it be our new game, to hide constantly to survive? I wondered if our training was nullified by the Chippers traveling in packs. Was the blue or the green glow more intimidating, when the blue glow felt like a checkmate for one of us every time?

"Maybe we should barricade one of these rooms?" Samuel whispered, nudging us further into the building. "If we leave now, it's certain death for us."

"Since when has Martha Noirytz played it safe?" Ava's tease cut through the tension, a smile tugging at her lips even as her eyes remained serious.

I shot back a look, half-exasperated and half-fond. "I'm not playing it safe," I hissed. "It's suicide out there." My gaze swept the room, locking on each member of my apocalypse family. "I'm not leaving until we find more information, or those monsters are gone." My voice cracked with a mix of anger and determination.

Samuel gave a slow nod, his shotgun poised like a cane at his side. Calian, more reserved but no less fierce, mirrored the gesture against a trash can.

"Alright then," Samuel said, his voice low. "Let's make this place a fortress."

We snuck back to the lab to fortify it, pushing heavy desks against doors and turning every entrance into a barrier. The metallic clangs and scrapes of furniture against the floor echoed around us, a dinner bell to any Chippers close enough to hear.

"Keep your guns ready, and make sure they're loaded," Calian reminded us with a light jab at me. "We don't know if they'll try to find another way in."

Every muscle in my body tensed as we worked, the fear of an ambush lurking in every shadow. But as desks lined up like brick walls at each door, a hint of safety wrapped around us. It was fragile and temporary, but it was something.

"Good enough, I suppose," Ava said, inspecting our handiwork. Her approval felt unsure, but was still enough to calm me some.

And with that, our little group dispersed, scavenging the chaos of papers and equipment that littered the lab. Deep down, I prayed that with extra time and nowhere to go for the foreseeable future, we may find exactly what we needed.

A desk stood in the corner, partially shrouded by darkness, like it held secrets it wanted to keep from view. I had an inexplicable pull toward it, my legs moving almost of their own accord while Calian and Ava shuffled through other parts of the room, their voices a low murmur in the background.

"Martha, let me know if you find anything," Samuel said from his spot next to the hallway door. His words felt comforting, reminding me he was there, but I shrugged them off. I needed to focus.

"Will do," I whispered back, pushing papers aside as I scanned for important words. The desk held stacks of papers, next to a stack of thick textbooks. It could take me days to comb through the desk alone, but what else was I supposed to do?

A flicker of color caught my eye amid the sea of white paper: a photograph. My heart hitched, and I pulled at it, removing it from the pile with careful urgency. Profiles stared back at me from the sheet, faces frozen in time. I leaned closer, my breath catching as recognition sparked within me.

"Guys…" The word stumbled from my mouth, but not loud enough to gain their attention. My fingers trembled slightly, clutching the document as if it might crumble to dust. Those people… they were more than just profiles. They were clues, perhaps even answers.

"Find something?" It was Ava, her footsteps soft as she approached, concern etched across her features as she peered over my shoulder.

"Yeah, I think so," I replied, though my voice sounded distant to me, drowned out by the rush of blood in my head. "Looks like… profiles."

Her gaze sharpened, and we poured over the paper. The search for answers narrowed to the details on the page. The room closed in around us, every sound magnified, from the scratch of paper, the faint hum of building ventilation, to the collective breaths of our small band of survivors.

"Could be important," she inched closer, her hand on my shoulder. I nodded, the weight of responsibility settling upon me. We'd found something crucial. I could feel it in my bones.

"Let's show this to Samuel and Calian," I said, preparing for whatever surprises lay ahead. With the profile clutched in my hands,

I stepped away from the desk, ready to delve deeper into the mystery that held us captive.

My fingers trembled as they traced the contours of familiar faces lined up on the white paper. Monica Noirytz, Peter Noirytz, Ava Noirytz. The shock of it was cold and sudden, an icy plunge into waters I hadn't known existed. Why were our profiles in such a haunting place? What connection did we have to the birthplace of our zombies?

"Martha Noirytz," I whispered, staring at my face. The brown eyes I'd seen a million times before in the mirror as I prepared for the day, or in the car window as Dad drove me to school concerts or Ava's soccer practices. A twelve-year-old girl who should've been worrying about school dances and friendships, not survival in a world that had turned its back on humanity.

I couldn't speak. The words were lodged somewhere between my heart and my throat, tangled with the fear that clutched my chest. How did we end up there? Why us? My mind spun with questions, each one a thread in the web of this nightmare.

"Martha?" Ava's voice sliced through my paralysis. Concern laced her tone. Her hand tightened on my shoulder. I couldn't look away from the paper and my mind ran wild with questions.

"Why is our family on this paper?" Ava's question read my mind. She was caught in the same circle of questions as I was. "Who would do this?" Her voice cracked, her motherly facade crumbling as she grappled with reality. The vulnerability in her tone reminded me that despite everything, she was just a kid too, thrust into the role of protector.

"Mom… Dad…" I said, ignoring the haunting reminder they weren't on the planet anymore. I slipped back into the innocent, weak girl I'd tried to escape through the whole nightmare, but I was helpless to fight it.

"Don't. We need to find out what asshole dragged our family into this mess," Ava assured me, but there was a tremor in her tone.

"Samuel! Calian!" Ava called, her voice steady as she summoned the boys. I folded the paper carefully, tucking it into my pocket as if it were a million dollars.

Footsteps approached, heavy and quick with anticipation. Samuel and Calian appeared behind Ava.

"I found something," I said, my voice steadier than I felt. "It's about us—about my family."

"Let's see it," Samuel said, his voice grave, shotgun still cradled in his arms like a baby.

In that laboratory, surrounded by spilled secrets and the echo of the ravenous undead, I questioned our future and now my past. As I unfolded the paper and smoothed the edges, unease filled me as my apocalypse family stared into the eyes of my broken family.

CHAPTER 17: SECRETS REVEALED

I tore through the remaining papers, frantically searching for an explanation as to why my family's faces stared back at me from a picture on a cluttered desk in such a miserable place. Our faces had rested with the chaotic papers the entire time, undeniably us with our names and personal information below, but what did it mean?

The more I dug, the less sense the world made. Graphs, numbers, and words tangled into a meaningless mess. Names and codes jumped out at me, but they may as well have been scribbled in a foreign language from what I could understand.

A surge of frustration bubbled inside me, burning with intensity. It wasn't just paper; it was someone's research on our family. A scientist had studied our family before they turned the world into an apocalypse.

I stood abruptly and my chair screeched against the cold tiles. I needed space, clarity, something other than this frustrating mess.

Moving to another desk, I found a fresh start to my search. I glanced back at the mess I'd left behind. Additional papers scattered across the floor as Samuel, Calian, and Ava tried to locate possible answers. A burning feeling that I'd given up too soon echoed in my ear.

Calian's brow furrow in frustration as he flipped through a stack of papers, his fingers moving rapidly. Samuel stood rigid, his eyes darting between the lines of text, searching for something, anything, that might make sense of the chaos. Ava sat in my seat and focused on each paper in total concentration.

Their confusion mirrored mine. None of the paperwork on that desk made any sense. With a collective, resigned sigh, the three of them abandoned the shadowy desk and scattered to new desks. Separated and refocused, I felt we'd have a better chance of discovering something important.

Calian moved off to the far corner of the room, his shoulders squared to a flipped desk in determination as he dropped to his knees and sifted through the mess of papers. Samuel gravitated to the opposite end, his steps labored. Their shoes slapping against the cold tile punctuated the eerie silence.

Ava, however, stayed close, settling at a flipped desk only a few feet from mine. The warmth of her presence became an anchor, even if she had become icy. Calian, with a fleeting glance toward where Ava sat, offered a small loving nod before turning his attention back to the task at hand.

"Anything?" Ava's voice rang out in curiosity.

"Nothing yet," I replied, unable to keep the edge of defeat from seeping into my words. "Just more questions."

She nodded subtly. "Keep looking, Martha. There's got to be something here."

"Right." I tried to portray conviction in my response, but it felt hollow, even in my ears.

"Martha," Ava called, her voice tinged with urgency. "Look at this!"

I rushed to her side with bated breath. But when I peered over her shoulder at the document in her hands, my initial surge of optimism faded. It was another piece of the puzzle, yes, but a piece of a

Martha's Notebook

different puzzle. The pages had specific information on each member of the board. Information that could be relevant, but we need additional information on the Chippers.

"Hey!" Calian's voice echoed from across the room, laced with a mixture of shock and revelation. "Ava, check this out!"

I followed behind Ava to hear the revealed secrets. Every line of Calian's body was tense with discovery. He pointed at an image, a grotesque mimicry of biological forms intertwined with mechanical precision. "It's… it's like they modeled these microchips off a parasite, the Horsehair Worm," he said, his eyes wide with horror.

"Parasite?" The word numbed my tongue like poison. The thought of those microchips burrowing into spinal cords and minds like worms in rotten fruit sent a shiver down my spine.

"Exactly," Calian confirmed, tapping the paper emphatically. "They engineered them to control the brain electronically through signals and pulses. The three microchips hijack motor functions and override the brain so the controller can take complete control of the host, a.k.a. the Chipper."

Bile rose in my throat as my stomach dropped like swallowing a fifty-pound weight. Those microchips weren't just controlling people, they'd erased every piece of the person they used to be.

A triumphant shout from the opposite corner drew our attention. Samuel, his face animated with excitement, waved a stack of papers above his head. "Guys! You won't believe this!"

We converged on him, Ava trailing a step behind, weariness etched in her features. Samuel slapped the documents on the desk in front of us, a marketing brochure unfurling under the fluorescent lights. The glossy pages boasted vibrant images of ecstatic people plugged into sleek, futuristic devices.

"Look." Samuel's finger traced lines of text that promised a revolution in entertainment. "They advertised these microchips as the next big advancement in virtual reality. They told volunteers it would

Martha's Notebook

be unlike anything they'd ever experienced, all for free, if they signed up to have the microchips installed."

"Free setup included," my voice cracked. Free or not, the price was far too steep. The entire campaign reeked of manipulation, of a con so vast it had destroyed the world.

"Virtual reality…" Ava mused, her lips pursed in thought. "More like virtually enslaving everyone who bought into their lies."

"Exactly," Samuel agreed, his ecstasy dimmed. "They sold dreams and delivered nightmares."

"Nightmares that we're left to navigate," I whispered, unable to shake the chill that clung to me. Our reality, warped and twisted by the very technology that promised to elevate it. And somewhere in the threads of deceit and ambition, our mother's truth lurked. A shadow we inched closer to unveiling.

My fingers trembled as I sifted through a nearby stack of papers, the whisper of secrets hidden within. Papers fluttered to the floor like fallen leaves in an autumn storm, each one adding to the chaos around us.

"Martha," Ava's voice broke through the rustling paper. She clutched more documents, her eyes wide with a mix of fear and revelation. "Look at this."

I scrambled to my feet, crossing the space between us in a heartbeat. She handed me the papers, and I scanned the contents. My stomach clenched as the words took shape in my mind. "Mind control at the flick of a switch?"

"Exactly," Ava said through gritted teeth. The room collapsed in on us. "The government and Onakele Enterprises could just… turn people into puppets whenever they felt the need."

"Volunteers…" I chuckled, my thoughts racing back to the glossy brochure. *They weren't just volunteers for a groundbreaking virtual reality experience, they were guinea pigs in a far more sinister plot.*

"More like victims," Ava corrected, her protective instincts flaring, and she placed a comforting hand on my shoulder. "This is too much to hear. I don't know how much more I can take."

Nodding, I stumbled back to my desk as my stomach fell ill. The search continued, however. Every document hinted at a potential key to unlocking the hell our world had become. Then, amid the scattered reports and files, I found mention of "DHIA" emblazoned across a technical manual.

"DHIA," I exhaled and traced the letters with my finger. "Groundbreaking Artificial Intelligence System." My pulse quickened. It was no ordinary microchip. The government that swore to protect us had designed and implemented it.

"Martha?" Ava leaned over my shoulder. Her gaze locked onto the papers in my grasp.

"DHIA," I repeated, meeting her gaze. "That's the system running the microchips. It's an AI system, Ava. Artificial Intelligence and the government are behind the microchips."

"AI is controlling the Chippers? Why is it trying to murder us? What did we do?" Ava's voice shook, and her anxiety mirrored mine.

"That's a new question to answer. I feel like every question we answer spawns new questions."

"With or without more answers, we need to shut this AI system down, no matter who or what stands in our way," Ava declared with a sparkle of doubt in her eyes. "Some things are becoming more important than answers."

Ava squeezed my shoulder, but it differed from her typical consoling touch. My attention focused on the AI system, though. No matter how much it hurt, DHIA held the key to the zombies that destroyed everything around us. We had to find it, understand it, and ultimately destroy it.

"Guys," Samuel's urgent voice cut through the tense silence in disbelief, "you need to see this."

I pushed off the desk and hurried over to where Samuel hunched over a desk that seemed as chaotic as our lives had become. His fingers trembled as they traced the lines of text on an official-looking document. His eyes darted across the page.

"Look at this." He pointed at a list of signatures, each one more elaborate than the last at the bottom of the page. Signatures that belonged to Onakele Enterprises board members, as well as those from its two sister branches. The words above their names declared an immediate shutdown of the DHIA AI Control Program, citing the system's unnerving evolution beyond its intended capabilities.

"It's too intelligent?" I asked, not wanting to believe in words. It sent a shiver down my spine. How could we fight something that was not just mechanical but intellectually superior?

"So, it's intelligent enough to consider us expendable." Samuel added grimly. "I wonder if they lost control of their own creation once it understood why it was created."

"Just like Frankenstein's monster," Ava chimed, mentioning one of her favorite stories. She held a stack of papers so thick it looked like a book. With a flick of her hands, the papers scattered across the desk and surrounded Samuel's discovery.

"Board members," she announced. "Profiles, pictures... everything." The pages featured formal faces that lacked the dirt, fear, and exhaustion we wore. They were the faces of people who had played god and lost.

As Ava flipped through them, a gallery of strangers stared back at us, each oblivious to the doom their decisions had unleashed on the world. We reached the section labeled "Onakele Enterprises Board Members," and a knot formed in the pit of my stomach. They were the scammers who peddled a false product for their personal gains.

"Look at them," I whispered, my throat tight with a mix of fear and anger. "They look so... cocky, smug." Behind those facades lurked minds that created and implemented the Chippers. Those monsters wouldn't be what they were without the Mion-Lach Republic and this... Onakele Enterprises.

Ava's hands shook as she turned the pages, and the muscle in her jaw clenched. Her eyes hardened with every unfamiliar face. We peered into the eyes of our enemies, the true villains behind our nightmares who we couldn't confront.

"Monsters in suits," Samuel's words echoed my thoughts.

"Monsters, we're too late to stop," Ava said. We realized then that the Chippers had simply gotten caught in the middle of a power struggle between greedy humans and an ultra-intelligent AI.

"There are a lot of dirt bags involved in this." Ava's words burned inside me as each page revealed new, vile people. "I want to see the face of every piece of shit responsible for this catastrophe."

So, we continued deeper into the stack of paper left by those who had considered themselves gods, yet still wanted more.

The glossy sheen of professionalism couldn't mask the absurdity of some of the board members' portraits. Ava paused at a page, and we all leaned in closer, our eyes drawn to a man whose mustache defied both gravity and current fashion. Our rage quickly transformed into mockery.

"Check this out," Ava chuckled, pointing at the picture. "It's like he covered two leaves in coffee grounds before super gluing them to the sides of his lip."

I snorted, the tension momentarily lifting from my shoulders as Calian joined in with a full-on laugh.

It felt like Calian released all the laughter he'd suppressed since the first day in that moment. "Looks like a wet candy bar dragged through dog fur," he added, wiping a tear from his eye.

"That's one impressive coffee filter. Does it filter coffee for the entire planet?" Samuel joined in, and for a brief second, he wore a smile I hadn't seen since we'd lost Jordan.

The next profile featured a stern-faced woman, her eyes sharp enough to slice through steel. "Oh, she'd definitely sue you for breathing too loudly," I observed, nudging Ava with my elbow.

"Her glare could probably turn you to stone," Ava chuckled.

We turned the page and came face-to-face with Karen: the portrait of every internet meme. She'd cropped her hair into that telltale bob, the emblem of entitled complaints and demands to speak to the manager.

"Wow," I said, "Karen really is a 'Karen.' It's like they're not even trying to hide it anymore."

"I bet she threatens zombies with a lawsuit as they chomp her outstretched hand," Calian joked, and we all erupted into laughter that felt strangely comforting amid the chaos of our reality.

Our shared moment of levity felt like a fragile bubble released in a needle factory. For those fleeting seconds, we forgot about being survivors and enjoyed simple bliss. But as quickly as it came, our laughter died out. The rage boiled back up, remembering who those people were.

"Okay, okay," Ava said, smothering a stray giggle on her lips. "Let's focus. These people… they know how to shut down the AI. We need to shut down the AI to regain a chance at a normal life."

"Right," I nodded, squaring my shoulders.

Samuel placed a hand on Ava's shoulder. "It doesn't hurt to enjoy these moments and take a break. We can indulge in a little more fun."

Ava nodded, understanding Samuel had a point. "This guy definitely gives 'intern' vibe."

"The enthusiasm of a golden retriever who just discovered he's going to the park," Calian added, trying to enjoy the moment with Ava.

"Ah, and meet the park owner," Samuel chimed in, pointing at the photo below of an older gentleman who resembled some of the Chippers' grotesque faces. His gray hair was wild, and his skin sagged from years of frowns. "Gotta be the big boss, right? Or maybe that's just his 'I'm disappointed in you, son' face."

"Let's skip her," I hurried as my gaze slid over a kind-looking woman with a soft smile. She seemed out of place among the stern faces, and a pang of guilt for mocking the strangers filled me. We were looking for answers, not picking apart lives we knew probably ended weeks ago.

"Next page," Ava announced, flipping it over. Her next words caught in her throat, and the room fell silent. My heart dropped to the cold tile floor, sensing something was wrong before my brain processed it. Ava stood motionless, her light blue eyes locked on the paper like they were glued.

"Did you find something?" Calian asked, concern consuming his features. He and Samuel leaned in, their playful banter replaced by tension.

"Martha... do you see this?" Ava whispered, her voice hollow. It took me a moment to find my voice, to wrap my mind around the familiar face staring back at us from the ink.

"It's—it's Mom," Ava finally forced the words to stumble out of her mouth. Her fingers trembled uncontrollably as they hovered over the image.

"Is this a joke?" Calian asked through gritted teeth, confusion lacing his words. "What's going on?"

"Mom?" I pointed. My hand shook as much as Ava's. There she was, our mother, Monica Noirytz, frozen in time on the page. The woman who valued finances over us, who wanted us removed from her life, immortalized as a key player in the nightmare that had ended her life.

"It is her…" Samuel's voice trailed off, unable to understand.

A heavy silence enveloped us, the weight of betrayal and confusion becoming a physical force. Our laughter had evaporated, replaced by the cold, hard reality that our mother had played a part in creating the Chippers.

My fingers traced the outline of my mother, the lines of her familiar face bringing forth a flood of memories. Her laughter echoing in our home, her stern rants about our homework and good grades. But it was no trip down memory lane. It was a silent acknowledgment of the villain she'd hid within.

"Ava, what's going on?" Calian's voice cracked. Betrayal masked his features.

I could barely swallow, the shock had constricted my throat. "It's… Mom," I choked out. The words tasted like copper in my mouth, and the glossy paper under my fingertips practically burned my skin. The reality of Monica Noirytz's double life haunted us weeks after we lost her. "Head of Research and Development for Project DHIA," a title that screamed betrayal.

Calian and Samuel exchanged a glance. Their expressions morphed from bewildered to infuriated in a matter of seconds. A storm brewed in their eyes.

"Your mom…" Samuel's voice held a tinge of hope for some mistake, a clerical error that would erase the truth.

"Monica Noirytz…" Calian's voice trailed off, a low growl replacing his usual calm demeanor.

They glared at us, Ava and me, like we were accomplices. As if we'd hid the grotesque secret all along.

"Guys, we didn't know," Ava stammered, her tone defensive like an animal backed into a corner.

"Didn't know?" Calian spat. Samuel stood silently, lips pressed into a thin line.

The room became constricting, the air hard to inhale. The walls closed in on us, trapping Ava and me in a moment of raw revelation. Our mother was the puppeteer of a project that turned humans into monsters for narcissistic gain. And there we were, her offspring, left to grapple with the aftermath of her ambition.

I caught Ava's stare, her eyes silently pleading, asking if I knew about any of it. Calian and Samuel stood rigidly, and their anger boiled in our direction.

"Ava," Calian's voice sliced through the tension, "Your own mother? How could she be a part of something that... that devoured the world?" Desperation filled his words as he tried to understand.

A mix of fear and confusion swirled in the pit of my stomach. I wanted to shrink away, vanish into the floorboards. An identical fear shook Ava's body. We had no words to alleviate the situation.

"Did you know Mom was involved? That this was her job?" Ava's whisper pleaded for ignorance, yet it boomed in my ears like thunder.

My lips trembled as I tried to form words, my voice a faint echo of my inner turmoil. "No, I-I didn't." I turned to Ava, seeking a reassurance of understanding in her eyes. "Did you?"

She shook her head. Her blonde and blue ponytail bounced like an innocent child, shaking away the fear. "She was always on business trips, sure, but I thought... I thought..." Ava's voice faltered, and I heard her doubt. Did we know, somehow? Did Dad know?

"Even Dad didn't really know what she did, just the company name," she added, her tone laced with a bitter edge of betrayal. "Every time I asked him what Mom did for work, he just shrugged and said she

Martha's Notebook

worked in research and development for Onakele Enterprises. When I asked what exactly she did, he'd blow it off and continue doing the dishes or whatever he was doing."

The boys exchanged glances. Their anger slowly dissolved into a shared sense of bewilderment. We were all victims, pawns in a game none of us had known we were playing. Samuel and Calian believed us having seen the turmoil in our family firsthand before we lost Mom.

"Look," Samuel finally said, his voice steadier but still tinged with the raw edge of disbelief, "either way, we're all stuck in the same mess. Let's... let's figure this out together."

Calian nodded, his earlier fury diminished into resigned acceptance. He ran a hand through his hair, a gesture to calm his anger and return to our shared mission. "Right," he agreed, albeit reluctantly. "We still need to locate the shutdown for the AI, no matter who's to blame for creating it."

Samuel's and Calian's hard expressions melt into something more vulnerable, their hostility giving way to a confusion that mirrored mine. They had been ready to blame us, but Ava nor I had seen the full picture of our mother's deception.

"Mom," I began, the words leaving a bitter taste in my mouth, "she did nothing unless it benefited her. Her work... it was always more about proving how smart she was, how important she was, or how much money she could make." My voice wavered, memories of her indifference slicing through me. "This... all this chaos," I swept my arm across the strewn papers, "it's exactly the grand scheme she'd be a part of."

Ava nodded solemnly beside me, her eyes darkening with resentment. "She loved her research more than us, more than anything." A storm brewed in her gaze. "Always chasing more power, more..."

Her voice trailed off, and realization dawned on her like a shadow creeping across her face. She clutched at the air as if trying to materialize the thought into something tangible. "The safe," Ava gasped and her eyes snapped to mine, wide and urgent. "That damned safe she wouldn't let out of her sight, claiming it would make her the most powerful person in the world."

A collective shudder ran through us. We remembered the safe, a constant presence in our mother's arms, an object of mystery we never touched. It had been with us at the hotel, the same hotel we fled from in the early hours of the outbreak when the world turned upside down and micro-chipped undead invaded our tranquil community.

"Wait." Ava lowered her head, thinking. "She hid it there. In the hotel. Before we met Samuel and…"

Ava halted her recollection, but the unspoken words hit Samuel as he dropped his head. The realization washed over him, understanding that one of the people responsible for Jordan's death had stood right in front of him at one point.

The revelation hung heavy in the musty air of the abandoned offices, a new piece of the puzzle slotting into place with a sickening click. Our mother's secrets continued to unravel before us, each thread leading to a darker and more treacherous path than the last. Somewhere behind us laid a safe that held answers we weren't sure we wanted to find after days of searching for them.

I blinked away the fog of shock. "She said we'd need her alive to find it," I repeated her words in a mocking tone. The safe, that cursed thing she'd clung to like a safety net, sat nestled in a hotel deep within Chipper infested mountains.

Ava's laugh cut through the heavy silence, though it held no humor. "She couldn't have hidden the safe well with how quickly she came back out of the hotel," she scoffed, her gaze distant, like she could already see herself rifling through the contents. "I bet I could find it."

We all looked at one another, exhaustion and disbelief etching our faces. "Maybe we should take a break," Ava suggested, her voice softer. "We've been through a lot. We need to relax for a moment."

The others nodded in agreement, relief flooding the room as shoulders dropped with deep exhales.

Taking a moment, I reached for my notebook. Its pages filled with hastily scribbled notes and questions. My hand shook as I uncapped my pen, ready to record every twist and turn of the day's discoveries. It felt grounding, necessary to document the madness we'd unraveled. If we ever made it out alive, someone needed to know how everything fell apart and the true villains behind it.

My companions found solace at abandoned desks, sinking into swivel chairs that once belonged to people who probably never imagined the end would be their doing. The chairs gave soft squeaks and groans as they twisted back and forth, the sound strangely comforting amid the stillness.

"Okay," Samuel finally broke the silence, his voice laced with fatigue. "What's our next move?"

"We find that safe," Ava replied without hesitation. The safe felt like a self-appointed mission Ava had placed upon herself as an apology for our mother's horrendous actions.

"Right," Calian chimed in, clasping his hands on top of his head, leaning back in the desk chair. "But we also can't forget what's out there. Those... things." His eyes darkened at the thought of the Chippers, the mindless drones hunting us with relentless precision.

"First things first," I said, a surge of resolve filling me. "We've got a lot to piece together. This Project DHIA, the microchips, our mom's involvement..." I scribed every point as I made them, cataloging each detail. It was a puzzle, and I was determined to put it together, piece by painful piece.

"Martha's right," Ava agreed, bouncing in her chair. "We need to understand everything before making a move. One poor impulse move and they could eat us."

"Then let's make sure we're armed to the teeth," Samuel added, raising his shotgun in the air.

Martha's Notebook

As they bounced ideas back and forth like ping-pong balls, I cataloged every idea, not wanting to miss anything of value. Every word spoken, every plan hatched, I captured it all. Because my notes might be the only legacy we'd leave behind.

The swivel of the chair beneath me was a momentary distraction from the weight of my situation. I scribbled furiously, my pen running across the paper like it chased the truth itself.

"We need to find that safe," Ava insisted. "If Mom hid something that important in the hotel, it could be the key to all this. Maybe she literally had a 'shutdown' key."

Calian nodded with an intense glare, focused on Ava's every word. "Yeah, but the hotel is days away even without Chippers interfering, and we don't even know if the safe is still there."

"Or we could head straight for Onakele Enterprises." Samuel leaned back in his chair and yanked a large map from the wall above him, one that detailed city streets and buildings of the entire Mion-Lach Republic. His finger tapped an imposing structure labeled "Onakele Enterprises." "If we can shut down the mainframe, maybe we'll cut the head off the snake, stopping every Chipper."

"Easy to say, hard to do," Calian countered with a sigh. "We're talking about infiltrating a high-security corporate building possibly crawling with those things."

I looked up from my notebook, weighing the gravity of each option. They both carried risks, immense ones, but also potential rewards that could change everything. My hands quivered, but I steadied them, determined to capture every word, every argument. It wasn't just a record of plans, but information for whomever held my book after we were gone.

Ava's gaze met mine, and I saw the flicker of fear she was struggling to hide. "Martha, what do you think?" she asked.

I swallowed the lump in my throat. "We need to decide, and whatever we choose, I think we should do it together."

"Let's vote then," Calian suggested, his hands clenched into fists. "Majority decides our next move."

"Fine," Samuel agreed, though reluctance shadowed his features. "But we're not splitting up. We stick together, no matter what."

Nods of agreement followed, and I jotted down their decision. The pen felt heavy, like it bore the weight of our collective fate. We were in it together.

"Alright, let's vote," Ava said. Her voice firm, rallying us like a commander before battle. "Where to first? The hotel or Onakele Enterprises?"

One by one, we cast our votes, sealing our path forward. With each name uttered, I etched it in the pages of my notebook, a silent witness to the choices that would either lead us to salvation or doom.

Ava took the votes. "Martha?"

"Onakele Enterprises," I said.

"Samuel?"

"Onakele Enterprises."

"Calian?"

"I think we should go to the hotel."

"Ok, and I think we should head to the hotel, too."

Ava appeared annoyed. "A tie. What do we do with a tie, then?"

Calian stared into Ava's eyes with a comforting smile and shot her a wink. "You know what? Maybe we should just go to the Onakele Enterprises. Like we said, who knows if the safe is still there?"

Martha's Notebook

Glancing at Ava, I expected a look of disagreement, but she nodded in agreement. "You're right, Calian. Let's all go to the Onakele Enterprises headquarters."

Relief hit me as I relaxed into the chair. Then a shrill, electronic scream pierced the air, followed by a symphony of equally terrifying sounds from just beyond the facility walls. My pen fell from my shaking fingers. The quiet thud against my notebook felt like a door slamming.

"Chippers," I whispered. Terror seized my throat as Samuel and Calian leaped into action, guns in hand, charging toward the reception area. Ava and I clutched our guns as the comforting weight grounded my nerves as we followed the boys.

"Behind the desk, now!" Samuel barked in a low and urgent tone. We complied without hesitation, crouching behind the makeshift barricade. The click of claws on exterior concrete resonated like a death knell.

"Martha, stay down," Ava hissed, positioning herself between me and the entrance.

I peeked out from our hiding spot. My breath hitched in my chest. The Chippers clustered just outside the entry doors, their movements erratic and purposeful all at once. It was as if they were communicating silently, each one a grotesque mirror reflecting the horror of this new world.

"Think they know we're here?" Calian's whisper cut through the tense moment.

"Can't tell," Samuel whispered back, his eyes never leaving the horde. "But we can't take chances."

In the dim light, I could see the strain in Calian's face, his jaw set in a way that told me he was ready for whatever came next.

"Stay alert," Ava said. She slid her pistol from her pocket. The weapon shook as she readied it at her side. Yet, there was no doubt in my mind that she would use it with deadly accuracy if it meant keeping us safe.

"Everybody, just breathe," I whispered, trying to dispel the panic that clawed at my insides. The very act of breathing felt like a challenge to the Chippers' existence.

Ava gave my hand a final squeeze before freeing us both to wield our weapons. We hunkered down, waiting for the nightmarish parade outside to pass or pounce.

The rhythmic pounding of feet grew erratic, drawing my gaze back toward the grim scene unfolding beyond our barricade. I peered over the edge of the desk in time to witness the horde's abrupt transformation. The Chippers, previously a churning mass of rage and decay, snapped into an uncharacteristic stillness. It was like a conductor had signaled for a sudden rest in their symphony of hunger.

"Look at their heads," Ava whispered next to me, her eyes wide with both curiosity and fear.

I followed her gaze, where, in unison, each of the twenty Chipper snapped their necks backward and their faces aimed straight at the clouds. Another chilling glow emanated from their microchips, casting an eerie blue blanket over the landscape that shone even in the bright sun. The sight was hypnotic, otherworldly, like a beautiful painting that contained a violent and terrifying background.

"Blue... Another upgrade?" I asked, more to myself than anyone else.

"Upgrade or not, this can't be good," Samuel hissed from my other side, his hands clutching his shotgun so tightly his knuckles lost their color.

We watched, transfixed, and the momentary calm shattered. The creatures' microchips flipped to green, and they broke formation, sprinting off with renewed vigor in random directions. Some ran in pairs or groups while other Chippers took off on their own. As if receiving their personal missions, they were a collective force that moved with terrifying purpose.

"Whoever, or whatever, they're after, I'd hate to be in their way." Ava's voice rang out with a mix of relief and dread.

"Let's hope it's not us they're hunting," I replied, trying to shake the image of the glowing chips from my mind.

Even with no Chippers in sight, Samuel crept from our hiding spot, caution in every move he made. With a careful motion, he edged toward the shattered front door, listening intently as he inched his head through a mostly missing pane of glass.

"Clear," he finally announced, stepping back to flash a thumbs up. His eyes held a glimmer of something I couldn't quite place. Hope?

We slipped from behind the cover, our weapons ready and our bodies rigid with tension. The absence of the Chippers' guttural snarls was almost more unsettling than their presence. Sweat pooled on my revolver's grip as we made our way back to the offices where chaos had spilled over in our search for answers only moments before.

"Back to square one," Calian announced as his fight drained from him and he slumped into a chair. "But at least we have a moment of peace."

"Peace?" I echoed, my thoughts racing as I surveyed the mess of papers and scattered remnants. "We still need a plan to disable this AI, DHIA, whatever we need to destroy?"

Ava quickly changed the subject. "What do you think those Chippers took off after? Could they be searching for us?" Her eyes were still enlarged and stared off into nothingness.

"Maybe they found a new target. A large group of survivors could have drawn their attention," Samuel suggested. His voice carried an uncertainty that mirrored my fears as I pondered their actions.

"Or maybe," Ava added softly, brushing a strand of hair from her face, "they're being called back… by the AI, or something with more control over them than we realized."

The weight of that possibility shrunk the room again. It felt like a constant stream of information that one-upped previous fears. If the Chippers were pawns, then who, or what, controlled them from the shadows?

"Whatever it is," I said through fear trying to silence my voice, "we need to stop it. I'm so exhausted of this nightmare and it needs to end."

Silence blanketed the room, and I realized I still clutched the notebook. My fingers worked methodically, tucking it into the side pocket of my backpack with care.

It wasn't long before Calian's voice cut through the eerie calm. "Hey, over here!" he called, an edge of excitement breaking through his stoic demeanor. We grouped around him, standing in front of a door slightly ajar. With a push, he opened it wide, revealing the contents within.

"Looks like we've hit the jackpot," he said, stepping aside.

The room was small but densely packed with military paraphernalia. A veritable arsenal that seemed out of place in the desolation we'd grown accustomed to. Racks of rifles lined the walls, pistols laid arranged in neat rows, and several shotguns stood at attention. Someone had stacked boxes of ammunition haphazardly, and to my surprise, I noticed grenades nestled in a cabinet like deadly eggs.

"Niiice," Samuel said before loosing a whistle of disbelief. He stepped forward to inspect a rifle. "This could change the game."

"Or at least even things up," Ava added as her hand caressed a shiny pistol.

In front of us sat the power to compete with our assailants. The power to defend ourselves. The power to take a stand. For a moment, the weight of our despair lifted, replaced by Samuel and Calian acting like children in a toy store.

"Grab what you can carry," Samuel instructed, his arms already filled with a rifle, two pistols, and extra ammo for his shotgun. "We need to be prepared for anything."

On cue, we sprang into action, filling our backpacks with ammunition and flinging weapons over our shoulders. With the added weight, I felt safer and safer.

Samuel scooped up the grenades, eyeing them with a mix of fascination and fear. "Never thought I'd be so happy to see these," he mumbled. "Hey Martha, mind carrying these for me?" His outstretched hands offered the nuggets of destruction.

"Of course I can." I unzipped my backpack and tucked them in, trying to nestle them into my hoodie at the bottom.

Ava chose last, her fingers running across each gun before stopping on a shotgun. She pumped it, then looked at Calian as he gave her an approving nod. She tucked it into her backpack, with the muzzle sticking straight out. Calian tucked three pistols into the bag, along with boxes and boxes of ammo.

After stuffing the rest of our backpacks, we left the security room behind. A new sense of safety and confidence followed us, the added weight giving security to our future.

"Looks like we've got a fighting chance," Ava said. She jostled her backpack as a smile grew with every bounce of the guns. Her words lifted a weight from the room, and even I felt a surge of hope.

"Let's not get ahead of ourselves," Samuel cautioned. "We need to prepare with more than just guns. We need food and anything else we can scavenge."

Ava and Calian shot each other an awkward gaze at Samuel's words.

Ignoring their unusual gesture, I spotted another map and approached it. My fingers traced the contours of mountain ranges and river paths. I attempted to memorize each twist and turn to ease our path. A stark red line marked the Underground Bridge, while black dots represented the small outpost and our current building.

"Look at this," I called, beckoning the others over. They crowded around me with piqued interest.

"It's all here," I said, pointing. "Our entire terrain... and there—" My breath hitched as my finger landed on a detailed map of a downtown. A building in the center, marked with a red flag with the letters 'Onakele Enterprises Headquarters' printed with chilling formality, caught my attention.

"Is that..." Calian began but couldn't finish the sentence.

"Yep," I confirmed. The name sent shivers down my spine. "That's where they birthed this nightmare. That's where we might be able to end everything."

"Or where we'll find more trouble," Samuel interjected, reminding us of the real possibility of it being more than we could handle.

"Either way, it's our best lead," Ava added, her gaze locked on the marked building. "And we've got to take it."

"Plus, we already voted on it," I joked with an exaggerated smile, trying to lessen the tension.

"Then it's settled," Samuel said. "We head for Onakele Enterprises, end this nightmare, and get back to our normal lives... as much as we can."

We all nodded, a silent pact forming. Our apocalyptic family had formed honest bonds, and we felt like a real family.

I paced, my boots scuffing against the concrete floor. "We can't just head out blindly," I said. "We need to be sharp and more ready than we've ever been."

"Agreed. Plus, we'll need boats." Ava pointed at the map, underlining the title with her finger. "It's not on our island. It's on one of the other islands."

"Seriously?" Embarrassment and annoyance shot through me. "Well, I guess we'll need to scavenge."

"Martha's right," Samuel agreed, nodding solemnly. His eyes dipped, understanding the time it could take to scavenge a working boat. Did the Chippers see boats as vehicles to eliminate from our world, or had they spared them?

"First off," Calian chimed in, tapping the map. "Have any of you ever been to… Ina Onar Island? I know I haven't."

"I've never even heard of it. Does it say how far it is?" Concern covered Ava's youthful face.

"It doesn't matter how far it is or how hard it'll be to find a boat," I said. "No matter what it takes, we'll find that city. And when we do…" My voice trailed off, feeling the weight of what the mission could take and how long it could last.

"First things first," Ava cut in, bringing me back to the present. "We stock up. Food, water, medical supplies, a boat. We make sure we're prepared for what awaits us on that island."

"Right." I nodded. It felt good to focus on something tangible, breaking things down into steps so we could focus on what was in front of us.

"We stock up first, then we battle the Boss Chipper," Calian added. A mocking expression lit his face as we all shared a laugh. It was a ridiculous name for the monstrous AI, but it helped lighten the mood.

Martha's Notebook

"Let's get moving," I urged, heading to the rear exit door through the hallway. Our laughter echoed off the walls, a sound so rare in the desolate world it almost felt taunting toward the Chippers.

As we approached the exit door, I felt different. It felt like a new chapter in my notebook and in the world was about to be written. Nothing would split us apart, even death.

"Ready?" Samuel asked, slinging his shotgun over his shoulder.

"Let's do this," I answered, my fingers brushed my trusted revolver still tucked in my belt.

"Wait." I froze. My gaze fixed on a metal cabinet tucked in the corner, its surface dull and unassuming. Yet something about it beckoned me. "What are those?" I asked, pointing at the stenciled letters that read 'EMP BOMBS' on the glass panel.

Samuel spun, and his eyes followed my outstretched arm. The color drained from his face as he recognized the significance of the contents. Without a word, he snatched a nearby chair and smashed it against the glass with a force that echoed through the building. Shards cascaded onto the floor.

"Are these good against Chippers?" I asked. "And maybe even the Boss Chipper?"

"Martha, these could be the game-changers we need," Samuel stated with glee. We scrambled to stuff the ten EMP bombs into my backpack, placing them atop the grenades as carefully as possible.

As the last bomb nestled deep into my bag, Samuel turned to me, his stature grounding us in the chaos of our reality. He kneeled before me, his gaze piercing the shadows and locking with mine. His hands were rough, but they held a gentle firmness.

"Listen to me, Martha," his stern voice vibrated against the walls. "We've been through hell these past weeks. Seen things no one should ever witness. But we're still here, we're still breathing, and we're still fighting."

He reached into my backpack and retrieved an EMP bomb, holding it between us like a magical lamp. "This nightmare," he continued, "this cruel, unforgiving world… We're going to end it, Martha. We'll stop the Chippers, take down the Boss Chipper, and bring back some semblance of life to this forsaken place."

My breath caught in my throat and the weight of his words settled deep in my chest. Samuel's determined stare didn't waver.

"Or we'll die trying," he concluded. It wasn't just a statement. He vowed we could end it ourselves.

"Okay," I replied, my voice steady despite the tremor inside. The metal was cold and dense in my grip. But with Samuel's unwavering gaze upon me, I felt a surge of courage. We would face whatever horrors awaited us together, as a family forged by loss.

Whatever reasons there were to create the atrocious mess, we all took the responsibility to clean it up. We would clean up the world together.

CHAPTER 18: EPILOGUE

Samuel turned to me in confusion. "I can't believe, after all this time, you still have that letter."

I unfolded the letter and read it again. A reminder to myself of how many things had changed.

> *Dear Martha,*
> *I'm sorry to leave like this, but we had planned on doing this much sooner, like the night we almost snuck off just before we found the outpost. Calian and I have different goals from you and Samuel. We understand we may never accomplish half of the things we want to, but we felt we needed to try. We don't want to place Samuel, and especially you, in death's path more than you will be. Good luck to both of you with destroying the Chippers, but we have some things we need to do first. We don't know how much time we have left in this world, but we're going to make it count.*
>
> *I love you with all my heart, sis. Please don't look for us. We will constantly be on the move and almost impossible to locate. Stay strong and know that I will always love you and Dad.*
>
> *Love you forever,*
> *Ava*

Gravel crunched under our boots as we slipped from under a highway and approached the on-ramp. Having our apocalyptic family cut in half had hurt, but what stung more was the fact that my sister had left me when I needed her. It had been so long I couldn't remember how much time had passed, but Samuel tried to keep up with time and believed it was around four years since the night we left the government outpost. I never knew Calian and Ava would sneak out that night to never be seen again.

"Isn't reading that letter over and over just torturing yourself? I don't think she left any clues or anything like that in her words." Samuel's words snapped me from my spiral.

"Still trying to make sense of why she'd do this. I can't believe she'd abandon me like that. I'm her sister. She told me we'd do everything together." My heartache was impossible to mask, even years later.

"I get it. Just don't get distracted, Martha," he reminded me without looking back. I adjusted the grip on my obsidian axe and felt the comforting weight of my revolver against my hip. My backpack, torn and dirty, hugged my body, filled with scavenged supplies and my trusty notebook. Samuel and I had bonded over the years, through Chipper altercations and scavenging houses for supplies.

I couldn't shake Ava's and Calian's gnawing absence from my mind. We had sat around a cozy campfire talking about plans and "what ifs." The next morning, I woke to a smoldering fire and only Samuel in sight, a void that echoed louder than the electronic screams of distant Chippers. No goodbye, no plan discussed, just emptiness. It felt like abandonment, a betrayal that stung more than any Chipper scratch. The disappointing letter felt like a punch in the heart.

"Can you believe they didn't wake us? Just a single letter torn from a notebook." My voice cracked as the pain attempted to hijack my voice. Samuel halted, then spun on his heels to share a pained expression. His eyes hung heavy with the same abandonment.

"I don't like it either, but Ava did what she thought was best for her and Calian. She's always been protective of you, but the letter sounds like she wants to follow a different path. One with a chance to regain what was stolen from her... a family." His words, meant for comfort, only tightened the knot in my chest.

"I've lost my entire family now. These zombies, Chippers, monsters, whatever you want to call them, they've officially stolen everything from me. We need to stop these things so no one else loses their family, too." The words spilled out of my mouth. "Leaving me is not protecting me, Samuel!" My hands shook, but whether from anger or fear, I couldn't tell.

Samuel sighed and closed his eyes, followed by his head falling. "We need to keep moving," he mumbled. "Standing here and fighting their decision won't change anything. You can't change Ava's decision, but you can change your reaction to it."

"Can I?" I asked, the ache for my sister resurfacing. Ava, with her blonde hair and blue streak that caught the light in better days, and those light blue eyes that held so much love and fear. She had been everything, and all that remained was a gaping hole where she should've been.

"Come on, Martha," Samuel urged, reaching out to squeeze my shoulder. "Let's find the headquarters and the heart of this AI nightmare so we can end it. For Ava and Calian. For Jordan, Elu, and your dad. For us."

I nodded stiffly, swallowing the lump in my throat. He was right; we needed to focus on the mission to stop the Chippers and save what remained of humankind. With every step, I carried Ava's will within me, the drive to make her proud, to become the strong woman she believed I could be.

"Let's go then," I said. "We've got an AI system to fry. We can find Ava and Calian after we stop the Chippers."

Samuel gave me an empathetic smile before spinning back around to resume his march. The shotgun glinted in the evening light from the holster on Samuel's back, with it crisscrossing his new sword.

The menacing sword always filled me with envy and safety. "What sword was that again? A samurai sword or something?"

"I don't completely remember, if I'm being honest. The tag underneath it said it was a Tamahagane steel sword or something like that. I think it said it was a samurai sword." Samuel reached up and unsheathed the sword. He carried it like a baby as he admired the craftsmanship.

"That house sure had some spectacular weapons. It was like an apocalyptic weapon store," Samuel continued as he chuckled maniacally, like a spoiled kid in a toy store.

"I'm surprised no one had raided it before we got to it. But better for us, we got the first dibs on weapons. I wonder if it was some sort of personal weapons museum."

"Or just some crazy multi-millionaire's weapon collection. I'm pretty sure I couldn't have afforded a single weapon he had in his collection. Some benefits of a zombie apocalypse... I can afford things I wouldn't without it."

Samuel slid the sword back into its sheath just as our boots transitioned from crunching gravel to the hard asphalt. The steps onto the bottom of the on-ramp finally gave me some familiarity. After weeks of hiding under highways and ducking hordes of Chippers, we neared the city we'd searched for.

The minor downtown sat against the edge of the mountains, littered with two- and three-story buildings. An unusual architectural building broke through the miniscule skyline, highlighted with the name "Onakele." The view reassured me we'd reach our target within a day's walk.

I scanned the streets and buildings for any movement, calming myself with the wooden grip in one hand and the cold revolver in the other. Samuel marched ahead, removing his shotgun from his back as he scanned the area with me.

"We don't have much further," he announced with a fatigue in his voice from the long trip and the ever-present threats.

Our exhalations mingled, a visible testament to our shared relief. "We've made it," we said in unison, a small smile tugging at my lips despite the grimness of our situation.

"Yep, this highway has been our yellow brick road to Foscad City." Samuel pointed at the intimidating building at the heart of the city. "That should be the headquarters we're looking for."

"Great, just months and years of zombie-infested landscapes to get to this point," I responded.

A sign loomed ahead. A once-bright panel weather-beaten and rusty. Foscad City, 5 miles. Beag Town, 55 miles. Dermadta City, 91 miles.

"Hey, look," I called to Samuel, pointing at the sign. "We're closer than we thought."

"Still a long walk," he replied, squinting at the numbers. "But we'll make it."

"Of course we will. Just a casual stroll through apocalypse central." My attempt at humor fell flat, even to my ears.

Samuel didn't respond, but I caught the ghost of a grin on his face as he glanced back. It was enough to lift my spirits. A tiny spark in the encroaching darkness. We were survivors, after all. And we had a city to reach, a company to confront, and a future to reclaim.

"Martha," Samuel's voice broke through my thoughts, his tone cautious. "You think Calian and Ava could have stopped in one of those other towns?" He nodded at the sign we passed, his eyes scanning the horizon for movement.

Biting my lip, I felt a familiar pang of worry for Ava. "I don't know, Samuel." Fumbling through my backpack, I pulled out the crinkled map, smoothing it against a nearby tree. My fingers traced the lines and symbols, all leading to Foscad City.

"I don't know where they went, but I think you're right about that building," I said with more confidence than I felt, pointing to a spot on the map marked with a red circle. "That's the headquarters for Onakele Enterprises, and that's the headquarters for the Chippers."

"Right." Samuel's gaze fixed on me.

"Once we're in the city, if we can find the headquarters..." I hesitated, then lifted the heavy sash from my chest, letting the EMPs clink together. Six left, enough to take out the AI control center. "We could use these on the AI system. Shut it down for good." The words sounded hollow, even to me.

"Martha, do you think that'll work? Without... hurting the victims?" His voice was a mix of hope and dread.

"I don't know," I admitted, shaking my head slightly. "But we have to try." My hands tightened around the sash, the metal cold and unforgiving against my skin. "It's a chance we must take."

Samuel nodded, his expression set in grim determination. "Then that's what we'll do."

We quieted, each lost in thoughts as we resumed walking. The EMPs jostled softly, a constant reminder of the weight of our mission. We had miles to go, dangers untold to face, and an uncertain end. Clearly, we couldn't turn back.

We pressed forward, the unending stretch of pavement beneath our boots. I dared to glance at Samuel, whose eyes seemed trained on an unseen horizon beyond this desolate world.

"I hope Ava and Calian had the same idea," I whispered. "Stole their own map and are making their way to Foscad City."

"Maybe," Samuel replied, his voice a low rumble of cautious optimism. "I've been to Foscad twice for work before... before everything happened. It's not like cities in those old movies, with skyscrapers touching the clouds. Just a small downtown area, a scattering of five or six buildings huddled together like they're afraid of the sky."

"Small might make it easier to find them," I ventured, trying to believe my own words.

"Or harder to stay hidden," he countered.

As we continued, the silence stretched between us, filled only by wind whispering through the trees and the distant groans of the undead that had become part of the landscape, like the chirping of crickets or the rustling of leaves, commonplace and eerie.

"Once we get closer," I started again, breaking the quiet, "we'll need to scout the buildings carefully. We must figure out which ones the government and Onakele Enterprises used." My fingers subconsciously brushed against the EMPs, their presence both comforted and terrifying.

"Any idea how we do that without drawing attention?" Samuel asked, eyeing the lethal sash across my chest.

"Carefully," I sighed. "We can't afford to trigger any Chippers, or worse, any of those Upgrades. If this works, we'll most likely kill everyone with a chip in them."

"We can only do our best to save them, but those notes said there was no way to remove the chips without killing the host," Samuel stated firmly, remembering our horrifying time in the Underground Bridge and the horrors we learned.

"Right," I answered, though doubt gnawed at my gut. Doubt was a luxury we couldn't afford, not when every moment mattered.

"Let's keep moving," I urged, shifting the weight of the backpack on my shoulders. The road ahead was long, and time was a resource as scarce as food and safety. Every step took us closer to an uncertain fate, but backward wasn't a direction we could choose.

We trudged forward, the desolate highway stretching before us like a black ribbon through the wilderness. The sun was a harsh eye in the sky, scrutinizing our every step as if to burn the question into my skin: how far can AI really go?

I adjusted the sash of EMPs, their weight a constant reminder of the power we intended to dismantle. "Samuel," I began, my voice barely above a whisper, "if it's AI, how advanced can it really get?"

"Too advanced," he murmured, his gaze fixed on the horizon. "It learns, Martha. It adapts. That's what makes it dangerous."

A chill ran down my spine despite the heat. Somewhere out there, unnerving circuits and code plotted against flesh and blood. "What if... what if it's already learned about us? About the EMPs?"

"Then we'll adapt too. We have no choice." Samuel's determination was a balm, even if reality left us treading dark waters.

A rustle in the nearby brush stole our attention, and I drew the handgun with reflexes honed by years of survival. My finger hovered over the trigger, my breath suspended.

"Easy," Samuel warned, stepping ahead with his shotgun ready. "Could be a deer."

"Or a Chipper," I countered, my heart pounding against my ribs.

"Clear," Samuel's voice cut through the tension as he nudged a branch aside, revealing nothing but the wind's plaything, a tumbleweed caught in the thicket.

"Right." I holstered the gun, but I couldn't shake the fear. If the AI had learned enough to predict our moves and attacks, then what hope did we have?

"Listen," Samuel said, turning to me with a seriousness that emphasized the lines in his aging face. "The Chippers... they're still human underneath. We can't forget that."

I nodded, but the lump in my throat made it hard to speak. "We won't forget. But the AI…" The thought trailed off, lost on the breeze.

"Martha, whatever happens, we can't let it win. We can't let it strip away our humanity."

"Is that what you think it's trying to do?" My voice sounded small, even to my own ears.

"Maybe." He shrugged, his eyes distant. "Or maybe become so advanced it doesn't need humans at all. Replace us or control us completely."

"Then we won't let it," I said, finding strength from somewhere deep within. "We can't."

"Exactly." Samuel reached over and squeezed my shoulder. "You're not just fighting for your survival, Martha. You're fighting for the soul of humanity."

"Then let's make sure we win," I replied, my resolve hardening like steel.

We continued down the highway, two silhouettes against the sprawling decay of the world. Each step was a statement, a declaration that we wouldn't go quietly—that we'd fight until the very end.

And as the shadows lengthened around us, I realized it was more than a battle against a mechanical foe. It was a war for every heartbeat, every breath, every life that still clung to hope in a world overrun by nightmares.

"Hey, Martha. I was just thinking about something…" Samuel began, a question that sparked a new set of fears. "In a typical zombie movie or story, the zombies transfer their virus or whatever by biting others. You can't transfer a microchip through a bite…"

"True." I replied.

"So, why haven't the Chippers' numbers diminished? It seems like their numbers have even grown in the last year or so."

As the question washed over me, my entire body shivered. How could a zombie horde grow without the ability to multiply?

Martha's Notebook

To be continued…

DEDICATION

This book is dedicated to my wife, my daughter, and our two dogs. I want to thank them for all their constant support, laughs, and licks. Through the many doubts, ups, and downs I've faced over the years, they've always been there to keep my spirits up so I could finish this book. Without my family, I would have never made it this far.

ABOUT THE AUTHOR

An author, illustrator, producer, and electrician residing about thirty miles outside of Denver, Colorado, C. Fulster loves spending time with his family, hockey, food, and writing. From his sixteen children's books written under his pen name, C. Fulsty, to his animated short film, The Happy Statue, to his handful of animated feature scripts, C. Fulster loves learning and creating new stories.

C. Fulster focuses most of his time on animated and children's stories but has gained a fresh interest in writing sci-fi novels. His animated short film, The Happy Statue, has won sixteen film festival awards from the Swedish International Film Festival, Global Film Festival (Los Angeles), Florence Film Awards, London Movies Awards, and many others.

With many goals in mind, C. Fulster plans to have one of his feature film scripts turned into a movie along with having it win awards. He is very driven to reach his plethora of goals and consumes dozens of book on his path to grow as a writer and turn his writing into a true career for himself.

Have you enjoyed immersing yourself into our zombie world?

If you enjoyed this book, we'd love to hear about it in an honest review. Book reviews help spread the word about our book and can help grow our community of sci-fi, horror, and zombie lovers.

If you're looking to indulge your zombie appetite even more, feel free to check out our website at **cfulster.com** for merchandise and the continuation of Martha's journey through her post-apocalyptic world.

Will Martha find her sister? Will she stop the zombie threat? Dozens of new threats and twists await you in the second installment of our trilogy.

Thank you for reading.

Martha's Notebook

Made in the USA
Monee, IL
04 October 2024